The Marshal of the Borgo

A CAPTAIN SCARPONE MYSTERY BY JOSEPH D'AGNESE

Captain Matteo Scarpone is a modern-day Job. A man more sinned against than sinning. Once a cool-headed logician and the pride of Rome's carabinieri, he's devastated when disaster rocks his world.

He is a lost man. Beaten. Shaken. HAUNTED.

Shunned as an embarrassment, he is exiled to a tiny village in the sticks—a hamlet, a burg, a *borgo*.

But in this land of vineyards and olive groves, life is far from idyllic. Murder, witchcraft, and hate taint the soil once tread by the Etruscans.

Now the young captain must unravel a series of murders that pit him against a cynical evil and force him to use a power that he has long denied.

Praise

"Joseph D'Agnese does it again. On the surface, this novel is just a murder mystery. But there is so much more just beneath the surface, and to mention it all would give too much away..."—**Robert Swartwood, *USA Today* Bestselling Author of *The Serial Killer's Wife***

"An engaging story well told. That's what *Borgo* offers—and what genre readers want."—**Loren Eaton, *I Saw Lightning Fall***

"...A *tour de force* of literary tone."—**Lars Walker, author of the Erling Skjalgsson historical fantasies**

THE MARSHAL OF THE BORGO

A Captain Scarpone Mystery

JOSEPH D'AGNESE

NutGraf Productions LLC

THE MARSHAL OF THE BORGO

NutGraf Productions LLC
Printed in the United States of America
First edition: May 2014
Cover design by Damonza

With thanks to Denise Kiernan and Kathryn Temple.

www.josephdagnese.com

In the middle of my life's journey
I found myself in a dark wood
Where the one true way
Was obliterated, decimated, and utterly lost...

—Dante
Inferno, Canto I

Chapter One

The dead man walked out of the bay trees at dawn. He was completely naked. Pink blotches covered his body. His eyes were dark and seemed to burn. He picked his way through the tall grass as if he were afraid of hurting his bare feet. I watched him carefully as he shambled through, and was privileged to observe the moment when he realized that he no longer had a sense of touch. He froze, and almost cried aloud. His face had the look of a child who has felt the splash of water for the first time.

He looked up and saw me sitting off a ways from him. Fear crossed his face: What's happened to me?

I gave him a smile and waited. Before long he was moving again. He strode across the ground faster now, his feet, skin, and privates impervious to the assaults of the earth. He stepped out of the tall grass and stood there puzzling out his next move.

It's not my way to give them any sort of hint in these moments. They usually figure it out for themselves.

The wind shifted, bending back the grass. He looked which way the wind blew and saw the house, the barn, and the rows of crops. He nodded at me and headed for the grapes. In a while he was gone. He had disappeared into the mist lying low over the vineyard.

I was alone again. I crouched low above the damp grass and waited for the day to begin. I could smell the dew and early rain. I could see the drops like crystals on the grass. But I could not feel them. Not the dew, not anything. This is my blessing, and my curse.

The earth is so still at these times of day. I have waited hours like this, waiting for you people to rouse yourselves. The earth never seems so beautiful, so still and fragile, as when you are not in it. These hours are bliss for me.

The door of the house opened and the woman came out. She kept her hands in the pockets of her apron as she walked, fearful of exposing her hands and part of her arms to the chill of the day. She walked briskly up the side of the hill outside her door, and stopped to take in the view. This was her morning routine, something she liked to do when her boy had not yet stirred from his bed.

She watched the fog, like me.

From where she stood, she could see the mountains to the east, and the great reservoir lake called Corbara, and the hectares of grapevines in distant fields. Normally the view strengthened her, but today she was preoccupied. Her brow had been wrinkled since she left the house. She dug in the apron and came up with a letter. For now, its contents are known only to her and to me. It was something about her mortgage resetting. It was not a large amount—another 89 euros—but each month, she'll pay more to the bank and less to herself. It was enough to make her wonder yet again if this stubborn dream of hers was worth it.

She had dark eyes, clear olive skin, and long dark hair that spilled to her shoulders. Highborn and beautiful, she had had what most would call a fortunate life. She had traveled the world and returned to this village to make something of her father's land. The parcel consisted of twenty-seven hectares filled mostly with grapes, a stand of olives, and, for the first time in her life, debt. It rankled her to be at the mercy of others, even an entity so impersonal as a bank in Orvieto.

A car door slammed. Startled, she stuffed the paper away.

Her workers milled around in front of their cars, nibbling on food they'd brought. There was coffee, bread, cheese, and maybe even a bit of salty cured meat wrapped in foil. One or two of them caught sight of their *padrona* and waved. *Buon giorno!* For a moment, their voices carried easily from where they were, down by the road. But when they spoke to each other, she could not hear them precisely. Their voices reached her like the sounds of herd animals, eating and milling about and chattering to each other.

She turned her head and I could see her better.

I am drawn to this woman, my beautiful Lucia.

My purpose on this earth is somehow bound up in her, though I don't know how or why.

I receive no instructions. No spoken word has sent me here.

I don't know how long I've lived or where I'm from. Am I an angel or a demon? I honestly don't know, for I've never met another of my kind. I know only that my Lucia needs me, and I must use what powers I possess to bring her happiness. But already this task seems doomed.

She scanned the line of trees between her property and the next. And just like that, she spied the birds. Eight or nine of them circled overhead in an unhurried yet determined configuration that can only mean one thing.

Lucia flinched.

I knew her thoughts: Her mind flew back to the day she witnessed something similar. She was just a child. A cow of one of her father's tenants had wandered into a forbidden field and ate something green—she couldn't remember just what—that made its stomach grow fat with gas and burst. They found the poor creature on its side, a kind of sickly, blood-tinged foam oozing from its wound while carrion birds wheeled in the sky, waiting. All the neighbors ended up buying the meat, as it could not be sold at market. It was tainted, though it still represented a calamitous loss for the family.

Lucia turned and screamed toward the house.

The door opened and out ran Magda, carrying Lucia's son. The housekeeper ran up the hill, carrying the child. The two women spoke briefly, gesturing at the sky. Magda, it was decided, would go for help. Lucia would take the boy. Yes, come to Mamma, Leonardo.

At four or five years old, the boy was too old to be held by either woman. I have watched him for months now, and don't care for him. He was a nice enough boy, just spoiled. Today he was dressed like a prince, and his chubby, delicate fingers played with a toy car. He was cranky because he'd been ripped from his breakfast.

Lucia rocked him while Magda ran down to the foreman, who was using a pocketknife to inefficiently carve a piece of bread on the roof of his battered Fiat. Magda, an unpretty woman with a nearly shaved head of black-and-white hair, has not spoken a word in fifty years. And so she gestured wildly. The foreman tried to comprehend. Yes. He understood. He was wanted on the hill.

He ran first to Lucia, then to the line of trees and brambles dividing the two properties. He dressed carefully each morning so that no one would mistake him for a migrant. And yet he failed. His face was sunbeaten, a look that marked him forever as a man of the fields.

I tried to read his thoughts but they were closed to me. I caught only his scent: unwashed smokiness cloaked in a light shirt and jacket. It would be hot here today but the morning was still cool.

He ran to find a way to cross the ravine between the two parcels of land. After a few minutes, he discovered that the trees and brambles were impassable. He was forced to run almost to the road and double back into the neighboring field. In a while, he made his discovery and called his mistress on his mobile phone. He was a poor man, but he carried a phone in his pocket every single day.

"Signora Lucia?"

"Yes? Tell me everything. What is it? A cow? Livestock?"

"No, Lucia, much worse."

He spoke of his discovery, and uttered a single word.

Her heart leaped to her throat. She hung up without thanking him. Then she called the local police station, and repeated the word herself.

"Omicidio," she said, panting, though she herself had not moved from her spot. "I want to report a murder."

Chapter Two

Everything he touched died. Plants mostly, but other things too. He tried mightily to shake the truth of his affliction from his mind. He tried not to dwell on the past. Which was why he buried himself in the news of the day.

Every morning since his arrival in Castelpietra, one of my other charges, Matteo Scarpone, had sat in the front window of the Bar Fleming, and flipped through newspapers. His presence surprised villagers returning from their August vacations.

What annoyed me most about Scarpone was that parts of his mind were hidden from me. But that didn't mean I had given up on him. I am still here, watching his every move.

He fussed with a glass of warm milk marked with a dollop of espresso coffee. Yesterday he managed at breakfast to sip about three-quarters of his cup, but his guts roiled all day. This morning he felt he must mix the milk with a bit of *cornetto*, a jam-filled pastry. But his lips didn't seem to know what they were doing. They worried the pastry to crumbs, which sprinkled down the front of his uniform while his eyes were distracted by an article.

According to that morning's *cronaca nera*—the so-called crime news—a sixty-eight-year-old man in Puglia had murdered his seventeen-year-old lover when he caught her together with her new paramour, a man three years his senior. A woman in Naples had wounded her husband after he mocked her preparation of his favorite appetizer, *filetto di bacala*. According to the officers who responded to the scene, she had sliced him as deftly as she had the fish. The gutted husband was in stable condition. Up north, outside Turin, a marketing executive being sued by his firm for embezzlement had hanged himself in his study. This alone would have been a tragic development, something to be forgotten, except for the fact that the dead man's wife was rumored to be sleeping with the dead man's attorney. And so the local magistrate was investigating.

Scarpone tore out each of these gems and carefully folded the remaining newspapers. Later, at home, he would preserve the articles in the pages of his scrapbooks. He found the cronaca nera oddly comforting. Other people read these pages as a way of reassuring themselves that such things couldn't happen here. Scarpone, instead, thought: "See? It happens everywhere."

This morning, Scarpone had missed a few spots in his beard while shaving. Ironically, this had happened because he had been too busy studying his looks in the mirror. You would not think this of him, but he was a vain man. He was not bad looking. His hair was cut short against his skull, a pleasing mixture of black and gray bristles. His nose was sharp and finely tapered at the end. He was handsome, like many of the men in his family.

But I could not deny that he had changed greatly since I began monitoring his movements. His eyes had receded into their sockets, and an unpleasant pallor had settled itself across the whole of his skin. He was once a strongly built man. Now his flesh hung limply on his bones. In fact, this morning, in the stuffy air of his furnished apartment rental, he had used a kitchen knife to gouge a new hole in his leather belt.

Compared to my beautiful Lucia, he looked feeble, lifeless, and alone.

I love this man. I have followed him for two of your years. But I must say that in the month since his arrival in the borgo he had done little to deserve this love. The natives didn't see him the way I do. The man they saw was uncomfortable in conversation. He read his papers and made a mess of them. It was painful to watch him eat or drink. The locals have offered on occasion to buy him his morning coffee and pastry—this was common courtesy—but he always declined.

In the morning, he told them, my constitution is delicate.

This was true, but after a few days no one believed it anymore. He'd only been in their midst a few weeks, but they were already fed up with his excuses, and now ignored him entirely as they took their breakfasts.

The farmers who patronized the bar ordered a shot of espresso, followed by a small glass of wine. They stood at the bar and made small talk. They watched the car races on TV and the reruns of the soccer matches.

The barman, Alessandro, flirted with the girl from the pork store who came in each morning to have her coffee and cornetto before she opened her uncle's shop. From years of helping her family cook the daily roast pig, her pink-striped uniform and her own flesh was impregnated with the smell of rosemary, fennel and salted pig's fat, and of greasy, crackling skin. All the men—young and old—found her intoxicating.

Not Scarpone.

Alessandro, the proud barman, would occasionally cast a disdainful eye toward my captain. He was especially irritated by the officer's daily appearance, but didn't know how to put what he felt into words. Two years ago, when Alessandro had first opened the bar, his family and friends had presented him with a multitude of potted plants. Touched by their generosity, the barman had situated the plants in the south-facing windows to catch the sun.

For twenty-four months the plants had thrived beautifully. Now, in the last month, since the coming of the marshal, the plants had begun to wilt and die.

Alessandro would have been shocked to know that Scarpone had also closely observed these plants, not to mention the ones dying on his own balcony at home, with great interest. They were all part of a bizarre experiment my captain was conducting.

Each time he touched a plant, he whispered: "I condemn you."

The months-long experiment had grown out of his own self-pity. That the plants later died was all the proof he needed. See? he told himself, everything I touch dies. What more was there to say? I am a cursed man.

The phone rang.

Scarpone fitted his Bluetooth device into his right ear and reached for a pair of reading glasses made of pale red plastic. The glasses were too small for his head, yet for some reason he enjoyed wearing them.

"Sir?" said the tremulous voice on the other end. It was the voice of Enzo Lamiscia, a young soldier at the station. "We have a situation."

Enzo tried to explain, but his voice hung up on a single word, a word that seemed to have struck fear in many people this morning. A word no one likes to utter in a small town.

"Did you say homicide?" said the captain.

The word washed over Scarpone like a warm bath. A grin crawled onto his face.

"Did you hear me, sir? I'm sending a car for you."

Scarpone was already moving. Those in the shop would later say that they had never seen him move so quickly.

Now, if you were to fly over the borgo, as I have done, you would see that the southern tip of the village stands a few hundred meters above the floor of the Tiber River valley. Narrow sidewalks and two roads are cut into the hill. The tip of the borgo is shaped like a V, like the prow of a ship that is pointed south to Rome.

The captain ran out of the historic district, newspapers tucked under his arm, toward the open end of the V. It was the last week of August, and the borgo was slowly coming back to life after the long holiday. It was still early morning, but a number of people already lined the *decumano*, the old Roman road that led straight through the heart of town. People opened their shops, drank their morning coffee, set up stalls, unfurled their awnings. The bakeries and coffee shops were already remarkably fragrant.

The citizenry stared as the gaunt captain limped by at an awkward clip.

What's gotten into him? they wondered.

He did not acknowledge them. His eyes were fixed on the road ahead. A small police vehicle zipped down the cobblestone street.

Scarpone jumped in. The car made what all onlookers recognized as an illegal U-turn, and then it flew out of sight.

The inside of the car smelled like a cigarette filter. Scarpone struggled with the seat belt.

The uniformed, thick-lidded bear at the wheel grunted.

Scarpone smiled awkwardly. He was embarrassed. He had not had enough time to get to know his men very well. "Remind me of your name again."

"Belluzzi, sir."

"Well. Drive carefully, Belluzzi. The fog's thick."

"This?" the big man said. "This is nothing."

As my captain settled into his seat, his eyes focused straight ahead.

A child stood in the middle of the road.

A boy dressed entirely in gray.

Scarpone slapped his hand on Belluzzi's thigh.

"Jesu, Belluzzi. The brakes!"

The big man slammed on them, but not fast enough. The car whipped through fog—*punching right through the child's body.*

Punching through *nothing.*

The car lurched to a stop. Both men rocked. The big man craned his head to look behind the car. "Is something wrong, sir?"

Scarpone scanned the road ahead of them. Nothing.

Jesu. It was *just* there. That thing. *That thing with dead eyes.*

"Sir? Did you see something?"

Scarpone forced himself to smile. "No. I'm sorry. You must excuse me. It was just...the fog."

He patted the man's thigh, and gestured for him to keep going.

The cobblestones of the old town ended, and the Fiat slid gratefully onto asphalt. Belluzzi gunned the engine and the car rocketed first past the remainder of shops and apartments, and finally shot down a country road. This was the Orvietana, the nimble, pretty highway that cut through this country on its way north to the city of Orvieto. Farms passed on the right and left. Skeins of white mist rose from the fields. The earth seemed as if it were warming up for a run at another fine summer day.

The car went about two miles before Belluzzi considered braking.

He was drawing close to what looked like an abandoned field with a boarded-up stone farmhouse rising in the center of it. Another police car sat parked at the end of the long driveway. Belluzzi slammed on the brake, pulled the car off the road and ratcheted the parking brake.

My captain stepped out and studied the landscape. The field was covered with tall, uncut grass. A tobacco tower rose not far from the house. The land dropped away behind both structures, giving the impression that they stood at the end of a steep slope.

The captain marveled at the pasture below. It was late in the season, and everything that grew here had turned brown. Here and there were dots of faded red color. Old poppies fluttering in the breeze. The winds came out of the east, skated across that distant lake and tossed the dried grass like waves upon the sea.

Belluzzi cracked his door. That's when the two men heard a gunshot echo across the field behind the house.

Chapter Three

Later that morning, when her mother was at the shop and her father on deliveries, the girl sat in her basement workshop pouring water into a flat soup bowl. Siouxsie and the Banshees blasted into her ears. She took a small cruet and tipped it over the bowl and allowed three drops of olive oil—just three—to hit the water.

She bent over the bowl and looked. The droplets were still small.

She looked at the newspaper on her workbench. The regional section was folded open to the picture of a man. An awful photo of a man staring into a camera as if he wished he were somewhere else.

The girl held the idea of this man in her mind as she made the sign of the horned hand—pinkie and forefinger extended. She closed her eyes and dipped those two fingers into the water and oil and swirled them around the bowl. She sighed heavily, breathing her power over the liquid.

Then opened her eyes.

Each of the droplets of oil had expanded vastly. They nudged each other around the bowl, jostling for space.

She felt a dull throb at the front of her skull.

My God—his pain is so great.

Next she took the pair of scissors and separated the two blades. She pressed one blade to her forehead. First horizontally, the way a dead man lies. Then vertically.

She closed her eyes as she felt cold steel against her forehead.

Again the pain. *My God—what happened to you?*

Her father didn't like to find her practicing like this. He liked the money her skills brought in, but he had no patience for the craft itself. He thought she was merely going through a phase. The craft was the domain of old ladies, not pretty young girls who ought to be out flirting with boys on the decumano.

She had better things to do than consort with those losers. She *knew* she was young, she *knew* she was beautiful, she *knew* what those idiots wanted when they looked at her. She could see it in their eyes.

She had no use for them. Unless there was a purpose.

The Albanian had been that way. Ignoring him, egging him on, teasing him—had been such a pleasure. She'd played him along until it was just the right time. He'd been so eager to grab her, to whip himself out of his pants, to let her touch him. The first time she slipped her hand through his fly, his cock had jumped in her hands.

Like a snake.

A snake?

She laughed quietly to herself.

But the time hadn't been right. So she'd toyed with him. Put off taking action until something had changed in the borgo.

A man had come to town. A man of justice. A man whose pain was so great that her oil drops kept growing. Look at them: one monstrous drop had consumed all the others.

She looked at the picture in the paper again.

A man in pain. *Angoscia.* She had not counted on that.

"What happened to you?" she said to the newspaper.

I walked past her and peered at the photo in the paper. It was the photo of a man in uniform, looking too small for his clothes.

The photo of my captain, Matteo Scarpone.

The girl whirled, eyes stabbing the darkness. She, more than any of the humans I have ever encountered, sensed my presence. She knew I was there—but could not see me.

I had to watch this one. She could be trouble.

"Who's there?" she hissed. "Who's there?"

Chapter Four

Belluzzi was down the hill first, his weapon in his hairy fist. Scarpone stumbled down after, certain that he was going to shoot himself or his man. He did not so much fall down the slope as slide. The grass was still wet with dew. His ankle twisted at the bottom of the hill, just where the ground evened off.

I'm going to kill myself, I heard him think.

A strange tableau awaited them in the lower field. The corpse of a young man lay on its side in the grass, completely naked and damp with dew.

At a glance it was hard to see what had caused his death. His face looked mauled.

A few feet away lay the body of a large carrion bird, blown to pieces. Blood, feathers, and gristle littered the ground, and had spattered the man's corpse.

Still farther away, a young soldier sat on the ground weeping, his legs outstretched in front of him. His Beretta lay between his legs, a trail of smoke curling upward from the barrel of the gun.

"I'm sorry," the young soldier croaked when he saw the others. "I didn't know what to do. I didn't know what else to do."

Belluzzi holstered his gun and uttered an obscenity.

Scarpone took a while to catch his breath and put some weight on his ankle. The injured foot felt rubbery, as if instantly asleep, but he did not think he was hurt badly.

The young soldier, a slender, blond Florentine, mistook his superior officer's silence for a reprimand.

"I didn't know what else to do," he repeated, and launched into his story.

Dispatched by the officer on desk, he'd arrived at the scene expecting to find a corpse. But when he picked his way down the hill in the fog, he beheld a terrifying sight: a carrion bird had descended and was feasting on the soft flesh of the man's face and throat. "I tried to shoo him away," he said to Scarpone.

"But he wouldn't go," said Belluzzi.

"He hopped around. Hissed at me."

"They're vicious," said Belluzzi.

"He would not yield his ground," said the young soldier.

"You had no choice," said Belluzzi.

Scarpone made a show of holstering his weapon. The other two men stopped talking and watched him.

"Belluzzi, why don't you shut up and go up to the road?" Scarpone said. "Stand patrol. No one comes down here."

"Shouldn't I stay?"

"What did I tell you?"

The Neapolitan glowered and stomped back up the hill.

Scarpone waited until he was out of earshot to talk to the seated, weeping officer. "What's your name, soldier?"

"Iucci, sir."

"You fired your weapon, Iucci. Okay, fine. I understand this. But now there will be questions. Reports. You defiled a crime scene, and now I'm going to have to work this scene with one less man."

"Am I discharged?"

"Don't be ridiculous. You're desked."

"Damn. Excuse me, sir. I hate the desk."

He reached for his weapon, but Scarpone waved him off. "Leave it. We're going to need it. Get up and go wait for instructions. Help Belluzzi. There may be gawkers."

Scarpone watched the man's wet rump disappear up the hill. Then he stood for a while listening for the sound of his men's voices. Interesting. The land dropped below the abandoned house and tower into a bowl in the earth. From where he stood, Scarpone could not see, much less hear, traffic or the men talking.

Now he turned around slowly. Once in the bowl, the terrain flattened out into what looked like good, arable land, except for deep gullies that cut across the field in several spots.

His hands grazed the tops of the dried grass and he could feel the ridges of the blades, sharp as knives. If he was not mistaken, farmers always cut grass in the summer to make hay. Why hadn't that been done here? True, the farmhouse was abandoned, but abandoned farmhouses were rife in this country. That didn't mean people wouldn't try to earn a profit where they could.

He squatted and studied the dead man. His skin looked as white as stone, except for his lips and fingertips, which were blue. His lips and eyelashes were thick and sensuous. Both eyes stared at the copse of trees that lay to Scarpone's left. The man's left cheek and throat were pierced by a couple of jagged, bloodless holes. The vulture's handiwork.

The grass around the body was trampled.

Scarpone saw wildflowers popping out of the turf and heard the sound of trickling water. A few feet from where the man lay, water rose to the top of a low stone enclosure, spilled over the sides of the rock, and cut another gully in the dirt that ran away to join a stream farther down the slope. A rusty, cast-iron crucifix rose from the back of the enclosure.

The water led to an impassable hedge of thorny wild blackberries that lined the banks of a creek between this parcel of land and the next.

Scarpone turned back.

The scene seemed so peaceful. If not for the presence of the dead man, this was the sort of place you'd want to sit and sip a glass of wine.

He tapped the thing in his ear.

"Enzo, I need you. Come as quickly as you can."

"Excuse me, sir? I'm on desk."

"I'm sending Iucci to relieve you. I need you here."

"But sir? With all respect, Iucci isn't qualified to be on desk. And I'm not much good in the field."

"We all must stretch. I'll see you here in ten minutes."

"Very well, sir. I've taken the liberty of contacting the pathologist. We have an agreement with the Orvieto hospital in Ciconia."

"Surely you mean the Ciconia Hospital?"

"No, Orvieto."

"The hospital is in Ciconia, right?"

"Yes."

"Then it's the Ciconia Hospital."

"No, it's *Orvieto's* hospital. It's just situated in Ciconia."

Scarpone hung up abruptly.

He trudged up the hill, leaving the body behind. Iucci sat on the hood of his vehicle, his hair disheveled. Belluzzi leaned against his car, a cigarette in his lips, a bored expression on his face.

"Whose land is this?"

"This land—"

"The land on which the man lies dead."

"It belongs to the *azienda.*"

It was a word used to describe agricultural companies, not unlike a *hacienda* in Spanish-speaking countries.

"Which one?"

"Cortese owns it. He's rich."

"What's the name of the firm?"

Scarpone waited. Belluzzi puffed away.

"You heard me."

"Oh—the name? Madonna della Sorgente."

"Sorgente? Madonna of the Spring, as in spring water?"

"Yeah—you saw it down there. The one next to the dead man. It's supposed to be a holy spring. Something like that. Never runs dry. You'll see this weekend at the Assumption festival. The ladies come out here to pray, there's a pageant in town, and then everyone eats. You'll like it."

Cars zipped down the country road. Some slowed to take in the apparently fascinating spectacle of three cops conversing on the highway.

A beige, fluffy herd appeared, marching up the asphalt in a long, bleating line. The men smelled the animals before they could discern what they were.

"Sheep," said Belluzzi.

Behind the dusty creatures trailed a sunbeaten man dressed in rags, followed by a stubby, tailless dog.

The dog ran ahead and snapped at the sheep, who spilled off the asphalt and down the path as if they knew the place well.

Scarpone waved his arms at the shepherd.

"We can't have this," he yelled. "I can't have sheep on my crime scene." He turned to his men. "Can you take care of this?"

Belluzzi flicked his cigarette and pulled himself away from his vehicle. He dug a whistle out of his ceremonial pouch and gave a deafening blow on it.

The shepherd and dog flinched. But the sheep kept clattering downhill.

"I don't know what I'm supposed to tell them, Captain."

"Tell them…tell them that this is now a place of death."

Belluzzi guffawed but did as he was told.

The shepherd did not tarry long after hearing this news. Man and dog ran after the shaggy, shit-bedecked beasts and headed them off. Soon the sheep were marching back up the road.

"Peasants," Belluzzi said. "You can always count on superstition."

Chapter Five

Everything you may have heard about the borgo is true. It's renowned in the area for its wine, but that's not saying much. Nearly every borgo in this region is known for its wine.

Madonna della Sorgente, the biggest grape and olive producer in town, was housed in a walled compound just outside the historic center. The stone walls enclosed an asphalt courtyard for men and trucks. The long building that hugged the courtyard on one side held some offices and some old bottling machines. In the old days, the firm used to sell table wine that was sold in squat bottles wrapped in wicker. You know the type.

The azienda's machines had long been in disrepair because the firm didn't bottle anymore. Like a lot of agricultural firms these days, Madonna della Sorgente acted as a broker between the smaller farmers and the buyers in the region. As each harvest came in, the azienda bought and sold grapes, juice, and olives, not to mention everything from wheat to sunflower seeds.

The front office was run by two men who were fixtures in the coffee shop, though I doubt my captain had come out of his funk long enough to notice them.

Adriano, the overseer, was a young man in jeans and work shirt. Even if he weren't hearing about a strange death on the firm's property, he'd be wearing a befuddled expression on his face. He always did.

These days, I had noticed that he was preoccupied with the notion that he would never have a son. Two weeks ago he'd become the proud father of a beautiful baby girl. Girls were nice, but darling as she was, Adriano's daughter would never grow up into a son. She would inevitably become another man's wife and another man's daughter-in-law. Sons, good sons, took over their family's businesses. In this town they still observed the quaint tradition, enforced by local statutes, of holding family lands in trust for the firstborn son. A father could not sell a large quantity of property unless his firstborn son—or a duly appointed representative for that minor child—gave his assent. Though he had no business to speak of, the overseer's sonlessness troubled him enough to persuade his wife that they should try to have another child. The sooner, the better.

"Was he murdered?" the overseer said to Scarpone.

"We don't know. We can't say at this point."

"But he was naked," another man said. "Surely that's strange. Even a person who is about to drop dead of natural causes doesn't go traipsing around a mile or two from town stark naked."

This was Damiano, the firm's bookkeeper. I'd often found him to be one of the more hilarious men in the coffee shop. Indeed, when the men in the shop wanted to mock him, they called him the "grape-counter." He had teeth the size of candied gum, and hair tinted red-brown. A terrible dye job. From one of the pockets of his suit jacket fluttered a necktie, which he carried but never put on.

The overseer stood as he spoke to Scarpone. The wall behind his desk held a corkboard pinned with articles clipped from viniculture trade magazines. Above this was a white ceramic crucifix limned with gold leaf. Next to that was a map of the local territory with the azienda's properties outlined in red. It was framed behind glass. Stickers depicting symbols of various crops—olives, wheat, sunflowers, grapes—studded the outside of the glass. Scarpone noted that the majority of the stickers surrounding the borgo were grapes.

Scarpone studied it for a while, then pointed. "This parcel here. The land isn't so much fallow as it is abandoned. Is that correct?"

The men nodded. "I'm told that it's regarded as something of a community property."

The overseer clucked.

"That's not strictly true," the bookkeeper said. "The land belongs to us. To the count, that is. But because it's in a dip, it can be difficult to work. It's hard to bring trucks down there. But we've allowed the townspeople to use it as a base camp for the *cinghiale* hunt every fall."

"I thought it was illegal to shoot wild boar?"

"Well, of course you need a permit. The season lasts three months," the overseer said. "Please don't let people hear you say we allow the casual shooting of boar on our land. We'd be in a lot of trouble. It's absolutely illegal to shoot wild boar any other time of year. As everyone knows, they're national treasures."

The two men laughed. Yes, technically, wild boar were a protected species. But as they had had no natural predators, they ran wild, ruining crops, and were the bane of every farmer's existence.

My captain forced himself to laugh with the other men. The effort paid off. *He's not so bad, this police marshal,* I heard the grape-counter thinking. *He's a regular guy, after all.*

"No," the overseer continued. "And come Christmas, we host the pageant on those grounds. The grotto there is perfect for recreating Bethlehem, with donkeys and cows and the manger."

"And the water?" Scarpone said.

"The water? Oh yes, the miracle. The sorgente. The water never stops flowing there. In the thirties, it saved the town from drought. But we don't have that issue any more since we tapped into the reservoir at Lake Bolsena."

"So you're not using the property in any way right now?"

"We store some equipment in the old tobacco tower, but beyond that, no," the overseer said. "But I will call around to the field hands to check."

The phone rang and the young man pounced on it. A meek, deferential tone crept into his voice. "Yes, sir, right away, sir. The marshal is here waiting."

He dropped the phone. "He'll see you now, Marshal. It's right up those stairs to the top. Is there anything else we can help you with?"

Scarpone looked where the overseer had pointed—around the

corner of his office, through the dingy white plaster room that held the bookkeeper's desk and files and fax machine, to a dark narrow staircase that looked as if it ascended into a goat's intestinal tract.

"Just one thing," Scarpone said to them. "I didn't mention the man was naked. How did you know?"

The overseer blushed. The bookkeeper shrugged.

"I don't know," the bookkeeper said. "It's all over town."

Chapter Six

The man waiting for Scarpone at the top of the staircase was a short, older gentleman wearing slippers on sockless feet, white suit pants, and an exquisite shirt opened at the neck. He was well into his sixties with a sizable paunch. His white-gray hair was parted in the middle and feathered back in a long-gone hairstyle.

His hand was outstretched.

"Come in, come in," the count said. "At last we meet, Marshal, but under such terrible circumstances! Can I offer you a drink? A coffee? A soft drink? Mineral water? Something stronger to alleviate the shock of such a distressing discovery?"

Scarpone waved these all away. The man led him to a marble-tiled office. A pair of double doors behind the man's desk opened onto a balcony. My captain saw a chair and cafe table out there, overlooking the courtyard of the azienda. A view of hills and farmland which looked south toward Scarpone's home city.

"Of course," the count said. "Why would you need to fortify yourself? You're a professional. An expert from Rome. No doubt these things are commonplace in your neck of the woods."

The count made no attempt to sit, but stood behind his empty desk, which looked like something you'd pay to see in a palace. Inlaid wood of various colors, topped by a leather blotter fitted with thick paper. The desk bore an old rotary-dial phone and a picture frame showing a family of four. A younger man who had to have been the count, a handsome heavyset woman, and two children—a dark-haired boy and girl.

"Your family's been here a while, I take it."

The count laughed, displaying rows of remarkably white teeth. "My family literally built the borgo. The stones you see in the historic center? They came from my ancestor's castle."

"Must be…nice to have such a lineage. Or at least interesting."

The count shrugged with some forced modesty. "All those things are in the past. What can it possibly mean today? We live in a republic. Despite the title, I'm nothing but a simple farmer today, Signore."

"Now then. I'm told that the land is scheduled to be used for the festival this weekend?"

"Ah, no. The pageant's here in town. But there's always a group of women who go down to the sorgente to get water for the priest to bless."

"I'm afraid that can't happen this year. I can't have people down there until we clear up this matter. Unfortunately, I don't know when that's going to be."

The brown flesh over the man's eyes furrowed. A pause.

"The ladies will be disappointed," the count said. "But I suppose it can't be helped. Perhaps—and this would solely be up to you and your excellent judgment, Marshal—we could arrive at a compromise?"

"I'd be happy to have one of my men fetch the water, if that would help," Scarpone said. "But to convince everyone of the wisdom of this decision I'll need to rely on *your* most excellent influence."

The count beamed. His mouth opened wide. Then chuckled.

Well, aren't we a couple of astute bullshitters, his laugh seemed to say.

"I'd be happy to use whatever meager influence I have at the church," the count said. "I'll call the priest as soon we conclude our business."

"Your firm doesn't use that property?"

"That's right. It's always been special to my family and the borgo because of the holy water. But the truth is, it's a bitch to plant. When it rains, the water runs down the cliffs and washes out the grapes we set out. Gullies cut right through it—"

"I saw."

"There you go, then. One of these days I'll find an engineer who isn't a big thief to terrace it off. But in the meantime, we are fortunate to have bigger parcels we can work. It's nothing—what, two acres or so?" He shrugged and made a face.

"The structures are empty?"

He laughed girlishly. "You know, dear Marshal, I don't even know. We keep machines all over the borgo. My overseer is the man to ask. But tell me—this fellow you found dead. Everyone's talking about him. Who is he?"

My captain whipped out his phone and hit a button.

"We are men of the world, I presume?"

"But of course."

"You are not shaken by death?"

"Who is not, dear Marshal?"

Scarpone held up his phone. The count leaned over to look at the photo on my captain's phone. The bluish face of a dead man.

"My God! How terrible. So young. Some poor family will hear terrible news from your lips today. My soul, it cries for these people."

"I'm sure you're too kind, Count—"

"Cortese."

The older man brought the heels of his slippers together in an attempt at a courtly click.

"But you don't know this man, Count Cortese? He's not one of your workers?"

"No—I assure you, dear Marshal, I've never laid eyes on this man in my entire life."

My captain descended the staircase in silence. I searched in his mind in vain, and saw no hint that he knew he'd just heard the first lie of his day.

Chapter Seven

Belluzzi did his best to keep inquisitive drivers from blocking traffic, but this was difficult to do while lounging, immobile, against the side of his police car.

"Everyone wants to know what happened," he said when Scarpone wandered back. "What should I say?"

"What do you *want* to say?"

"Piss off and keep driving."

"So tell them that. No—wait." Scarpone paused while a sad smile came to his lips. "Why don't you tell them the truth? A man has been found dead. We don't yet know if he was murdered. And your stupid captain doesn't know if he'll ever discover the truth—"

Belluzzi's grin was tremendous. "You're good, sir."

"As always, reveal no pertinent details. Just make us look like idiots. People think we are, anyway. But sooner or later, someone will call to tell us something we don't know."

He saluted his man and descended into the great earthly bowl of death. This time, what looked like a small party tent had been erected over the corpse. A fat officer prowled the larger field, walking slowly through the tall grass, his eyes peeled to the ground. As he walked, he beat the ground with a leafy branch cut from a nearby sapling.

A young, nervous policeman paced the ground in front of the tent, speaking animatedly into his mobile phone. He was short and possessed a wide skull covered with dark ringlets of hair. A pair of modish blue plastic spectacles were perched on his nose. Despite his height, he was remarkably fit. It was well known at the station that Enzo Lamiscia rode a bike to work from two towns over every morning and was a habitué of the local gymnasium.

He slammed his phone shut as his captain arrived.

"Why is there a tent?" Scarpone said.

"It's difficult to explain," said Enzo, rolling his eyes.

Someone else said: "Are you the marshal?"

Scarpone turned to find himself staring at a striking young woman whose eyewear was nearly as severe as Enzo's. She was dressed entirely in a suit of white Tyvek. White booties. White hairnet. White latex gloves. She stood over the corpse, which, Scarpone noted with regret, was still dead.

"May I say that you have incompetent buffoons working for you?" she said.

"Captain, may I present Claudia Cavalcanti," said Enzo, wagging his head. "Pathologist."

Scarpone pronounced his name and, with the count's gesture still in his mind, bowed. A ridiculous gesture in this age, he knew, but he didn't want to shake her hands and thereby force her to change her gloves.

She ignored his introduction. "Do you realize that this dead bird must now be treated as part of the crime scene?"

"I expected as much, which is why I collected and stowed the officer's firearm."

"And then I am told that a herd of sheep trampled the upper path."

"We chased them away. They never got down this far."

"But this is all extra work, Marshal, as if we don't have enough as it is."

Scarpone asked where his own technicians were. Couldn't they lend a hand?

"I don't want *their* help," the woman snapped. "They began collecting samples before I arrived on the scene. They may have moved the body before I pronounced it dead—"

"What killed him?"

"I have certain theories which shall make their way into my report."

"Signorina—"

"Dottoressa."

"Very well, Dottoressa Cavalcanti. I beg your indulgence. Please tell me how this man died."

She made a mouè of disdain and embarked on a litany of suppositions. The upshot: It wasn't clear. After extracting a promise that he would not touch the corpse, she invited him into her tent. The body had been rolled over onto its back. The man's genitalia were now fully exposed. The side of his body had turned black from descending blood.

The pathologist used a tongue depressor to indicate various points along the corpse. "You see these? Here, and here, and here and here?"

At each point, the pale skin bore the angry, puckered marks of raised, red puncture wounds.

"You see? He has no other wounds besides these and the ones on his throat and cheek, which were no doubt inflicted postmortem. If your man is to be believed, the last two were made by the carrion bird."

"But the bird didn't inflict these others."

"No. They're probably snakebites. Or insects. I can't say."

"Not to presume," said Scarpone, "but I've also seen stun guns leave similar marks in the flesh."

She was silent.

"It's weird, isn't it?" continued Scarpone. "Normally, when you find a naked body, you have to assume it was dumped. But snakes and insects or whatever you're suggesting sounds like a perfectly natural death. As if he was attacked *here*. If so, why was he naked? Are we to assume he walked here naked, and then was set upon by snakes? Or, if it *was* a stun gun, was he stripped naked somewhere else, attacked, then dumped? I suppose we're just waiting for the toxicology results?"

She nodded, still trying to assess his logic. "If I may say, Marshal—"

"Captain," said Scarpone.

"Captain. You should not have permitted the man who discharged his firearm to leave the scene."

"Someday, when I have the luxury of more than a handful of men to patrol a farming community this large, I'll follow protocol. Why the tent?"

"That was not my idea," she said, unable to hide her scorn.

"I see," he said, not bothering to ask more. "And my technicians? Where are they?"

Enzo had been hovering nearby, fussing with his phone and notebook. "The cave, sir."

"Cave?"

"The grotto."

"Show me."

They left the pathologist and walked across a fresh path trampled by foot traffic. The dry grass swayed. It was turning out to be a beautiful, hot morning, marred only by the presence of the dead man. Enzo beat the ground with a stick.

"When was the last time you had a murder in this town?" Scarpone asked.

"I couldn't say," Enzo shrugged. "I've only been here five years."

A rocky hill covered with gnarled trees and shrubby vegetation rose out of the grass on their right. Leading the way with his stick, Enzo walked toward a large opening carved into the rock. The ceiling of the cavern was about three meters high. The back of the cave was completely flat, with ancient chisel marks still visible in the stone. Here and there, the roots of above-ground trees had penetrated the chamber, creeping across the walls in search of moisture.

On the sandy floor of the cave was a thin, ratty mattress that was being inspected by two men dressed in Tyvek. Both wielded flashlights.

Enzo laid his stick against the wall and reached for his own flashlight. The air inside the grotto was noticeably cooler. My captain shuddered as he jutted his chin at the men in an unmistakable gesture that said: "What gives?"

"We canvassed the area and found this," said the smaller of the two.

"Have you found his clothes?"

Both men shook their heads.

"They could be anywhere on four acres of land," said the smaller man.

"Yeah, but isn't it likely that he kept his clothes nearby? Is that how you see it? He's homeless or a migrant, maybe? He takes to sleeping here, living here, cooking here—"

"Having sex here," finished the other man. He had a face like a horse. He was down on one knee in the sand, flashlight in one hand, tweezers in the other. From the tip of the instrument dangled a used condom.

"Is it fresh?" said Scarpone.

"Not in my job description," the horse-faced cop replied. "I just bag this filth."

Scarpone slowly dropped to his knees. He winced once, and reached out to Enzo to guide himself to the earth. The old wound in his abdomen stabbed him so hard that he imagined his old stitches would burst anew. Once on his knees, he crawled along the edge of the mattress. His three subordinates watched silently.

The mattress was not, as he'd originally suspected, a relic of a bygone era. It was of fairly recent manufacture and had been outfitted with sheets as well. At one point, halfway around the thing, he stopped and sniffed the sheets.

The men looked at each other.

"I hate to say this," Scarpone started.

"Please no," said the horse-faced cop.

"Yes, I think you're going to have to take this mattress in as evidence as well."

"Damn it!" Horseface cried. "Where in hell are we going to put a mattress?"

"We have the van," his partner offered lamely.

Scarpone steadied himself on the cave wall as he rose.

"There's no way around it," he said finally. "The mattress is clearly evidence. We can take it up with the pathologist if you want, but I fear it may be relevant."

"She can go screw herself," Horseface said, cupping his crotch.

"Enough!" the captain barked.

The men fell silent.

Scarpone staggered a bit and stalked out of the cave.

Enzo found him a few moments later resting his back against a tall rock, squinting into the sun. What little shade there was came from a scrawny peach tree sapling that grew wild between two rocks above them.

"I'm going to need some water, Enzo," he croaked.

Enzo said he had some juice in his vehicle.

"Be honest with me, okay?" said Scarpone. "Does anyone here have any experience investigating murder?"

"I can't really say. There hasn't been one in all the time I've been here."

"Where are you from, again?"

"Turin, sir."

Up north. Figures, Scarpone thought. Enzo probably believed that everyone he met here was a barbarian.

"No strange deaths in the time you've been here, then?"

"There are always deaths, sir. It's a farming community. Someone always falls off a ladder or out of an olive tree. There are domestic disputes. Children die."

"Children?"

"Teenagers. You know, from drugs. I hate to say it, but the town is not exactly squeaky clean."

But what town was squeaky clean? Scarpone thought. His supervisor, Fausto, had told him nothing about the place before assigning him here. He'd simply indicated that it was the usual provincial shithole, and so far his superior had been right. The people were nice enough. It just wasn't home.

Still: it was beautiful. In front of him was the field he'd admired just that morning. The fat cop was still combing through the grass.

"We'll need drinks soon, Enzo. Water. Nothing else. This could take a few more hours and it's getting hot."

They agreed that Enzo would phone one of the markets in town to have some bottles brought over. When the young man scurried off, Scarpone became irritated that he hadn't thought to insist on that juice now.

Shit, he thought.

The sun was higher now. The fat cop saw Scarpone hanging out and picked his way over to him, waving his stick in front of him. He was a genial gent with a whitish beard and blue eyes, a local by birth, and a true marshal by rank. If anyone knew the dead guy, he would.

"It could be one of the foreigners, but I can't be sure. They all look alike," he said.

"You have got to be kidding me."

"It's true!" the fat cop insisted. "I dunno, they all look…like they don't belong. There's this look of wonder on their faces all the time. Like they're afraid they're going to be found out."

The fat cop reported that the only thing he'd found in the field was an empty mineral water bottle not far from the corpse. The pathologist had taken it into evidence.

"That's another thing," Scarpone said. "What's with the stick?"

"Snakes," the fat cop explained. "Gismonda made a big deal about it. He always does, but we figured it pays to be careful."

Scarpone told him to search the grounds around the house and the outbuildings. "And while you're at it, you might want to keep an eye out for the poor bastard's clothes and car."

"His car?"

"Or his scooter. Follow the logic, er…" He paused, searching for the fat cop's name.

"D'Orazio, sir."

"D'Orazio. Okay. So either he was dumped here or he came on his own. The mattress in the cave suggests he was accustomed to coming here on his own. How did he get here if he didn't have a car or a scooter?"

"He could have walked."

"Sure, but where are his clothes? You see? Either way, we keep coming back to that."

"I'll keep looking."

When D'Orazio left, Scarpone bellowed into the cave for Gismonda, not precisely sure which soldier that was. Horseface appeared, wearing goggles.

Scarpone reached out like an invalid and snagged the sleeve of the man's coveralls and drew him close. He did not have the strength to do much else. "What's this about snakes?"

"What, she said something? That bitch! Sir, I want a complaint lodged. I wish to denounce her. It's *our* case. We work the scene, right? But the minute she gets here, she start giving us orders. But I told her, look, bitch, you can't just work under the trees in this season."

Scarpone swatted the side of the man's head. Gismonda shut up.

"May I say something as your superior? Your path through life will be made a lot easier if you watch your language. I don't want to hear another word from her about you, and vice versa, is that clear?"

Gismonda hung his head and murmured something akin to an apology.

"Now what's this about the trees?"

"The body was under a bay tree," Gismonda said. "This time of year, you don't want to stand under trees."

"I stood under that tree this morning."

"Madonna mia! That's dangerous, sir. You could have been hit by a falling snake."

"Next you'll tell me snakes fall from the sky."

"I don't know why it's so, sir, but my grandfather taught me this, and I have always taken it to heart."

"I've never heard of this," said Scarpone.

"Well, no offense, sir, but you're a Roman. A city man. You wouldn't know about this. Hence the tent. I insisted on it."

"What species are these snakes?"

Gismonda hadn't a clue, so Scarpone was left to take the question up with the pathologist. "I have no idea what you men are saying about me behind my back," Cavalcanti said, initially ignoring his question. "I'm no hick, but I can't profess to be an armchair zoologist, either."

"Where are you from?"

"Perugia."

"Beautiful city. You must miss it."

He knew that there was no quicker way to anyone's heart than telling them how much you adored their city. The woman smiled and told him a few things about herself. She in fact tried to go home every weekend to see her family, her fiancé, and her beloved school chums. It was only about an hour from Orvieto, if you did it right.

The pathologist was an easy read. I glimpsed her heart as easily as the grass, the sun, the corpse itself. She avoided telling my captain other things.

Like how her boyfriend often came on Fridays to visit for the weekend, and though she enjoyed having him, she resented how he wasted their time together watching sports on her magnificent flat-screen television.

Like how much she hated being away from home.

Like how she would fly back to Perugia in a second if she could find a decent job which exploited her skills.

Like how she often considered renouncing her profession altogether and working in her uncle's restaurant back home in dear, glorious Perugia.

She said none of these things, which were all in her heart. Instead, she merely said, "Do you know Perugia?"

"I haven't been there in years," he said. "I love the main street. The energy! The street life!"

Scarpone had never set foot in the city in his life.

"Corso Vannucci! Yes, yes exactly. It's the place to be. Ah, but Rome is grander—"

"It's filthy!" he said, saying what everyone expected Romans to say. "I'm glad to be out of it."

This too was a lie.

"No, no, no!" said the woman. "It's glorious. One of the truly great cities of the world!"

He shook his head dramatically, as if trying to put the splendor of Rome out of his mind. "Let me ask you a question, and please—this is not to cast aspersions on your work, which I happen to find exemplary. It's only because I feel we're starting to develop a *buon rapporto*—"

She eyed him hungrily from behind her glasses. "Yes, yes?"

"Did you smell the body?"

"Smell it?"

He nodded. And waited. She was nice looking, her makeup notwithstanding. But he did not know what aroused him more: the stirring presence of female sexuality, or the wonderful feeling that a decent case had finally come his way.

"I...*did*," she admitted.

"Shall I tell you what you smelled?" he asked. "A scent of lavender, used either as a cologne or perhaps a—"

"A body lotion!" she exclaimed. She grabbed his arm in a sudden gesture of intimacy and led him to the corpse, which was now resting under a tarp. She waited for Scarpone to ratchet himself down to his knees, then pointed to the dead man's pale clammy skin.

"You know when you use suntan lotion at the beach? The lotion goes on wet but then dries. Then, what happens? You go in the water and it becomes slimy again. Well, so it is with this. The morning dew left it wet."

"That's why his skin looked white but strangely so," Scarpone said.

"Creamy, even."

"But what is it?"

"I don't know," said Cavalcanti. "But it covers much of his body. I've taken samples."

"Take more. For yourself."

He was thinking that the case would ultimately pass to a provincial coroner or medical examiner, someone he had not yet met and thus did not trust. The evidence would be wrested from Cavalcanti's hands. The only way to protect their turf, to ensure that they would be able to continue their investigation in a timely fashion, would be retain their own stash of certain critical pieces of evidence.

"I'll do exactly that."

He needed to go. "Carry on, Dottoressa. And just so you know: I've ordered some water for us."

"You are too kind!"

As he left, she waved to him as she would to a lover. A new one, not her own.

I am a natural-born bullshit artist, Scarpone told himself as he walked away.

Enzo phoned as he ascended the hill.

"Sir? Calls are pouring in at the station."

"Ah, so young Iucci has managed to figure out the phone system, has he?"

"The mayor and magistrate have called repeatedly. I don't know how people find out about these things so quickly."

Dear Enzo. Why had he not anticipated such a thing?

"They want you to call, sir."

"Do they have my personal mobile number?"

"Apparently not."

"Then why would I call them back?"

He rang off with Enzo to find that Belluzzi was gesturing for him. The traffic appeared to have tapered off.

"Sir? It worked!"

The man's stubble looked as if it had grown two inches since morning. Scarpone pulled off his hat and swabbed his scalp with a handkerchief. His legs were exhausted from trying to find traction in the damp grass.

"Did you hear me, sir?"

"Water!"

His throat felt caked with dust.

The burly man reached for bottled water in his car and handed it over. The liquid tasted warm and stale, but Scarpone gulped it thankfully.

"Grazie."

"Prego."

"Your ruse, sir? It worked. One of these gossipy shits called to say that one of his neighbors has been missing for two days. He went out to the supermarket and never returned. The guy's mother hasn't known what to do. Didn't report it because she's probably illegal. *Capitano,* do you hear me? We have the dead man's name."

Chapter Eight

Arbend Demaci's mother lived in an apartment building in a newer section of the borgo. The pink stucco structure looked freakishly modern at first glance, but proved drab once you entered the courtyard. Scarpone was the first to the mother's door, followed closely by Enzo and a soldier named Puzio, whose childhood on the nation's eastern border had apparently imbued him with a gift for languages.

The Albanian woman was well into her fifties, and dressed carefully in a housedress over what looked like a man's trousers. Like so many of the migrants Scarpone had encountered here, she smelled strongly of woodsmoke, as if she'd spent her morning warming herself around a campfire. She'd been up since well before dawn, and had come home from the fields for lunch.

Puzio's words came out haltingly, as he tried to wrap his tongue around words that did not come easy in any language. He had uttered only half of his sentence when the woman screamed and began beating him with her fists.

Enzo and Scarpone tried to pull her off, but Scarpone was too weak to restrain her effectively. He lost his balance and toppled to the floor. Luckily, D'Orazio, the fat cop, propelled the woman to the couch. She fought him every step of the way.

She sat at the edge of her seat and reached around D'Orazio to grab Puzio in a hysterical bid for more information. Each time Puzio let another morsel of bad news drop from his lips, she flailed against D'Orazio.

Scarpone picked himself off the floor where he'd been thrown and watched.

Remarkably, I knew what he was thinking.

Signora, my heart is with you. Do you hear me? I feel for you, more than you will ever know.

On the balcony, he and Enzo pulled themselves together. "It's the worst news a mother can ever hear," Enzo said in a small voice. His curly hair was a mess. "I've already called the clinician."

The doctor appeared in minutes. Not bothering to remove his hat, he marched into the apartment, reached into his bag, jabbed the woman with a syringe, and massaged the fleshy part of her upper arm until she slid onto the couch.

The apartment filled with people. It was a small space, narrow in spots where it should have been roomy. The remains of the woman's lunch sat on the kitchen table, wrapped in an odiferous shroud of coffee and grease. A small countertop TV blared away. A neighbor came who spoke the woman's tongue, and it was from her that they extracted the bulk of their immediate information. The mother was well known to a number of foremen in the region. Her son may or may not have worked with her. This was murky.

Scarpone wandered back to the bedrooms that sprouted off the eat-in kitchen. The rooms were certainly not spacious, but the son had managed to cram a mattress, a desk, and a good deal of clothing in here. There were music CDs, newspapers, posters, and a mess of electronics.

Something was off.

The sound equipment looked nice. Too nice.

Scarpone's phone throbbed in his pocket. He ignored it and stepped to the closet. Clothes, more clothes. And shoes.

Again, something was off.

He looked at the shoes and tried to think clearly but this was difficult, as a noisome racket was beginning to emanate from the rest of the apartment.

Think. Look and think. What do you see—and not see?

I see shoes. And more shoes. I see a closet of fine dress shoes. I see stylish, ridiculous sneakers and tennis shoes.

I *don't* see work boots.

He stepped back and studied the whole of the closet, then spun slowly around to examine the clothes lying on the floor.

I see nothing resembling work clothes here, he told himself, though I might be mistaken.

The place would have to be searched more carefully, the bedclothes analyzed as carefully as the mattress they had pulled out of the grotto.

Can it be, he wondered, that this migrant mother had done so well for herself that she'd managed to turn her son into the embodiment of one of our own slack-assed teenagers?

The phone rang insistently in his pocket. More noise from the apartment. What the hell is going on? He stepped to the door and poked his head around the corner.

Jesu, more people.

The pathologist, aided by technicians Gismonda and Puzio, was there with her gear. The doctor was writing out a prescription and using exaggerated gestures to communicate with the woman's neighbor. Enzo was on his phone, walking in circles, presumably talking to Iucci back at the station.

Meanwhile, outside the apartment a maddening scene was brewing in the small parking lot that the apartment building shared with the hardware store next door. Customers who wanted to leave the hardware store now found their way blocked by the police vehicles and Puzio's van. Customers wanting to pick up caulk or wall fasteners or a bucket of window plaster before siesta now found their entrance to the parking lot blocked as well. Many had simply double- or triple-parked on the residential street, blocking the police vehicles from pulling out.

Thanks to the mysterious power of small-town gossip, word of the young man's death had spread to the legion of citizens hurrying home for *pranzo*, the afternoon meal. Families now gawked from the balconies of the nearby buildings. Figures paused in doorways. The hardware store employees who had gone out to the parking lot to yell at the cops now openly gaped at the commotion brewing in the upstairs apartment.

Scarpone withdrew into the dead man's bedroom and took the call.

It was Saviano, the public prosecutor. "I know you're busy, but do you have time for a short talk?"

"It'll have to wait."

He clapped his phone shut and stuffed it in his pocket.

As he was shooing people out of the apartment, Scarpone was stopped by the doctor, who handed him a sheet of paper. "Are you in charge? Then you should get this. It's my bill. I would leave it with the patient but these foreigners look for any reason not to pay."

Chapter Nine

Sometime later that afternoon, my Lucia was in the fields with some of her workers. It was a busy time of the season, when the grapes were close to harvesting and every vine on her land had to be touched by human hands. It wasn't work you could leave to just anyone. Even when the migrants knew what they were doing, you had to keep on top of them.

Lucia was inspecting grapes in one of the rows when the light changed. She looked up to find a thin man in uniform standing at the end of her row. His eyes were sunken, his skin almost cadaverous.

He introduced himself and asked if she had a moment. She followed him out of the row of grapes.

She was self-conscious, fussing with her hair and the apron she'd worn all morning.

Watching her, I wondered the cause of her distress, but then I realized: Despite the gossip that was rippling through town, she still didn't know the full outcome of her phone call that morning.

"So, it's true?" she said. "Someone's dead?"

She said this to his back. Scarpone turned to find that she was terribly close to him. His eyes roved over her hair and eyes.

My God, she thought, I am such a beast today.

"I assumed you knew," he said. "You phoned it in, didn't you?"

"Well, yes, but I didn't see him. My man went."

"Yes, I heard that. But I wonder how you knew to send him to look. That can't be obvious." He gestured at the landscape. "The bay trees obscure your view of the adjoining field."

She pointed at the sky. "The birds."

"Ah."

"Who is it? Who is dead?"

Scarpone held up his mobile phone. "I have a photo I'd like you to look at, if you feel up to it. I would be grateful for your assistance."

"A picture of the dead?"

"Yes."

She shuddered. "Let's go inside."

He was grateful to get out of the sun. He'd walked from town after mapping out next steps with his men and the pathologist. Seeing the dead man's mother had jogged something in D'Orazio's mind; he thought he'd be able to locate the dead man's ex-girlfriend.

Some of his men were canvassing neighbors. Scarpone did not expect this operation to yield much, but it would fan the flames of rumor, and maybe something useful would blow their way.

Lucia's kitchen was cool. Magda stood at the sink, washing the boy's face with a washcloth. She attempted to excuse herself and the boy when she saw her mistress return with a carabiniere officer.

"No—please stay," Scarpone said. "Maybe you can help."

He sat and gratefully accepted a glass of water, which he drained in one gulp. Water was the only thing he could drink without troubling his stomach. Some days, it was all he ingested.

His eyes took in the boy, who stood by the sink. A cute boy. Dark hair. Dark eyes. A face that was strangely familiar, though he could not immediately think why.

Scarpone scrolled through the photos on his phone. Undoubtedly, the best image to share was the one in which he'd cropped out the gruesome wound at the man's throat.

He looked at the boy.

"Leonardo, go play," Lucia said.

The boy scampered off.

Scarpone raised the phone at arm's length. Both women flinched. Magda took the phone from his hand, glanced a second, and shook her head no. She did this so effortlessly that Scarpone did not catch on that she could not speak. She handed back the phone and left. Lucia was more deliberately careful.

"It's a terrible photo."

"Take your time."

"I don't know him, but I could be wrong."

He seemed confused by her response.

"If I saw him in life..."

"Ah yes," he said.

"He could be one of the foreigners," she said. "I would know almost anyone else."

Of course she would, he thought.

"I have lived here almost all my life."

Scarpone clicked the phone shut. Her shoulders dropped.

Lucia went to the kitchen counter to wrangle some pastries left over from that morning. She started some coffee, though he insisted several times that he could not stay. But of course, once she had started the coffee, he was obligated to do just that. It would have been rude not to.

She confirmed that this was her land. He asked for the names of everyone in the household, which he wrote carefully in his notebook.

Magda Ognazzi.

Lucia Anderson.

Leonardo Anderson.

Charles Anderson

"Leonardo is your son?"

"That's right."

"Is Signor Anderson at home?"

"No," she said. Then her face crinkled. "He's away on business."

"Do you expect him home this evening?"

"This weekend. He's in the United States. It's complicated. He's American. He comes and goes. We're still trying to sort out his citizenship."

"But your son was born here?"

"The States."

"A pretty international family."

She smiled awkwardly. "My husband and I met when I was studying in a viticulture program in California."

"So you're both growers?"

"In a manner of speaking, yes."

"Ah. But you say you were from here originally. What is your family name?"

"I'm sorry—why are you asking all this?"

"It's customary."

She rose to pour them each a cup of espresso. She took her time pouring and then looking for spoons. Scarpone heard the foreman outside, yelling to some workers. He thought he heard a truck rumbling somewhere. He watched her stare out the kitchen windows for a moment, trying to ascertain what was going on outdoors. She was tall, thin, and strong, and he liked the way her shape looked against the light.

When she came to the table, she said, "Charlie runs an American beverage company. You could drop my vineyard into all of his and it would completely disappear. This land has been in my family for centuries. Just sitting there, you know, the way so many fields do."

"I've never understood that. Wouldn't land be valuable in some way?"

"Grapes are extremely high maintenance. Olives too, especially when you're starting out. Even more so, if you're trying to grow them as organically as possible, the way we do."

"I understand that, and please, I'm just a city man with no experience in these matters at all. But wouldn't these abandoned fields we see around here bring a profit even if their owners planted wheat or corn or even sunflowers? Crops that don't need all that maintenance?"

She waited a bit, probably expecting him to sip his coffee. When he didn't, she drank hers in one long sip and licked her lips. "You'd think that, wouldn't you? But the truth is, these days, everything takes money. Just planting those seeds means hiring a man to plow and sow. And most families can't see spending that money, especially if they no longer depend on the land for a living. So the land stays in the family and it makes nice pictures for the tourists." She paused awkwardly, glancing at his cooling coffee. "This is our second harvest. We planted the first lot of grapes when I moved back from Australia about five years ago."

"Australia too? You've done a world tour in wine."

She blushed. "Well, I'd never been outside the country before that trip. Charlie's program runs through the American growing season, March to September. When I got out, I thought, why not try Australia? You know their summers come during *our* winters."

"So I've heard."

"We'll do our first bottling next year. I hope you'll come to try the first crush of the harvest. The *mosto* is always a harbinger of things to come. Would you like sugar?"

Now it was his turn to be nervous. He had accepted the coffee but had not raised the possibility that he would not drink that coffee. He sat stirring sugar into his cup as she watched him.

"Do you like wine?"

"Yes," he said. "At least, I used to. I'm a little delicate these days. Even coffee—I'm afraid, is not, is not, *correct* for me."

"You're the new marshal, I take it. The man they sent in from Rome? I'm sure I've seen you in town, but who talks anymore?"

He didn't know if she was joking. After all, who *didn't* talk? It was all anyone seemed to do. He raised the cup to his lips and held it there, simply smelling it. The liquid was strong, its blackness so deep that it threw up a scent like licorice.

Once, he would have thought this smell indescribably delicious. Now he wanted to gag, but he fought it off admirably.

In front of them was a plate of leftover breakfast *cornetti*. Plain but smelling strongly of butter. Lucia cut a piece of the nearest one and nibbled on it.

"Those smell good," he said. "Normally they're behind glass. You don't get a chance to smell them until you've bought one."

"These are fresh. The bakery delivers them every morning."

This is something you must understand: Bakeries don't deliver. Or rather, they don't deliver to just anyone. Scarpone had never heard of such a thing.

"You should try one. They're nice, even for an afternoon snack. The ones in the bars? Half the time they're refrigerated for weeks. Or frozen, then heated."

"Yeah," he said. "My guy microwaves them. A lot of them do it, even in Rome."

"You know," she said, "I like Rome."

Ah, the captain thought. She has mastered my own tactic. Suck up to them via their city.

"Do you?" Scarpone said.

She slid one of the cornetti in front of him. Hers was already done. She was saying something about loving to go to Rome with her girlfriends. But now they were scattered and married with children, and those days were gone. She spoke as if she were a woman who was not herself burdened with a business or motherhood.

Scarpone could not say no to the pastry. His lips tasted butter and flaky moist bread. He was not conscious of any repellent odors. He sucked the cornetto down greedily, realizing that he'd skipped breakfast and the lunch Enzo had bought for him.

As he brushed away the crumbs and drained the coffee, he thought: My God, I've just eaten.

"These people," he said, "the migrants. You hire a lot of them?"

"What choice do we have? Our own people are not exactly lining up in droves to work the fields."

"And they come from where?"

"Mine? Everywhere. Croatia. Bosnia. Morocco. Pick a country."

"Russian. I was told the town was predominantly Russian."

"Russian or Romanian. But you—Marshal...*Scarpone,* is it? Marshal, most of the people in our town don't know a damned thing about it. They meet someone with a strange accent and they assume they're Russian. Most of them wouldn't know a Russian if he was staring them in the face."

His coffee was done, and so was hers. He'd eaten and drunk everything all the while listening to her speak. He thought about reaching for another piece...

She saw his eyes glance toward the center of the table.

One cornetto left.

She reached for the knife, cut, and lifted half of the pastry to his face as if to feed it to him. She stopped mid-motion, ashamed.

"I'm so sorry," she said. "My son. You know...you have a baby and then it's like second nature."

He waved her excuse away and popped the rest of the roll in his mouth. It went down without a hitch.

He knew he should go.

"We have several unfinished things on the agenda, Signora."

She looked at him innocently. "Yes?"

"Your land is the closest to where the body was found. I'll need a list of the people who work for you. The list of people who were here this morning when you found the man, and copies of everyone's identity cards and work permits."

She stiffened as she collected the cups and plates.

"You can't possibly think—"

"The body of a man lies dead a few hundred meters from this table, and you think none your people know anything about it? We have to consider it."

She just nodded. Her silence told him that their interview was over.

"I'll need to talk to your man," he said, rising from the table. "The one who found the body."

"Of course. He's the foreman. In the nice jacket."

"One other thing. If *he* saw the body, why did you say it was murder when you phoned it in?"

She shrugged uncomfortably. "I only reported what was said to me."

"Ah." He thanked her as he headed to the door.

She tried to salvage their farewell by offering him another coffee. He declined. A moment later, he was out the door and striding down the gravel road to have a word with the foreman.

From Lucia I sensed nothing but worry. But that worry was too scattered to comprehend. She was worried for herself, her son, her workers, her land. I didn't see the point of lingering.

I hurried out and caught up with my captain. The foreman was congenial but unhelpful. Yes, he had run and found the body. Yes, at the time it was untouched by the carrion birds.

"Why did you think it was murder?"

"Pardon? Oh. Yes, I suppose that's what I said. I don't know, Signore. I know that land and I know it's not often worked. What else could it be when a man is lying out like that, naked, for all the world to see him?"

When you humans talk, I can feel the heat under your skulls, and feel the fogginess in your minds when you're distracted. That's how everyone was that morning—my Lucia, the foreman, my captain.

The captain was most certainly distracted—by the woman, by her stubbornness, and by something else.

She did not give me her surname, he thought. Did she think I wouldn't notice?

Did she think I wouldn't just ask someone in town?

Did she think I am a fool?

Well, of *course*—they *all* think we're fools. Toy soldiers, ineffectual clowns, marching around aimlessly in our colorful costumes.

He left, but not before using his mobile phone to photograph the license plates of all the vehicles in the driveway.

Walking back down the road, he tried to think. The walk out had taken him about forty minutes, about twenty minutes a mile. But his health was not at its best. Arbend Demaci had been a healthy man of twenty-four. If he had walked to the abandoned farmhouse from town, he probably would have done so in a shorter amount of time. But would he have done so?

Scarpone mopped his forehead and paused to catch his breath.

He looked off at the view to his left. At rolling hills and tall trees and the mountains beyond. The sky was red over the Umbrian hills.

God, it was so beautiful.

So beautiful, indeed.

And so alive, he thought. *How can it be that all these things are alive?*

A blue Mercedes whipped past him on the road, honking wildly.

He took a deep breath and kept walking.

Think: if the dead man didn't have a car, then he walked. If he walked, he didn't walk naked. If he drove, he didn't drive naked. So someone had been there. Someone had driven him, or met him, and then taken his possessions.

And okay, say it *was* a completely natural death. Say he *was* bitten by a snake. What the hell was he doing wandering around a field naked?

Who took his vehicle and clothes?

Clearly, there were questions, but instead of getting answers, he was getting bullshit. The conversation with Lucia Anderson reminded him of so many he'd had, both in his line of work and his personal life. In the span of seconds, he and my beautiful Lucia had each displayed intimacy, charm, sensitivity, caring, inquisitiveness, and even a conspiratorial naughtiness—and yet he had learned absolutely nothing. Moreover, he was left with the suspicion that someone—the housekeeper, the foreman, or the padrona herself—had lied to him.

Cazzo, he griped to himself. Balls, balls, balls.

By no small coincidence, the road back to town passed by his apartment house. He needed to get back to the station but he was hoping he'd be able to duck into his apartment for a second to freshen up.

The blue Mercedes which had passed him minutes ago was now idling in the driveway of his landlord's house. A silver-haired gentleman in a dark suit stuck his head out of the driver's side window.

"You've been avoiding us, Matteo."

"If it was so important, Saviano, why didn't you pick me up just now?"

"I figured you needed the exercise." The older man flicked a cigarette to the gravel road. His car radio was still blasting.

"I thought wealthy magistrates had chauffeurs," Scarpone said.

The older man chuckled and put the car into drive. "Are you aware that you mumble to yourself when you're alone? You don't think people notice but it's obvious. Curtail that behavior. It makes you appear insane. Get in."

Chapter Ten

Scarpone sat waiting while the mayor concluded a call with a Milanese dottoressa who was in the region to lead a symposium on the ever-important issue of globalization. The mayor was attending this evening's talk, and was trying to angle a post-meeting date with the dottoressa. Judging from Mayor Cicoria's florid language, Scarpone assumed the woman was attractive.

How many years of my life have been lost to this bullshit? Scarpone wondered. Will I ever get a chance to earn those hours back?

Saviano sat beside him. His skin was heavily lined, a road map carved by nicotine. His hair was gray, lustrous, and leonine. He'd smoked two cigarettes in the car on the short hop to town, and now sat impatiently bouncing an unlit cigarette and lighter on his lap.

"Where are we?" the mayor said finally, clicking his phone shut.

Scarpone made a brief report: "Arbend Demaci. Age twenty-four. Occupation unknown at present. Cause of death, unknown."

"That's it?" said Cicoria. "I heard he was murdered in a field."

The magistrate cleared his throat. A smoker's phlegmy rumble. "I would caution you and anyone with whom you speak about using the word 'murdered.' At this point, all we have is a man dead in a field. We don't know what happened to him. For all we know, he dropped dead of a heart attack. For all we know, he killed himself. Matteo, am I right?"

Scarpone nodded wearily. The old magistrate was correct.

"But would you believe we've already gotten a call from the newspaper?" said Cicoria. "What are we supposed to tell them?"

Under his breath, Scarpone murmured a sentence which contained an obscenity. Cicoria's ears perked up.

"What my friend the good marshal means to say," began the magistrate, "is that for the moment the bulk of the details must, out of necessity, remain confidential."

"But why? People will expect to know. It's a matter of public safety."

The magistrate smiled. He had spent his life mired in other people's embarrassing details, and possessed extraordinary patience.
"Wait a second," said Saviano. "Maybe we should back up and tell you how an investigation is conducted. In essence, until the marshal finds proof that a crime has been committed—"

Oh, my dear God, thought Scarpone, this isn't happening.

He looked at his phone. He'd been away from his men for about two hours. On a day like this, that was not good.

"Demaci?" the mayor said after a bit. "That's not one of our names. Is the dead man a foreigner?"

The word he used was *straniero,* a word that could just as easily mean *foreigner* as *stranger,* even a stranger in one's own country. Scarpone, as much as he was a natural-born citizen of this country, would always be a straniero in Castelpietra.

The magistrate cleared his throat and chuckled slightly. "Well, technically, he *was* a foreigner. He's dead."

The mayor still seemed to be struggling with an unknown fact. "An illegal alien? One of the *clandestini*?"

"It's too early to know what his status was," Scarpone said quietly. He was half-hoping that inconclusive answers would bore Cicoria and end the meeting.

"The town's full of them!" the mayor went on. "They come out of nowhere. Like dogs. Or rats. Was he Russian?"

"Albanian."

"Even *worse,*" said the mayor ruefully. He swiveled his head to look squarely at the old lawyer. "Did you know this?"

The magistrate shook his head.

The mayor tossed a pen on the desk and adjusted his seat to lean back more comfortably. "Shit. I thought it was one of ours. An *Albanian*? Why didn't you say so? It's not our problem, then, is it?"

"He still died in our country," said Scarpone. "Call me crazy, but we're still somewhat obligated to look into the cause of death."

"Yes, of course. Certainly. *Absolutely*. But it doesn't have to be a long investigation, does it? Isn't it a well-known fact that a lot of them are mixed up in crime? They kill each other half the time."

Scarpone stood up. "You know, I should get back. This is not a productive use of my—"

The mayor gestured toward the door. "Go," he said earnestly. "Wrap it up, by all means. My concern was that this would somehow interfere with the pageant this weekend. But if it's not one of ours..." He paused, searching for the right words.

The village's annual festival was in honor of the Assumption of the Virgin Mother. Because that feast day came in the midst of the summer holiday, the pageant and festival were always celebrated on the first weekend in September, when people were sure to be back from vacation.

Scarpone spent a few minutes trying to clarify that he could in no way predict when his investigation would conclude. This triggered one of the mayor's signature philosophical discourses. "I respect that," he said, tilting his head to stare at the ornate but crumbling ceiling. "But aren't investigations guided in part by the will of the people? By the desires of the populace? The tax-paying populace? And is anyone going to care if another Albanian is dead? God forgive me for saying so, but with resources scarce, a man in my position must say what others don't have the courage to say. Am I right?"

Scarpone shot a look at the magistrate: *Get me out of here.*

The old man pulled himself up out of his chair. Except for his white shirt, he was dressed entirely in black, down to his thin necktie, luxurious jacket, and silk scarf. He reached behind his chair for an ebony cane that was topped with an eagle's face, which looked much like his own.

"We understand you clearly, Signor Mayor," said the magistrate. "Your wish, your greatest desire, would be for a speedy investigation."

"Grazie, *Avvocato*," the mayor said, bowing his head slightly from behind his chair.

"I suppose it's too late for the pageant. But you know what a thing like this can do to a town? It scares off tourists. Paralyzes the industry. And in a global economy we cannot afford—"

"So right, Signor Mayor," said the old lawyer.

"You are most kind."

The mayor gathered up some papers for his next meeting. Some pressing matters to discuss with the village's civil engineers about the extension of the local aqueduct.

He waved to them both as he headed out to the hall: "I'll wait for your reports, then, Marshal? Text me? Okay, grazie, ciao. Ciao!"

The old lawyer leaned heavily on his cane, as if the act of standing was painful. He watched the leader of their borgo disappear, and waited a second or two before shaking his head.

"What an ass. I need a cigarette. Let's take the elevator."

Chapter Eleven

Enzo phoned as they were riding down.

"Sir? I've examined the dead man's documents. They appear to be in good order. A bonafide work permit. The mother's too."

"So they're not illegals, then?"

"No, but Iucci's calling Viterbo to confirm. But it's probably already near closing time. If that office is not open tomorrow, we'll have to do it Monday."

The door of the city hall opened onto the town's largest and, some would argue, only piazza. There was nothing picturesque about this communal space, a fact many citizens lamented. There were no cafes decorating its edges. No elegant or festive shops. No breath-taking tourist attractions. It was nothing more than a sea of asphalt used as a glorified municipal parking lot. A small park on one side of the square was always filled with old men taking in the view from the promontory.

"The medical examiner will see us tomorrow," Enzo said. "I can go with you and the dottoressa, if you like."

"Good."

"But I'll need to leave early, tonight and the rest of the weekend. Church affairs, sir."

Enzo's religious piety was not normal in a man his age. For the few weeks Scarpone had been here, Enzo's position as a deacon in the church had never complicated the station's schedule. But they'd never had an unexplained death before. Scarpone knew it was the festival weekend, but Enzo and his young wife didn't even live in Castelpietra. Yet he had somehow burrowed his way into church affairs here.

"Any word on the dead man's girlfriend?"

"She hasn't bothered with him in months, sir."

"*Months?* How can she be called his girlfriend, then?"

"Former girlfriend. It's complicated, sir."

"In what sense?"

"She's about six months along, sir. Demaci is the father."

Scarpone hung up.

The magistrate had leaned against a stone wall that looked east to Apennines and lit his cigarette. The drop behind him was a good ninety meters to the farmland and road below. He nodded a chin at the men across the piazza and observed, "All my life I've watched old men congregate in that park. My grandfather wasted the last two decades of his life there. My father too. By rights, it's my turn, but it is not to be. Why? Because it's the Russians' park now. Or the Romanians'. I don't know which. In the span of one man's life, we've been invaded."

Scarpone had come to like the old man. In just a few weeks they'd worked together on three increasingly banal cases. An adolescent shoplifter. An errant husband. A case of public lewdness and drunkenness. And now this.

"Something has been on my mind," Scarpone said. "Something one of my men said today. You worked cases with my predecessor, Vitellone, didn't you?"

"Who else would have?"

"Have there been some cases recently of drug deaths? Children dying of overdoses?"

Saviano picked a bit of tobacco from his lips and flicked it. "This is true. But they weren't children. At least, not what *I* call children. Teenagers. Just at the tail end of their schooling."

"But deaths?"

"Yes, overdoses. Heroin, if I'm not mistaken."

"How many?"

"Four or five."

"Four or five!"

"Does that figure alarm you?"

"Jesu, Saviano, I thought you were going to say one, maybe two. Five is an epidemic."

"You haven't been looking at the figures for the region. Per capita, yes, it's high. But we're lucky compared to some of the other cities. They've turned into slums. At least we still have a decent community here. People still work here. But this is the past. The case before you has nothing to do with drugs. And the young man in question is nearly a decade older than the boys who died."

"Can we speak frankly here a second?" Scarpone asked him. "What do you expect me to do in this case?"

"Go where it takes you. I'm not as big an idiot as our friend the mayor. But I am a nationalistic fool. A patriot. I love this country and I'm befuddled by what's become of it. But I do appreciate something most people don't."

"Which is what?"

"We bitch and moan about these people invading our towns and villages, but we ignore the facts. *We* brought them here. We need *them*. We live off them. We eat because of them. And we grow fat and lazy because of them. Whoever thinks the ancient Romans are dead and gone is lying to himself. For this reason, I think we have to be mindful that we don't offend the *stranieri*. There's a fine line being walked here. Do you receive my meaning? We can't have them thinking that this is an unsafe borgo to settle down in. If they get that impression, God help us. They'll go elsewhere and our food will rot in the fields and orchards. Our bank accounts will be bare, our businesses bankrupt, our apartment rentals empty. And we'll starve. You and I, we must practice strict justice on both sides. You get me? Otherwise, we are showing favoritism."

Scarpone nodded.

The magistrate had just one other question: "Do we know yet if it's murder?"

Scarpone shrugged. "All we know is that it's weird."

Chapter Twelve

A town like this is deathly still at night, except for the trains. The northbound tracks sit on the western side of the Little Tiber River, which leads all the way down to Rome and which the people call the Teverina.

The Teverina's position at the side of the tracks means that the nighttime occupants of Florence-bound trains can glimpse the moon in the water as they snake their way north.

That night I watched my captain fritter away his time in bed. In the manner of all insomniacs, he lay in bed as long as possible, because he could not give up hope that he might at last fall asleep. It was not to be. So he sat up, pulled on the red-framed reading glasses that did not fit him well, and flipped open the case files he'd asked Enzo to pull.

Three years ago:

Egidio Tubecchi, 16, deceased, heroin overdose. Son of Maddalena and Eusebio, brother of Lorenzo, 12 years old.

Five months later:

Gabrielle Santello, 17, deceased, heroin overdose. Son of Arianna and Fulvio, brother of Gisella, 8.

Two months later:

Luca Dancione, 17, deceased, alcohol/heroin overdose. Only son of Gianna and Carmine.

Jesu Cristo! Okay, the town had problems. But how do you ignore a problem this big and move on with your life?

He tossed those files aside and flipped through photocopies Iucci had made of documents Scarpone had requested in the course of the day. Here was the sheaf containing identity cards. His eyes scanned the list of dates of birth and the countries of origin. *Lucia Anderson, 18/07/79. Magda Ognazzi, 09/08/60. Leonardo Anderson, 11/09/07.* And Lucia's foreman, *Enrico Timpone, 06/02/53.* All but the child had been born here. The rest of the names—a long, exhausting pile—were of foreign-born farm workers in Lucia's employ.

Scarpone stared at the ceiling for a while. Then tossed the pile aside. He began walking around the apartment. He resisted turning on the lights, hoping that the darkness would eventually lull him to sleep.

There was a television in the second bedroom, but he never bothered to use it on nights such as this. He didn't want to risk waking his landlord's family.

Unmarried carabinieri lived in barracks at the station. My captain rented a furnished apartment in a cinderblock farmhouse on the Orvietana, just at the bend in the road, where it reached town. The house, once rustic and beautiful, had been restored in the last twenty years to achieve utter ugliness. It was divided into three apartments. Scarpone rented the one above his landlord's. The other whole half of the house was occupied by the landlord's daughter and her family.

A crushed stone courtyard occupied the front of the property, from which grew a dozen or so spiky artichoke plants. The landlord had once worked as a farmer. Scarpone couldn't remember who had told him this. Though everyone in town, down to the last man, woman, and child, was a professional gossip, no one ever tattled on their neighbors so completely that you knew the whole of their history. Odd bits of information were always missing. Scarpone was constantly recalibrating his local knowledge in light of fresh details. For example: The landlord's house sat on a bluff overlooking a crowded, dirty farmyard and a barn filled with animals. Scarpone had been living in the borgo two weeks before he figured out that the landlord's son worked the farm.

For a while, he busied himself pasting his newspaper clippings into his scrapbook. When he was finished, his hands were still restless. He tore the newspaper scraps and began fashioning them into small paper structures. He folded furiously for a while, then rose to snag some yellow cellophane tape from the kitchen. He used the tape to mortar the corner of his paper building.

Where had he been today? The abandoned farmhouse. The dead man's apartment house. The city hall. One by one, he fashioned them all, while a feeling he could not identify chewed away at his insides. There was something still...unfinished. He carried the paper houses out to the living room, and placed them on the floor between the two sofas. He liked to think of the couch on the eastern wall as the hills of Umbria. The western couch was the hills of Lazio. In between, the big shag carpet was the valley of the Tiber.

He congratulated himself on a couple of things: The river was a thin strip of plastic he'd cut off a six-pack of mineral water bottles. The train tracks were pretzel sticks. *There* was the defunct train station. *There* was the four-lane bridge that would someday link Umbria and Lazio together at the plains on the south side of town. People spoke of the bridge incessantly, claiming that it would siphon tourists out of Umbria and into Lazio. As far as Scarpone could tell, his own model was closer to being finished than the real bridge.

On the Orvieto side, he'd built the traffic circle in the center of the main drag. He'd built a train station. And he'd used an empty cigarette box, suspended from a clothesline, to stand in for the funicular that took tourists up the hill to Orvieto and back. His diorama was only a few weeks old, but he thought it a thing of beauty.

Later, he opened the double doors to inspect the plants on his balcony. Of the eighteen, only two were still alive. He swatted them. "I condemn you," he whispered. He noted the time. It had taken the sixteen plants only two days to die. He would check the remaining two tomorrow night.

Then he stepped back inside.

It pains me to tell you that such endeavors occupied Scarpone in those nighttime hours. I fear that you will judge him as harshly as he judged himself. You see, while the nighttime man was proud of these creations and experiments, the daytime man, Scarpone the cop, found them embarrassing.

The two souls of this man ran on separate tracks, like the Milan- and Naples-bound trains.

Thankfully, there always came a time when the trains outside his rooms quieted and the moon rolled upwards and out of his window. The owls hushed themselves and the tile floor grew cold. The chill ran up Scarpone's legs and arms, and came to rest at the back of his neck.

It was night. He was cold and alone in a city that was not his home. When that moment came, he crept back into bed, pulled off the red glasses, and lay down to sleep.

As he was drifting off, he remembered that he had not built Lucia Anderson's house. Maybe tomorrow night. The taste of her cornetto was on his lips. This pastry had been the only thing he'd eaten that day, and it had not come up.

The alarm was set to wake him in just another hour. This was fine, even preferable, for one good reason: he did not have to dream.

Chapter Thirteen

The medical examiner studied the body intently as the pathologist finished her summation. The older man murmured his approval, stopping occasionally to give what seemed like a delighted exclamation. "Excellent, excellent work, Dottoressa," he kept saying. But his body language suggested that he wished she'd shut up.

Was he impatient? Or was he threatened by the presence of this obviously educated young woman? Scarpone couldn't decide.

A night's rest seemed to have done the corpse good. Its skin had acquired a peaceful, bluish tone, except for the centers of the welts that rose violently from his flesh.

"*Allora,*" the man said at long last. "Let's unwrap the present, shall we?"

He revved the bone saw theatrically and went to work. When the dead man's skull popped, Enzo handed his notepad to Scarpone and fled the room.

Scarpone caught up with him an hour or so later outside headquarters in Viterbo, the provincial seat. The younger man sat on a bench in front of a fountain. Before moving to the region, Scarpone had never been to Viterbo. It was a city of hot spring baths, shopping malls, and antique shops. A playground of the ancient popes, a city of pale stone churches built by the northern people who'd ground the

Romans to dust. Pale, elongated faces of the dead Visigoths lurked in the architecture.

A number of cops milled around, smoking, chatting on mobile phones, joking with each other, either in the piazza itself or in the alley leading to the loading dock where they had taken the body inside.

"I know I'm supposed to be okay with it, but I'm not," Enzo said peevishly. "It's the most ghoulish—the most sacrilegious thing I've ever seen."

Scarpone said some words of consolation, but Enzo wasn't listening.

"I don't *want* to get used to it. Not ever. It's wrong. It's barbaric."

"Not to him. He's dead."

"I was trained in accounting. This is not my forte. This is not what I signed on for. A good person, a decent person, would not stand for..."

He drifted off without finishing, and did not meet Scarpone's gaze.

"Look, Enzo. If I may: the case files you pulled for me. Did you work those cases?"

The young man seemed perplexed by the sudden shift in conversation. "Why, yes. But they weren't major investigations, you understand. The deaths occurred over the span of three years. I was fairly new here myself. Marshal Vitellone knew the families and knew what he was doing. Each time, we looked into the source of the drugs but it was obvious that they were coming from outside the borgo."

"How did you ascertain that?"

"I don't recall. For some time now there's been a brisk trade on the school grounds. That's why we run so many patrols through that area during the school year. You know that road between the two secondary schools, where parents drop off the kids?"

Scarpone knew it. The brick walls of the two schools were festooned with graffiti. The older kids parked their scooters along the exterior wall of the middle school and used the broad stairwell as a hangout, even at night.

"Where do the drugs come from? Here in Viterbo?"

"Typically, yes. It's a big city, and there are lots of highways and foreigners. Montefiascone, too, I've heard. But we never got lucky intercepting any. Then again, we can't just stop anyone we like on the road. There are some nightclubs farther south, way past where they're building the bridge, where drugs are known to be sold."

Scarpone grasped the problem, though he didn't know how to put it into words. The best tips on drug rings came from insiders or users you leaned on. As the borgo became more and more filled with foreigners, that street-level knowledge was becoming increasingly walled up behind an impenetrable language barrier. Foreign-born kids distrusted cops more than the local kids did.

A shadow fell over where they sat. A young recruit was there. The head of the provincial command wished to have a word with Scarpone. The *commandante* was dining in a small eatery just off the piazza. If the captain would be good enough to follow—

It was impossible to say no. But it was inconvenient. Scarpone's men were his only ride back to the borgo. It wouldn't be kind to have them wait. Not on a Friday. Enzo spoke up: "Go—I'll wait. Belluzzi can take the dottoressa back to Orvieto. I can drive you when you're done."

Scarpone insisted no. He knew Enzo had rehearsal that night for tomorrow's pageant. "I can take the bus back."

"Sir, with respect, the bus is a bullshit ride. It'll take you a minimum of two hours to get back."

"I don't know how long I'll be."

"Sir?" wheedled the recruit. "He's right this way."

Chapter Fourteen

I watched Scarpone thread his way to the back between a long bar and a smattering of tables. He passed a low table that bore the remains of the day's grilled vegetables: sliced eggplant and red peppers submerged in a garlicky, golden bath of olive oil. The walls of the restaurant were covered with junk—mismatched oil paintings, water-stained etchings and photographs, faux armor and weaponry, flecked mirrors in various frames. Some of the shelves above the tables held books that no one had touched in years.

The place was empty except for a bored hostess who ignored Scarpone when he walked in, and a burly man in uniform who sat at a table in the rear, just to the left of the kitchen door. He had blunt features, hair swept back revealing a widow's peak, and a massive forehead studded with clogged, blackened pores. Scarpone had to wonder if the man had once boxed. His nose was as docked as a show dog's tail.

Wielding a fork, the man was laying waste to an au gratin dish filled with a blisteringly hot dish of crepe-like pasta drenched in a cheesy white sauce.

"Ah," said the commandante. "At last I have the honor of addressing Matteo Scarpone. Or is it the great Scarpone?"

Scarpone expected a laugh to follow, but one did not. Nor did an invitation to sit. The man prattled on, oily sarcasm creeping into his voice.

"Which is it, then? Scarpone, or the great Scarpone? Perhaps, 'Scarpone Grande, Pride of Rome's Force'? Our meeting has been long delayed, though through no fault of my own. Too much going on at your station, I gather?"

"We've had an unusual death," said Scarpone.

"Yes—but that's two days old, at the most. I'm referring to the weeks prior to this moment in which I have not had the pleasure of making your acquaintance, nor the presentation of your documents. Oh, I know it's a formality these days, but when I joined the force we observed the niceties. One hand washed the other. A soldier came to introduce himself and pay his respects. That station of yours may be small, but it's a plum prize. A just reward for a soldier returning home from the field. That's the way it's always been. A prize for returning Viterbo or Bagnoregio men. In all cases, men from the great region of Lazio. And my command has always selected these men. Until now. Is this a glimpse of the future, do you think?"

"I'm sure I don't follow, sir."

"Playing dumb does not become you. You have your concerns and I have mine." He held up his fork. "Look where I am: I'm backed into a corner here, way up in the sticks. Ask anyone who lives in Lazio outside of Rome what the real political and financial problems are, and straightaway they will tell you: Rome takes all the money. That bridge in your neck of the woods? Why do you think it's taken six years to complete? The Teverina is not wide at that point. A bridge there would be close to the A1 highway. You wouldn't need to get off in Orvieto and double back 14 kilometers. Such a bridge in the flatlands there would be advantageous, and bring prosperity to your borgo. But why is it being finished now, in 2012, instead of 2006? The answer is plain: the arrogance of Rome. So I guess I shouldn't be irate that the bosses in Rome would ignore my advice before naming their man."

He brought a fist down on the table so heavily that it jolted the tableware. A waiter appeared with a plate of three nicely browned sausages. Commandante Rombelli speared one with his fork and bit the end thoughtfully. The interior of the link was violent pink.

"Me, I have to interpret what this means. Is this a sign that Rome will now presume to dictate to Viterbo? Is that it? Will Viterbo no longer have any say in the governance of her affairs?"

Scarpone shifted his weight. "Sir? May I speak? If it's any consolation, I wasn't even conscious when the decision was made."

Indeed, the bosses had ruled while he was still lying unconscious in a bed at Salvador Mundi Hospital. No one had bothered to tell him for weeks after that. In fact, during his convalescence at home, when he was trying to teach himself how to walk again with his injured hip and patched abdomen, some lackey had been instructed to clean out his office and box up his possessions. His promotion had been postponed indefinitely, pending an investigation of the events in Termini and the shooting just outside the Vatican walls. Scarpone was to be ushered out of the city, reassigned as far as they could send a man and still have him be within their immediate jurisdiction.

"I know all about that," sniffed Rombelli. "You may think that by coming here you have escaped an embarrassing past, but you forget something. These small towns that you Romans despise are incubators of intelligence. If I want to know anything about anyone, I have only to ask. I am a Viterbo man. This is my country, and you are a straniero, Roman."

He seemed satisfied with his speech. He munched on his sausage, and for a while the air was filled with the sound of crunching skin and squirting fatty juices. When he finally spoke, it was as if a new man had arrived.

"So what was the coroner's finding?"

"That's pending the toxicology report. He's leaning toward accidental death but I think I can persuade him to see the complexity of the case."

"Of course," said Rombelli, nodding and chewing. "How disappointing that would be for the great Scarpone to preside over just another case of accidental death. How dull. How uninteresting."

"I don't want to go into it right now, but there are certain features of the case that are too weird and too curious—"

"Hah! I was warned of this," said Rombelli, chiding him with his forkful of speared meat. "Is this the trademark of the great investigator? Clinging desperately to that which isn't there? Seeing conspiracy around every corner?"

Rombelli had a good laugh. Sipped his wine. Impaled his second sausage. Wiped the lingering cream and cheese from his lips with a napkin.

"Would you care to sit?"

"No, sir. I'll stand."

"Stand then, and understand this. You've seen our lab. Our fine facilities. They are paid for with Viterbo euros. Isn't it enough that the natural-born citizens of our nation must subsidize the care of these clandestini in our hospitals, schools, and prisons? You won't get much more from Viterbo, Roman. I sincerely doubt that the case before you will propel you to greater fame. It's just another stupid, dead migrant. Your job is to close it and move on. *Basta. Finito. Chiuso.*" He paused. His mean eyes slid down the front of Scarpone's uniform. "Are you sure you will not stop to dine?"

A few minutes later, Scarpone was stalking across the piazza past the fountain, hoping to clear the smell of sausage from his nostrils. The bus back to the borgo hardly settled his stomach; it stank of the fish some of the passengers were taking home for their Friday meal.

He watched the landscape pass by the window. For some reason, he thought of Anna.

Though he probably didn't know it, his lips were mumbling to themselves.

Chapter Fifteen

They do this every week. The young Nigerian girl waits for him on Bernini's bridge of angels. Waits in a bright green print dress, the only one she has. She carries a purse, though nothing in it could be construed as a personal possession of hers. She carries nothing but the tools of her trade: condoms, some tissues, some lubricants. She crosses the bridge, keeping an eye out for the cops who patrol the tourist areas. Prostitution is not illegal in their country, so long as the woman is over the legal age. But it *is* illegal to solicit on the streets, or to hire a woman off them.

He is dressed in civilian clothes. They established this routine long ago. No uniforms. At all costs, she cannot afford to arouse the suspicions of the men who own her. There is no question what would happen to her if they found out.

He steps onto the bridge and waits under the angel with the crown of thorns.

Then Anna walks briskly off the bridge into the heart of the city. At the end of the bridge, she turns right and disappears into the rabbit's warren of old stucco buildings.

She does not pay for the room. She merely enters, nods to the man who sits behind the mesh screen grille in an office smelling of ass sweat and boredom.

She nods and goes to wait on the staircase.

Scarpone feeds some bills through the grille. The clerk passes him a key. Scarpone slips him a few additional euros because that's just what is expected. Not too much, not too little, enough to make the man forget him.

He rides the elevator up. She is already by the door. He lets her in. She rushes first to the bathroom, closes and locks the door. The room is dreary, just enough room for a bed, a television, and a set of low cubicles that is supposed to function as desk, bureau, and TV stand.

On the bed he lays a newsprint pad and some charcoal drawing sticks. Some Conte crayons, if he has them. He does not touch the bedspread. Force of habit. Too many years of his mother telling him not to touch filthy things in public places. This place feels like a bathroom in Termini Station.

He perches uncomfortably on the cubicles and listens to the water run in the bathroom. She needs this. It's her only time to wash. Wherever her captors keep her and the other eleven women, they have only a cold water hose to share among them.

He sits and thinks.

The day she first approached him, he was talking to some officers just outside the Vatican walls. A black woman barely out of her teens stepped up to them and said in a perfect accent, "Arrest me, please. I have no documents."

The other cops laughed. Ignored her. Averted their gazes so as not to meet her gaze. Returned to their cigarettes.

Scarpone watched her wander off, guilt scoring his heart.

It's a pain in the ass, one of other cops said. We arrest them and fill out the paperwork and they let them out again, so what is the point? No one cares. Why should they? They're not our people. Not our women. They're nothing.

Scarpone followed her.

Not here, she said, when he approached. Wait. I'll go around the corner.

She stepped into an alley not far from where the tourists queued for the Vatican Museums. He waited outside the alley and listened to her instructions from the shadows.

It wasn't until two days later, when he followed her to the hotel for the first time, that he learned the details.

Twelve women, four young men, and a series of bosses. The big man coming in once a month to take the money.

She couldn't tell him how much. She didn't know figures. She didn't know euros. She knew that her street name was Anna. He knew that he couldn't properly pronounce her real name.

The men holding her were Nigerian, her fellow countrymen. She was sold to them by her uncle. She knew the coffee place in Rome where they took most of their meals. She knew this because they sometimes took one of the girls with them to help them carry back the coffee and panini.

The women are black?

Yes, she said. Most of us are Nigerian. One girl from Ghana. Another from Cameroon.

Leaving the hotel that first day, he knew that if they arrested the men, proving wrongdoing would be difficult without the money.

They would need the money.

They would need the big man.

And even if they nabbed him, he would never talk. Surely he was controlled by the Neapolitans. Or maybe the Calabrians.

Can you describe them? he asked her.

I can show you, she said.

She gestured for a pen and his notebook.

Each time since then, she steps into the room after showering and smells like hotel soap. Her hair and body are still wet and she has merely pulled her shift dress over herself. It sticks to her body.

It makes him uncomfortable to be alone with a woman like this. He has not been with a woman in a year, though I cannot see why.

He gestures to the art supplies.

She smiles at this luxury. She takes up the charcoal, and for several minutes her fingers move as if channeled by God. The charcoal moves with precision. Scratch scratch scratch across the paper.

A skull, nose, chin, jaw, eyes emerge from nowhere.

It's the face of a black man with a tiny mole under his right lip. A beautiful, unerring sketch.

Over several visits to the cheap hotel, she does this again and again, building for the young captain a collection so precious that he must lock it in his supervisor's safe.

She gives him street names. She draws the men's hands holding keychains, weapons, notes. She draws their Fiats and *motorini*.

She draws the facade of the building where she stays each night. The building from which she emerges each morning to have sex with Scarpone's countrymen for money.

Her bravery quiets him. His eyes ride her charcoal as it skims across newsprint.

They do this every week.

Slowly she is giving him the building blocks of his case. In a month's time, the big man will come. And if his supervisor's patience and discretionary funds have not run out, and the magistrate is true to his word, Scarpone will have enough to justify a raid.

Keep trying, he whispers. Keep drawing.

The girl smiles. Her teeth are white. Scarpone doesn't know how she can keep them so clean. She sleeps on a thin mattress somewhere underground every night. He cannot imagine such a thing.

All she wants is a better life. To see her family again, her homeland, her mother's face, her village.

He craves many of the same things.

This is what his heart tells me. Try as I might, I know no more than that.

Chapter Sixteen

Bad night. Bad night again.

And when morning came, Scarpone sat at his kitchen table, holding a blanket across his chest as a hulking man traipsed through his kitchen with a trio of pale-orange plastic bags slung over his shoulder.

"Do you have light?" ranted Rolando. "Do you even know the meaning of the word illumination? Has your soul even been touched by the sun? Jesu, *there's* the switch—"

Light blinded them both. Scarpone, caught under the glare of the kitchen lamp, rocked back in his chair and regarded his visitor. Rolando was a brute of a man clad in faded denim.

It was impossible to say what color his jeans were, whether blue or black, because every inch of his clothes, not to mention every ringlet on his shaggy head and beard, seemed coated with a fine gray powder.

Stone dust caked the stitches of his garments, the undersides of his fingernails, the creases of his finger joints, and the lines around his eyes. Scarpone knew his friend was precisely the same age as himself, but Rolando had seemed to have gone gray decades before. Was it age or marble dust? Scarpone wasn't sure.

"You look like one of those peddlers we used to pick up around the Lungotevere in the mornings," Scarpone said. "All you need are some knockoff handbags and a piece of cheese."

Rolando grinned broadly. "I have cheese! Thus, I qualify! Is there a light over the sink? Where are the lights in this place? What kind of thief are you renting from? Has he conspired to leave us in the dark? What are we, Etruscan cave-dogs?"

He stooped, packages and all, under the valance above the sink. "A light switch. *Grazie dio!*"

He hit the switch.

"*Ecce lucem*, cockhead!"

"How did you get in here?"

"That fat swine you call a landlord let me in. I told him I was your brother."

Of course. Rolando had used that line for thirty-odd years, whenever it suited him. They were *like* brothers, having grown up in the same alley. Rolando's family was always a window away, a door away. At night the two boys had conversed by shouting across Vicolo del Cinque. They were rats of Rome, inseparable *amici*.

"You know, you should speak to him about this flagrant breach of your security. Next thing you know, a stranger will say he's your long-lost uncle and murder you in your bed. I gave him an orange. He was grateful. His daughter, however, regarded me with suspicion."

"It's seven in the morning!"

"She's probably an idiot. Which of these is the goddamned *frigo?*"

He was trying cabinet doors. As was typical, the kitchen was designed to conceal the refrigerator, to disappear it into a seamless bank of cabinets, as if it were shameful possession that needed to be ensconced behind more pleasing panels of laminated wood. Rolando found the fridge and pumped the air with victory. He dumped his parcels on the kitchen table and began hauling out vaguely perfumed items wrapped in plastic or gaily decorated waxed paper.

"What is all this?"

"This?" Rolando said. "*This* is an orange, you goose. And this? This is another."

"But who is open at this hour?"

"Are you blind? Do you know nothing? Are you aware that your newly adopted piazza is the site of a Saturday market? They were just setting up. It's no great shakes—just a greengrocer, a salami truck, and a tent selling women's underpants. Nothing to write home about, you understand, but the food's fresh, and good. The fish truck comes Wednesdays. You should look into it." He rolled the oranges between his fingers. "These blood oranges? They are your breakfast!"

"You go ahead. I'm not hungry."

"Bullshit. They're beautiful. When I saw these two babies in the market, I knew I must have them. Here, let me slice them up. Where are the plates in this house? Jesu, why must everything be a labyrinthine search in this place? Am I Theseus? Throw me a thread here. A dish, a knife, where are they? Oh. Here. Make room, will you?"

He slid aside the shopping bag.

"Okay, tell me the truth," said Rolando. "Have you gone through their things yet? Any depraved memorabilia lying around? I could never rent my furnished apartment to anyone. Too many filthy secrets. Here—Sicilian blood oranges. What else is there to eat on a foggy morning like this? With each bite you are chewing the ass of the sun."

"I told you. I'm not hungry. Maybe we could just go for some coffee."

Rolando's hairy head was ducked under the low kitchen lamp. With his yellow, tobacco-stained teeth and wild eyes, he looked like a male Medusa. He slapped a callused palm on the table and snarled, "Eat, cockhead, or I will slap *you*!"

Scarpone raised a slice to his lips. The fruit dripped an obscenely red juice from plate to mouth. It had been a long time since he'd eaten one. As children they used to go wild for these precious fruit, waiting for the Befana—a jolly hag—to bring them each an orange on the Feast of the Epiphany. Back then, the first taste was always a shock. You expected something so beautiful to be sweet, and it was, but it lashed you first with bitterness to see if you were worthy. Scarpone lapped at the juices. His tongue puckered at the astringency. It was cleansing. He nibbled at the tiny raindrops of flesh.

"Mmm."

Rolando nodded. "*Buono.*"

"Remind me why you are here."

"You invited me to the festival, which I thought a beautiful gesture. By the way, I have something for you." He dug in his pocket and slapped a roll of euros on the table. "The American girl pays your rent early, so now we have spending money for our adventures."

"Keep half. You might need to spend it when the heater goes or the toilet overflows."

"So that's what I am to you? A handyman? A rooter of people's filth? I am an artist, Matteo!"

Yet he snatched the wad of cash and stuffed in his pocket.

The fire went out of his eyes and he returned to unpacking, calmly detailing his every move since they had last seen each other a few months ago, just before Scarpone left for the borgo.

Rolando had gotten in last night from St. Petersburg—a cold place, a miserable hellhole, as beautiful and cold as its women—where he had gone to consult on some pieces in the former Kremlin apartments. A renovation job. Very lucrative, as they had plans to eventually open the rooms to tourists. They would spare no expense. Rolando's Russian was pathetic, but he had managed to get by. The food was sickening, though. Every meal seemed to consist of grease slathered on slices of brown bread. He thought he would die. The plane back was choppy and nauseating, with nothing but vodka to sustain him.

Great, thought Scarpone, he's been inebriated for twenty-four hours. When Rolando hit the tarmac at Fiumicino at midnight, Alana had been there to meet him, their two toddlers in tow. Exhausted, his bowels roiling, vodka on his breath, he nevertheless stuffed the entire family into the aging Ford and shot up the Via Cassia to lower Lazio where Rolando kept the larger of his two mosaic studios, quartered in the animal stalls of an old farmhouse. His family had been sleeping soundly when the great genius headed north to Scarpone.

Of all the people Scarpone had told of his impending move up north, Rolando was the only one who didn't sneer, who had in fact applauded the move. He had been coming north for decades to get out of the city. Marrying Alana had helped, of course. Nowadays most of his commissions were completed on the grounds of her family's old property, ten steps from his mother-in-law's house.

"Country life will do you good, if you let it," the madman had said. "Just think: We can see each other all the time."

Scarpone had rolled his eyes, mostly for show, as if the thought were appalling. But here they were.

"What is wrong with this refrigerator?" Rolando roared. "He screwed you on this, didn't he? Probably switched his own piece of shit fridge for this one the day before you took residence. I'll fix him. What a rip-off! Look, it doesn't work! Do you see what thieves men can be? Pig of a Madonna! You want to be good man, but how can you with these thieves abounding—"

He froze.

His glance was locked on the kitchen floor. He ratcheted his head to stare at Scarpone, who was helping himself to another slice of fruit.

"It's not plugged in?"

Scarpone looked. A shabby electric plug snaked from behind the cabinets to lie on the linoleum.

"It was like that when I got here," Scarpone protested. "I haven't had time."

Rolando shook his head, and rolled his eyes to heaven. "Do you see what I'm dealing with here?" he said to the ceiling. Then to Scarpone: "You make me sick. Okay, let's see."

He pulled himself up to his full height and peeled off his denim jacket. The armpits of his denim shirt were damp with fragrant circles of sweat. He hugged the refrigerator with a loud growl. Scarpone, thinking his friend would burst a testicle, leapt to assist him. But Rolando barked him away. The fridge meekly gave up its post against the wall. Rolando snatched the plug and ducked behind the fridge. A moment later, they heard the familiar comforting hum. Rolando wrestled the frigo back into place, and recommenced filling it with milk, cheese, and delicately wrapped sliced deli meats.

Ironically, in the end, the vast majority of his purchases were left outside the fridge. He placed garlic, onions, and lemons in a bowl in front of Scarpone. The countertop was littered with a selection of tomato cans and a vacuum-packed brick of coffee. The fresh mozzarella he left in a bowl, covered by a cloth napkin. Rolando dutifully scrunched up the plastic bags and stuffed them under the counter. He slammed the cabinet shut, and grabbed a few slices of orange off the table. He munched them loudly, smacked his lips at their tartness, and spat the seeds in the sink.

"My work here is done. Come, get dressed. I must have coffee."

Chapter Seventeen

The borgo was home to a legendary vintner whose offerings had been mentioned in a wine and food guide Rolando lugged around in his Ford. The man's cantina didn't open till later, so Rolando had a few other places in mind.

Like, for example, the wine co-op in lower Orvieto. It looked like a warehouse, which dispensed wine from a gasoline pump into two-liter glass jugs. The selection was limited to four varieties of local wine: two reds (dry or sweet), and two whites (dry or sweet). Rolando bought one jug of each. Then he steered them back south toward the borgo, but stayed on the Umbrian side, where they sampled the wine of a Swiss expat who'd been written up in the guidebooks. His was some of the crispest Orvieto Classico either of the men had ever tasted. His reds were good too, but they went for a ridiculous price.

"But if you don't mind my asking," Scarpone said, "who has the kind of money to spend like this on a bottle?"

"If we weren't on the highway I don't think I'd be able to get away with it," the small, dapper man said. "But in the summer we're inundated with English and Americans and sometimes the Japanese, who come through here on their way to Florence. If they like it, they buy a case."

For a second it seemed as if Rolando would spring for a bottle of the red, just as a novelty, but he replaced the glass, bought a few bottles of the cheap white, and saved his spouting for the car. "This is what we've become? A playground for the padrones of the world?"

"Where have you been for the last three thousand years?"

"No, no, hear me out, what is the point of our people making wine that will only be bought by tourists? There is something idiotic to the proposition, do you agree?" He dug the book out of his car. "Next stop..."

"I should drive. You've been drinking more than spitting."

"Anyone who would spit is a fool."

"Give me the keys."

"Are you serious?"

Scarpone stared at him with a pained expression.

Rolando tossed him the keys.

MASSIMO BALDINI WAS A NEAT, PRECISE MAN IN HIS sixties with a lean body and immaculately tucked shirt tails. Outdated aviator glasses. While his daughter and son-in-law marched Rolando through their offerings, the old man led my captain on a tour of the fermentation room downstairs.

For a long while Scarpone ogled stainless steel tanks and listened to a lengthy discourse on the perils of drought and hail, and the horrors of chemical softeners and chaptalization before asking the man a more relevant question.

Did the most celebrated winemaker of the borgo ever have any dealings with the dead man, Arbend Demaci?

The farmer frowned. He held up a forefinger. Instead of answering, he selected a bottle from the basement display case, took a pair of wine glasses, and led Scarpone out of the fermentation rooms into the sunlight.

They sat at a small wooden table.

Out here, Scarpone could see Rolando's car and the family's vegetable garden. A floppy Bracco hound pup ran between the aisles of the vegetable garden, chasing bees.

Baldini did the honors. Uncorked the small bottle and poured. I heard my captain sigh.

Why must there always be eating and drinking?

Why must there always be a lecture?

Why must we pontificate?

Why can't we give a simple answer to a simple question?

But he said none of these things. He sipped Baldini's red. It was fragrant and jammy, with a soft heat that wormed its way into the captain's chest and filled it with unexpected happiness.

"Listen to me, Marshal," Baldini said. "When I was a boy, a teen no older than my own grandchildren, I got up every morning and packed my rucksack and canteen. I laced my boots. I kissed my mother, and then I went into the fields to work with the men. There was no other option. Nothing. I could work the fields or I could go to school. We didn't have money for anything beyond public school, so it was decided for me. But if I didn't work, our family would have starved. My place was in the fields with my father and my uncles. I thank God that the children today do not have to make such a choice. But what we have gained, we have also lost. Lazy, every one of them."

Scarpone wished he could roll his eyes. "So you *didn't* know the dead man?"

The man frowned again. "I'm trying to give you context. This is important. I see your hands. Your arms, your face. They are not brown. You are an indoors man. A man of the city. This is true, yes?"

Scarpone allowed as much. His family had a small piece of land in the Castelli Romani, the hillside outside Rome. His aunt still lived there. He knew his way around gardens, he knew about the cycle of the seasons, but little else.

"This one, the Albanian, they tell me I should cry for him. I cry for his mother who lost a son. She is a good worker. I cry for *her,* as I do for all those who know what work is."

Jesu, this one was a philosopher. "Wait—you know the mother *and* the son?"

"I know everyone, Signore. No one works the fields of this borgo without eventually coming to me for work. I say this with humility, you understand, not out of self-aggrandizement. We do four thousand cases a year. We sell to the restaurants in the region, we sell to tourists, and we ship overseas to America. This is my pedigree. Ask anyone. Yes, the mother I would describe as a good worker, honest and fine. I was sorry to lose her. She's with Monteverde now. It's a good cantina just over the hill over your shoulder. If it weren't for the language difficulty, I'd say she'd be running their field operations in a few years. I wish Eladio well for having landed such a serious woman."

"The son?"

Baldini raised his glass to the sky and inspected its color. Scarpone was intended to sip. The captain sniffed the contents of his glass. The wine filled his nostrils. Then he sipped—

He is in a field. Laughter. He smells his mother's sweat as she works his aunt's garden. Her hands, her arms, her face all smell like fragrant, damp soil. He is in his father's workshop. The smell of shellac and glue. The tap of the hammer against the tacks. The satisfying whish as the rattan is pulled through the growing chair seat. Then, a second later, he is a grown man, walking through a forest clouded with fog.

—and let the wine roll around his tongue.

Here, in a nutshell, is the captain's problem: these visions will not leave him alone. They are there on the edges of his mind, his heart, each time he takes a bite or sip of food.

He detests them, fights against them. In an effort to suppress them, he is slowly starving himself.

These visions are the best clues I have to understand him. To understand my purpose here. Each time he fights them, he fights me.

"Signore," my captain said. "This is..."

"Yes?" Baldini waited. He tried to hide it, but the corners of his lips were turned up in expectation of a compliment.

My God, my captain thought. If I could read the stock market the way I read faces, I'd be rich.

"Signore, your wine is indescribable."

Baldini sat back proudly and nodded. His hair was gray but thick. A shock of it resisted any attempt to comb it, so it stood straight up.

"Yes, thank you," he said. "This is our aleatico. We sell it in those small bottles. Ordinarily, I'd say you can help yourself to any bottle we have here, but I'm afraid I can't be generous with this vintage. It's my best seller."

"Compliments."

"Thank you. Thank you." He reached for the glass. "Have another sip."

"But the son, Signore?"

The man's hand froze mid-pour.

"Excuse me?"

"You did not answer my question about the dead man, Demaci. You were about to say?"

"Ah well. For the sake of his mother I gave him three chances. Finally, she too conceded it was a waste of time. Uninterested. Always on the phone. I tell you, he is not a worker. He is another thing entirely. For one thing, I don't allow smoking in the fields. If you make excuses in the spring when it's wet, then you're taking a risk in the summer when the fields are dry."

"Where did he work, then, if not for you?"

The old man shrugged.

"He was a different kind of worker."

"And what kind is that?"

"It pains me to tell a mother this about her dead son. And you, Signore, you're forcing me to speak against my better Christian nature."

"I am not the boy's mother."

"Then why ask?"

"I seek only to avenge his murder, if it comes to that."

"Why would you ever do that, Signore? He was a blot on the earth. A bum. Now: Will you have another glass?"

Chapter Eighteen

That afternoon Rolando dragged him across the Tiber and up the Umbrian hills to investigate one of the newer entries in the guidebook. A place some of his Roman friends had either raved about or mocked. Scarpone reminded himself that he knew nothing about business. He was a flatfoot, the son of a chairmaker. But seeing the place for the first time, he was convinced that he came down on the side of the haters.

The place looked like no cantina he'd ever seen. It was called Tiber Goat. The name seemed to be a misnomer, since one could barely see the Little Tiber River from where the winery's restored villa sat on that Umbrian hill. Vineyards lined the hillside for thousands of hectares, as far as the eye could see. Standing here, looking west toward his borgo, Scarpone lost even the glimpse of the A1 highway.

But this was the normal part.

A line of tour buses filed into the parking lot and disgorged armies of tourists toting cameras and hats and sunglasses and shopping bags. They spilled off the buses and flowed toward him, a rapacious mob in search of...*something*. Just what, he didn't know. It couldn't be wine. This crowd of garishly dressed humanoids seemed too rabid to appreciate wine.

Scarpone stepped inside the tasting room. The room was air-conditioned to the point of frigidity. The light was blinding, like he'd just stepped inside one of those monster *supermercati* in Milan. Here was a fountain spouting wine. A long wall of tasting counters. And shopping. Massive amounts of shopping. Over-the-top shopping. Wine holders, wine openers, pot holders, key chains, trivets, cruets, salad dressing, olive oils, glassware, pitchers, and packaged meats and cheeses. And everywhere the sound of cash registers zinging.

Rolando was at the counter, sipping.

"You said you were only going to inspect it quickly," Scarpone reminded him. "You can't possibly want more wine than you have now."

"Have a drink. It's not bad. But it's exactly what you'd expect: industrial wine. The co-op is fresher, and simpler, as always."

"Then why drink it?"

"Two reasons. One: I can't resist. Two: I'm fascinated by success."

Evidence of that success was abundant. People waited their turn in a queue to tour the fermentation rooms. When they exited the double doors at the end, they were handily funneled into the second part of the gift shop, a small cafe and a demo kitchen where they could watch a woman demonstrate how to make bruschetta with salsa from a jar.

A trio of interpreters was translating everything the faux chef was saying into English, Dutch, and German.

Oh yes—there was no doubt of it.

They had landed in America.

Once again, the double doors off to the side opened and a fresh infusion of wine enthusiasts concluded their tour. They scattered to the four winds, pouncing upon the tasting counter and the keychains. For a while Scarpone played the game he played in Rome: identifying tourists by their clothes. Americans in their white socks and tennis shoes. Dutchmen in their sandals, backpacks, and unstylish hats. Brits eying the wine and wishing it were beer.

And when the crowd dispersed, Scarpone spied Lucia Anderson talking to a tall man in a plaid, short-sleeve shirt and khaki pants. A handsome man. A slightly older man in his early fifties. A straniero.

Scarpone stood watching them interact.

They know each other. First-name basis, obviously. But he's not carrying a bag or a jacket or a camera.

So not a tourist, then.

Which was indeed strange.

The man's hands were on his hips. His tan, his crisp shirt, and his pressed pants exuded consummate confidence.

Moves like he owns the place, Scarpone thought.

He turned his attention to Lucia. She, I think we can all agree, was stunning: stylish hair, sunglasses, a sweater, a bag, gorgeous shoes, and a blue dress cinched with a buttery leather belt.

Watching her, Scarpone felt the way he had while drinking the aleatico.

When she turned and spied him staring at her, her face registered shock. Then delight.

Warm delight.

THE MAN WHO LOOKED AS IF HE OWNED THE PLACE *DID* own the place. Or part of it anyway. He was my Lucia's husband, the wine executive from California. The flurry of various languages made the ensuing introductions too complicated to follow. The boringly named Charlie Anderson had something to do with a beverage conglomerate with holdings in Napa or Sonoma or both.

"The problem is, Tiber Goat is *too* successful," Anderson was telling Rolando. "And that's something we couldn't have anticipated. The reception from the tour companies is mixed. Some love us. Tons of parking for the buses, and all that. But others are unhappy. We're still a trek from Orvieto. Some of these buses don't want to make the effort to get up here on these winding roads. We didn't anticipate that." His eyes spotted a young server filling Rolando's glass with the next wine. "Oh—we're proud of that one."

They had moved to a small table in the cafe area. Tourists filed through the gleaming sterility of the cafeteria like truckers at a highway Autogrill. A server hovered near their table with a selection of wines, two on ice. The label on every single bottle was emblazoned with the image of a cartoonish ram sipping from a wine glass.

"There's no need to indulge Rolando on my behalf," Scarpone told Lucia. "He's a fool."

"You're my friend," she said, "and he's your friend, and hence, he's Charlie's friend."

Anderson was laughing now, clapping Rolando on the back, speaking in a painfully slow tongue and occasionally asking Lucia to translate something the mosaicist said.

"The area's known for Orvieto Classico, but if you stop there," Anderson said, "you'll never exploit the, uh, maximum potential of the land."

"What's the dessert one?" Rolando said, sipping.

"That's the Dessert Blend."

"That's what you call it in America?"

Anderson shrugged. "Our customers don't know from the different grapes, so we have to keep it easy. This one has a lot of moscato in it. It's one of our bestselling boxed wines."

Rolando understood the word *boxed*, and tried valiantly to hide his disdain. "We tried an aleatico today."

"Oh really?" Anderson said. "Whose?"

"Baldini, across the river."

"Oh yeah! Great stuff. But we don't buy his grapes. He only grows enough of that varietal to cover his bottlings. To be honest, they're too precious and too expensive to be used in one of our blends. We asked him if he wanted to be part of our program, though. I've been thinking about moving into Lazio. The land's cheaper—no offense, Lucia, but it is. Next time, though, I wouldn't buy land on the side of a mountain, I'll tell you that. From now on, give me a nice piece of flat land, preferably near a highway. Hah!" He chuckled, handing Rolando a napkin. "Anyway—'allora,' as you folks say, Baldini turned us down cold. A lot of the old-timers here still object to large-style agriculture like this, I suppose."

"A lot of the new-timers do too," his wife said in English.

Scarpone and Rolando laughed after their brains had caught up.

"You can tell just by looking at the landscape," Anderson said, waving at the world beyond his frigid, air-conditioned window. "All these farms are typically made up of tiny parcels. It would take me forever to buy up another estate like this one."

"Thank God for that," Lucia said drily.

"You see, gentlemen? Let that be a lesson to you. You can't

change the way your wife thinks. I taught her everything I know. My prize pupil, Class of 2007. And she's been trying to forget it ever since."

More laughs.

He gestured at the glass in Rolando's hand. "You like that, Rolando?"

Rolando made a cartoonish face of ecstasy that sent them all into peals of laughter. Even the young sommelier in training.

What a comedian, Scarpone thought.

"You worked for him, I take it?" Scarpone asked Lucia. "That's how you met?"

"That's right. Charlie was one of my mentors. I was going through a rough patch at home, trying to decide what I wanted to do. I had signed up for his course, but the closer it came to the departure date, I just wasn't sure I'd be able to leave home for California. It turned out to be the best thing I ever did. I was in that program about eight months. Then he arranged..." She paused awkwardly here. "He arranged for me to broaden my studies at the vineyards in Australia."

"He has vineyards down under too?"

"A partner firm. I loved it there. You have no idea. A lot of our people have emigrated there. I would have stayed, but it had been two years. By then I had the baby. It made sense to come back."

Scarpone was silent. Thinking. "It's a game with these people, isn't it?" he said. "Moving juice all around the planet."

She shrugged. "Watch out, Charlie. The marshal here is particular about wine. But look, Marshal, he moves ten million cases a year, under fifteen different brands."

"Oh, Jesu!" Rolando exclaimed.

"At that rate, the entire world is your cantina," Lucia said. "But his cantinas are family-centric."

"Must have a big family."

She detected the sarcasm in his words. "This offends you, doesn't it? I don't see why."

He was about to deny it. Earlier today he had heard Rolando bitch about how stranieri had forever altered their nation's wine economy. Now Rolando, that big phony, was kissing the backside of a man who was the region's biggest invader. Scarpone lowered his voice and switched to his Roman dialect, hoping that Lucia would understand what he was saying but Charlie wouldn't.

"How is this different from making crappy mozzarella or crappy pasta and shipping it overseas to customers who don't know any better? It strikes me that this entire enterprise runs counter to what so many of the people in the borgo practice. You, for example."

"It runs counter to everything I'm doing, sure," she said. "But I don't have the land he does. I don't have the money he does. If I did, I don't know that I wouldn't be experimenting as much as possible. You know how hard it is to survive today unless you can get your wine outside our borders? We must export or perish. He's bringing prosperity here. They've bought up a lot of the lands here that were lying fallow and he's making offers to the co-ops and the smaller growers to buy juice that would otherwise go unused. Tell me this is wrong."

Her words were icy.

Scarpone had nothing to say.

"What are you guys fighting about over there?" Charlie said.

Rolando leaned over. "Hey," he said to Scarpone. "My new *amico* here says they're taking their son to the pageant in the borgo. We can make a party of it."

"I don't know if we should intrude," Scarpone said.

"Intruding?" Anderson said, waving the word away. "Are you kidding? It'll be fun."

Lucia averted her eyes from her husband. "You do what you want," she whispered to Scarpone, mocking his Roman accent.

"Look at these two, Charlie," Rolando said. "How serious!" He turned to the server. "Signorina, can we get some olives and some potato chips?"

Chapter Nineteen

The old Roman road leading into the piazza was lined with families. Twinkling lights bobbed on strings over their heads. Some people had brought small tables and chairs, others leaned against the square's buildings or leaned out of windows.

The three carabinieri on duty tonight tried to hold people back from the road but it was useless. Kids darted in and out of the crowds, chattering and clowning around as their mothers yelled.

An over-the-top dramatic score blared from speakers set on the green across from the town hall.

Down the old Roman road came the parade. A host of shepherds. A gaggle of Pharisees. A consort of gladiators in leather breastplates, some carrying wooden swords, shields, and spears.

"Who makes the costumes?" Scarpone whispered to Lucia, who held her son in her arms so he could see. "They look so real."

"Local man. Works in Rome at the movie studios. I think he has contacts."

Off to the side, Rolando and Charlie Anderson jabbered in their mixed tongue.

"This, right here? This borgo could become the next big thing in wine tourism," Anderson was saying. "They've got all the ingredients. Talented winemakers."

"Beautiful ones, too," Rolando said. "If you don't mind my saying."

"Hah! Not at all. And they've got the most important thing in the world: location. If they ever finish that damned bridge, they'd have the best of both worlds. The highway, the tour buses. Umbria's right over the river. Everything on their doorstep."

Rolando elbowed Scarpone. "It's paradise—if only the military police could control these damned crowds!"

The crowd pressed in to catch a glimpse of the condemned. Here were the two thieves, lugging their crosses, being faux-whipped by gladiators.

And here was a handsome, strapping Jesus, his mustache and beard stained with nicotine. He was a serviceable, hairy-chested Christ who fell three times, met his sainted mother, and had his face wiped by Veronica.

The crowd went wild, cheering. Jesus paused with the cross on his third fall so the crowd could take a picture.

The condemned men dragged their crosses into the piazza, the heavy wood thunking on cobblestones past the pork store, past the bank, past the church, past the fish and mozzarella stalls and the ladies working the fryers.

A minute later, Jesus, now dressed in his robes, appeared before the Pharisees. A soundtrack dubbed with dialogue blared over the loudspeaker. Jesus and his inquisitors mimed their way through the scene.

Jesus appeared before Pontius Pilate.

The crowd booed.

Pilate washed his hands.

"They do this every year?"

"As long as I've been around, yes," Lucia said.

"Shouldn't they do it in spring, at Easter?"

"They *can*. They do. But Easter came too early for togas this year."

"They've got the chronology wrong," Scarpone said. "Tried first, *then* the march to Golgotha."

"You're too analytical, Marshal."

Behold! Jesus and the thieves were stripped and nailed to the crosses, which lay on the grass in front of city hall. The crucifiers swung their hammers melodramatically, trying to time their blows to the soundtrack.

Thunk. Thunk. Thunk.

Now, the money shot: The crosses were raised. Red light bathed them. Spotlights threw up three enormous cruciform silhouettes on the old stone walls of the borgo.

The lush soundtrack swung into heavy, discordant rock.

"Jesus," Charlie Anderson said.

"In fact, yes," Rolando sighed.

Off the western cliff of the old town, fireworks burst in the night sky.

Then silence.

Mary the Virgin Mother appeared in front of the crosses, then disappeared in a fog-machine cloud.

The crowd roared and applauded.

The parish priest appeared at a microphone to say a few words.

The crowd ignored him and rushed toward the food stands.

"And now, oh God, let us eat fried cheese," Rolando said in his thick, mangled English.

Anderson guffawed, transfixed by the spectacle.

"It's so realistic," he said. "How do they get the men to stick to those crosses?"

"I'm sorry," Rolando said. "This is a state secret. It cannot by shared with foreigners."

The crowd jostled them hard. Rolando gestured menacingly at a few people, then calmly asked, "Are we eating?"

Anderson shrugged. "Sounds like fun."

Rolando waved a dismissive hand toward Scarpone. "I know *you* won't. How about you, *bellezza?*"

Lucia ignored him. She handed her son to her housekeeper, who led the boy wordlessly to the food stalls.

Christ, still crucified, now posed on the cross for people snapping pictures.

A couple of musicians tested their sound equipment on the bandstand overlooking the panorama.

"Care to take a walk?" Lucia said.

Chapter Twenty

She drew a scarf around her neck and left the sunglasses in her hair, at the ready, though it was dark enough now to see the stars. Her arm threaded through his, more out of necessity than any sense of affection. Her heels were giving her trouble on the shallow steps which descended from the top of the borgo.

In that part of the borgo, the houses were built of volcanic rock, and had clung to the cliffs for so long that cliffs and homes had become one. Some of the old apartments had been renovated, others looked as if they were crumbling. The only things that weren't stone were the wooden window frames and the pots of geraniums that hung from them.

Strings of red lights guided their way down the hill.

Everyone seemed to be running *up*.

Children dragged huffing parents.

A guy driving a Smart car took the shallow steps two at time, trying to dodge pedestrians and make his way up to the piazza. At one point he became stuck, and a quartet of men from one of the social clubs ceased their card game long enough to lift his vehicle onto the next tier of steps.

The bottom of the hill opened onto a gravelly patch of grass. From here Scarpone could see the lights of the distant highway. Off to the side of the lower road was an old, single-story chapel. A square tower rose from it. Its stained glass windows were all lit.

The perimeter of the chapel was lined with flickering red candles whose melted ends were pressed into the ground. The red dripping wax clung to the heavy gravel.

A queue of people at the door.

A shabby crone sat outside, accepting donations in exchange for candles. She had one eye, hair over her lips and chin, and was dressed in gray, with a habit over her head.

"You still have nuns here?"

"Not in the borgo. There's a home for old ones in Attigliano. They take care of the chapels in the area."

"So the chapel still functions?"

"Of course. And it always will, so long as people keep donating to maintain it. This is the church that was here in the old days, when the holy spring saved the borgo. They would never think to close it. Would you excuse me a moment?"

They'd reached the front doors. Lucia bought a red votive from the nun and headed toward the back of the church, toward a low arch that led into darkness.

Scarpone prowled what looked like an old ruin, walls made from a mix of brick and stucco and plaster. Centuries of layers here. The wooden altar was loaded with fresh flowers. The stained glass looked patched in spots; he could tell because certain colors were only mere approximations of their neighbors.

He watched a woman, arms outstretched, staring at a wooden statue of the Madonna to the left of the altar. The woman mumbled as tears streamed down her cheeks.

Families snapped pictures, tired fathers herded children. He stepped over to the low archway and peeked in. Lucia and a few other people were crammed into a room the size of an ancient prison cell. She knelt in silence over a stone slab, illuminated by her votive.

He pulled back to give her privacy.

He scanned the windows instead. The imagery of water was everywhere. Christ at Cana, turning water into wine. Christ with loaves and fishes and water. Christ walking on water. On the other wall, the Old Testament: the ark riding the waves, Moses parting the Red Sea, the Pharoah's chariots tumbling.

To the side of the altar, a huge depiction of the Madonna with water springing from her feet. Under the window was a small copper basin, from which visitors urged their kids to take samples.

One of the windows, neglected in all the ceremony, attracted him. It showed a ragged beggar, covered in sores, looking forlorn, reaching an outstretched hand to a crowd of people—rich men, clergy, and craftsmen, who all cringed, hiding their faces from him.

Scarpone heard a squeak and a shush.

A nun shuffled by with a broom, chasing a mouse.

She stopped to eye him looking at the window.

"Lazarus?" Scarpone asked her.

"Giobbe!" she said. *"Attento! Non toccare Giobbe. È maledetto!"*

Beware the touch of Job. He's cursed.

Chapter Twenty-One

Rolando and Anderson drank like fish until the night turned cool, and his wife took the boy home. In the end the American announced that he needed to look in on his cantina, and summoned a vehicle to take them all home. When the limo whisked the businessman off to Umbria, Scarpone had the pleasure of lugging Rolando up the steps to the apartment and stowing him on the couch.

Job still on his mind, Scarpone inspected the plants on his balcony.

They were now all dead. He'd need more plants to continue his research.

His phone lit up. He imagined it was the station, but a woman's voice greeted him.

"What are you doing tonight?"

"Who is this?"

"Can you not tell?"

The voice sounded young, female, slurred.

"Claudia? Dottoressa?"

"Are you free to meet?"

"Why? Do you have something to report?"

"Does it have to be about work?"

"Is it not about work?"

"*Why* does it have to be about work?"

"I'm sorry, I don't understand."

"I'm bored. I'm bored of this stupid town."

"Orvieto is stupid? Isn't that where you live?"

"Yes—*no*." She mentioned a town just outside the historic center, nearer the hospital. He'd driven through it once or twice. A town of residential homes and apartments and a tiny strip of shops selling luggage and camp equipment and the ubiquitous ladies undergarments.

"I thought you'd be with your family for the weekend."

"I didn't go. My fiancé was to visit but...we fought."

"I'm sorry."

He heard the sound of a burp.

"Are you sick?"

"Why don't you come meet me? For coffee? Or a drink?"

"It's late. The festival is still going on here. I need to stay up until they clean out the square. There may be a call from the station."

He looked inside his apartment. Rolando was dead to the world. His head hung to the side, drooling onto Scarpone's couch. The mosaicist's hands were deep in his pants.

"Forgive me," she said. "This was stupid. I'm an idiot when I drink. Some friends of mine were going to the discotheque on the highway. Just some people I know from the hospital. But I said no. I hate those places."

"As well you should. The accident statistics surrounding discotheque departures are alarming. Look—I should go."

"Matteo?" she said. "I'm not like this. I'm not. It's just that, I thought there was a moment yesterday when you...when you...I thought it would not hurt to call."

"When was this?"

"At the autopsy," she said. Then she added, "I should go."

"Please don't drive," he said.

"I won't," she said. Bite in her voice now. He was about to say something else, but heard the click.

Chapter Twenty-Two

This thing you humans do—this sex—confuses as it intoxicates me. The faint suggestion of it in the dottoressa's call arouses my interest in your ways.

That night, when the borgo finally falls still, I go in search of it.

Alessandro, the owner of the coffee bar, sleeps soundly and nakedly beside his restless wife. She is a young blond woman with pendulous breasts who clings to her man in the night, sighing and tossing.

She cannot understand how he can sleep well.

She has been with him since they were children together in the elementary school. Every dream of his, she absorbed and made her own. She waited dutifully while he served in the military. Then, later, when he announced he wanted to open the coffee shop, she watched as his parents presented him with some, not all, of the money he needed. Together, she and he took out a bank loan to mortgage the rest. Later, his parents gave the newlyweds some, not all, of the money they needed to buy their apartment. Then came a second mortgage.

And just today, hours before the pageant, Alessandro announced that he wanted to buy a used Volvo. They will need a loan to do this, too. Three loans in as many years! She doesn't know how he can live with such debt or have such confidence in their financial future.

Doesn't he know they will be in their fifties by the time these debts are paid off?

It horrifies her. She has her parents' fear of debt. But Alessandro feels he knows better. If we don't buy it with a loan, he tells her, the car you want today for fifteen thousand will be thirty by the time you have the cash in hand. So what are you waiting for? Buy now and live.

She loves him, she loves him, oh Jesu Cristo, she loves him. She just hopes he is being smart about this.

Now, in the night, she gently cups his genitals, feeling their heat. He had the biggest balls she has ever seen. Someday soon this cock will give them a child. Oh *Dio mio*, let him give me a son. Let it be a good son too, with his father's gift for hard work and diligence, but please, Jesu, not his capacity for debt.

In this closed space, I wonder if she can sense me intruding upon such a private moment.

A few doors away, the young girl from the pork store lies under the covers in the room she shares with her sister. As her sibling sleeps, the pork girl texts her girlfriends and alternately a boy she likes who lives in Bagnoregio. He was supposed to have come to the festival tonight, but he never showed. It makes her so mad, so mad, and as long as she has strength tonight she will give him a piece of her mind.

I watch her fingers fly across the keypad. Her bedsheet igloo is lit only by the light of her phone.

I extract myself from her room and take to the window. A lone car zips down the Orvietana and turns, heading out of the town. The driver, a businessman on his way back to Rome, is angry that the gasoline distributor is closed. Should he take the chance that he will find someplace open farther south, or should he head back to Orvieto and the highway entrance?

Even before he decides, a giant porcupine scampers across the road in the path of his car. The driver slams his foot on the brake.

He veers into the parking lot of the *supermercato*. The front of his Alfa clips the front of a shopping cart and sends it rolling into the roadway, straight for the plate glass window of the furniture store.

Crash.

To hell with them, he thinks, no one will know. To hell with this town, wherever the hell it is. I won't be here tomorrow.

The wind of his engine takes me swiftly out of town and off to Orvieto.

Claudia, the dottoressa, lives out that way. I train my thoughts on her and find myself in her bedroom.

Ah! After all that fuss earlier, she has found company in the arms and loins of a man whom I don't at first recognize. I watch them tumble and rut together on the sheets. She makes demands of him which he is only too excited to perform. But he is a born sluggard, and when his eruption is complete he falls dead to sleep against her freckled, naked body.

She reaches for her glasses and looks up at the ceiling. She still feels the affect of the alcohol. She hates the smell of her breath, the smell of her body, and his.

Every inch of her drips with sweat and dissatisfaction.

The man rolls, and I see his face.

It is Gismonda, one of the captain's men. Foulmouthed Horseface.

Over the rooftops I go, away from her and her sadness.

I see the terra-cotta rooftops and find the one that holds my captain.

Rolando is there in the living room, steeped in a cloud of wine-tinged flatulence.

In the next room, the captain sits up, flipping through the case files.

Eighteen months ago:

Domenico DelCillie, 17, deceased, heroin overdose. Son of Luisa and Antonio, twin brother of Patrizia, 17 years.

From the notes sent to Viterbo:

The sister alleges that the brother frequently lounged in the vicinity of the secondary school, where drug transactions are known to have occurred. (Patrols have been stepped up in this area. Traffic ceases briefly but recurs.) Parents not yet interviewed (sedated by physician).

In a later sheet, there was a long statement from the parents about how they sensed their son was acting strangely.

A sudden sadness grips my captain. He sets the case file aside. The red eyeglasses fit uncomfortably across the bridge of his nose.

He reaches for the newsprint and tape and scissors and goes to work fashioning miracles of his own creation out of today's newspaper. The steeple is the most difficult, he thinks. He needs to be able to mount it securely to the roof; he manages this with an abundance of yellow cellophane. And when he is done, he has a small replica chapel that he is itching to insert into his diorama. But that can wait till morning. Let Rolando sleep.

He closes his eyes and tells himself he can sleep.

But he cannot.

He collects the police files and tidies them into shape.

He thinks about Lucia and the darkness of that side alcove within the chapel. Somewhere in that ancient cell is an answer he needs to find.

Chapter Twenty-Three

Rolando spent time the next morning soaking his head in the bathroom sink. Scarpone heard throat clearings and intestinal rumblings. When it was through, the man emerged, smelling fresh, a spring in his step, his eyes bloodshot. "Coffee?"

At that hour, nothing was open but the small bar near the gasoline distributor. They sat at the plastic table outside and watched the owner arrange an outdoor display of laughably ornate plants and equally hideous fruit baskets.

"Signore," Rolando called to the man. "These trinkets are as ugly as sin. You think you're going to be able to sell them?"

"Mothers and wives love them," the man answered back. "We sell a sack of them every Sunday, but especially during holidays and festivals."

He was a sweaty man in coveralls.

"Really?" Rolando shook his head. He lowered his voice. "People are stupid," he told Scarpone. "Who can't find a plant or fruit when they need it?"

He proceeded to suck down three cups of espresso and a microwaved cornetto, then lay back in his chair and stared at the sky through his sunglasses.

"Ah, what can I tell you? It's a nice town but I fear that it is still a shithole. I am the only one who will look back on this sorry chapter of your life and say it enriched me."

"In what sense?"

Rolando dug in his wallet and produced the business card of Charlie Anderson.

"He wants me out there," he said, pointing across the Little Tiber River toward the hills of Umbria. "He wants me to do some installations. And when I'm done with their absurd Disney castle, he wants me to install more in California. Tremendous, right?"

"You think he's going to fly you to California?"

"Why the hell not? No reputable vintner can be without mosaics, am I right? It's part of the charm of these places. The tourists demand it, whether they know it or not. But seriously, we speak of bullshit. There's a more important matter at hand. Please, for my sake, take that woman. She is scrumptious."

Scarpone checked his phone: 7:45 a.m. "You need to get back home. It'll take you at least an hour, probably two, if you start hitting traffic on the Cassia."

"Screw the traffic. We're talking about love. About passion. You can't wallow in your bullshit pity. Women find it unattractive. I'm not saying marry her. I'm saying recognize what's right in front of you."

"I live here now. I can't do that. Besides, she's married."

"So what? Did you see the way he looks at her? He doesn't. He's all business. I know the type. And he's never home. He's here one day, California or Australia the next. She's ripe for a lover, believe me. And you—how long could you possibly be here? If those cockhead bosses of yours fart a different tune tomorrow, they'll want you back. The night before you leave, you take the woman again, and you part ways. You had your fun, she had hers, you move on. This is life." He checked his phone. "Hey—why don't you come with me? Alana has as much as insisted. We have plenty of wine now. Plenty of food. Have Sunday dinner with us, and come up tomorrow. To hell with this place."

Scarpone shook his head. "Can't. I have a few things I need to look into."

"Work? You're working on Sunday? Are you mad?"

"Go."

They were silent a bit, then Rolando stood and jingled his keys. Scarpone stood. The two men embraced and kissed each other's cheeks. "My brother," Rolando announced. "Be good, okay?"

Shaking his head, Rolando went over to grab a plant and a fruit basket off the display. He rooted in his dusty denim jacket and slipped some bills to the owner, who bowed.

"Last chance, Scarpone," Rolando said.

After the mosaicist's car disappeared, Scarpone pointed at the small plants. "I'll take ten of those," he told the man.

Chapter Twenty-Four

Scarpone parked on the grass in front of the old farmhouse, and popped the hatch. He stepped out and paused a moment in the doorway of the vehicle and looked out over the land. So quiet here in the morning.

Aside from the coffee with Rolando, he had not yet been to town. It would be coming to life soon, people streaming out of their homes, congregating in the piazza, dressed in their Sunday best, dressed not to go to church but to merely be seen in front of it. They would drink their coffees and converse with shopkeepers, chide children, ogle babies, embrace friends. Some would slip into the church while the priest intoned the mass. Others would wait until the mass was over and slip into the dark nave to inspect the decorations and to determine, as best they could, who paid for the flowers and altar cloths this year.

Later, they would congregate to listen to the music in the piazza, and grab another bite at the stalls before heading home.

He sat on the car bumper and pulled on thick rubber boots. Then tucked his pant legs into the boots. Such apparel would not protect him entirely from what he thought was there, but they would have to do. He had nothing else.

He slammed the trunk and headed for a tree. A slender acacia sapling already dripped with dried pea-like shells. In the spring, when those flowers bloomed, their scent was ambrosial. Honey on the wind.

He studied the configuration of the branch for a while, then used his knife to break away a branch—leaves, flowers, and all.

He waved the branch in front of him. It looked like the ones slaves once waved at Cleopatra. Or Caesar Antony.

He slapped the grass as he walked down the hill. The grass was wet. Some large birds cawed and fluttered from the trees. Across the valley he saw rows of neatly terraced olive trees.

The flailing tired him, but he kept it up until he reached the bay tree where they'd found the body. He swatted the ground and the branches above him, just to be safe, and waited. Nothing.

He bent and inspected the well. It looked like a stone chimney growing out of the ground. No more than two feet high. A crucifix fashioned of rusty cast iron rose about two feet out of the back of the stone. The spring water trickled over the lip of the manmade enclosure. The exterior of the well had been repatched with successive layers of stucco over brick. He was tempted to lower his lips and sip some water, but it seemed unclean to do so. He cursed himself for not having brought anything to collect water with. A small plaster Madonna, faded almost to white, was fitted into an alcove in the bricks, and hidden by grass. A few strings of faded plastic rosary beads dangled around her neck.

He stood now and tried to judge the distance.

The water was not far from the grotto. From here to where his men had found the mattress was a dirt path, long worn down to the stones.

He thought about Demaci lying naked in the grotto. At first thought, it seemed outrageous. But in Rome he'd found young couples copulating in cars, in alleys, in the backs of churches. The most obvious, sordid places. It was what you did when you were in your teens, twenties, thirties, and still lived with three generations under the same roof. According to a report he'd seen in the paper recently, at least a third of the nation's adults still lived with their parents.

So: If you were lying with a woman in that grotto and you wanted a drink, would you walk all the way here, naked?

It seemed unlikely.

The stones and sharp grass would cut your feet. You'd at least put on shoes.

But you'd walk here naked, with shoes on your feet?

No—it's too far to walk naked.

Even in the dark?

Especially in the dark.

So you'd pull on pants and shoes. Then why didn't you? We found your water bottle, but not your clothes. Where are they?

He bent again to the Madonna's alcove. Something caught his eye, tucked behind the figure of the lady. Something brown and crinkled. He tried to move the statue, but couldn't. The Madonna was mortared to her shell. Instead he used his penknife to pick away at the object and extract it.

It was a sheet of notepaper. A woman's handwriting.

Madonna mia the doctor says the cancer is back I have not told my husband. They want me to do the testing again. I cannot bear it but it must be done. I cannot say no. I want to live. The children need me. Pray for me Madonna hear my prayer.

The more he looked, the more of these entreaties he found, tucked into the crevices of the spring's enclosure.

Madonna, pray that my husband gets the job and we can pay for the wedding.

Madonna, pray for my mother who comes to you now. Let the pain not be great. Welcome her into Paradiso and let her meet Jesu.

Madonna, madonna, madonna. Pray for this, pray for that.

His mind discounted them immediately as not part of his case.

Still, it showed the power of these waters. It showed that people still came here. That it was part of the culture.

So tell me, Demaci—why would you choose this place to make love?

Chapter Twenty-Five

Since her return from Australia, it had become Lucia's custom, on Sundays and holidays, to spend mornings with her father. And afternoons with her mother and her mother's lover, the Englishman.

Her father had been on his best behavior. He'd come to accept that this was the only way she'd ever remain in his life. He had to make concessions.

That didn't mean that he didn't push his luck.

"Nanda is making lamb," he said this morning. "I can't possibly eat a whole leg myself."

This was her chance to decline and say that it would not be possible. Then came *his* chance to wheedle her into having one drink. She saw no harm in it.

The old man stepped from the kitchen to the living room and then to the dining room to find the fine glasses, which he passed to Nanda. He insisted that she wash them carefully while he ran down to the cellar to find just the right bottle.

While he was gone, she heard her son playing alone with some new toys in her father's living room, rolling his trucks back and forth on marble tile. The old man was good for that—always showering the boy with trinkets with an eye toward the child's eventual usefulness.

She just wanted to get out of there and get to her mother's in Bolsena. Weekends in Bolsena meant celebrating with some foreigners who'd paid Lucia's mother to teach them regional dishes. The foreigners stayed at a small pensione in the city overlooking the lake, but by fall, God and the contractor willing, she and her mother would board them at Villa Montelacqua, her mother's new agritourism venture, bought with her mother's patrimony, what the lawyers had been able to extract from the count's fingers, and the generous offerings of her mother's lover, the Englishman. Lucia dreamed of the day when she and her mother would treat their patrons to a double experience. Meals at the vineyard, a crash course in harvesting and winemaking, and meals and cooking classes at the olive grove overlooking the lake. As soon as the *agriturismo* was finished, the former Cortese women would not be stopped.

All things considered, she thought her mother had done well for herself. By the time the divorce came through, messy as it was, she already had immersed herself in a business of her own, making herself impervious to the count's future recriminations.

My Lucia wished to be this way herself, but she knew that she carried too much of her father's anger, too much of her brother's recklessness, stubbornness, and wanton stupidity to ever call herself her mother's daughter.

The older she grew, the more she felt there was something lingering under the water at Bolsena, and under the soil at Castelpietra. Something she could not understand or fathom or reckon with properly. Whenever she quarreled with her mother, she chalked it up to the old fears, the old worries. They were women in a world where men called the shots. They were presumed useless at birth. Who the hell were they to start businesses of their own, and to succeed at them?

She felt as if a stone had lodged itself in her throat. Tears welled in her eyes, though she did her best to hide them.

Yes, yes, that was it. Some creature—a hideous worm perhaps—had burrowed itself into her land. It lurked under the soil, the vineyard, and the house, and would undermine her best intentions. Either it was the old fear—I am worthless, I deserve nothing, I deserve everything he does to me—or it was something else. It would only grow like a cancer and destroy her plans if she did not root it out.

She was drying her eyes when her father returned with four or five bottles, just in case the one he opened was off. Then, slipping on his spectacles, he made an elaborate show of asking Lucia's assistance in reading the labels and assessing the probable quality of the contents. "Do you remember if *this* was a good year?" he said.

And then it was her turn to recall what she could about some random year in her childhood. How the weather had started cool and warmed up beautifully and all things had gone well until the hail fell and destroyed the crops. Or how the grapes had to be harvested earlier one year, though they were still of good quality. And how wintry a year had been until May, when they ended up getting too much rain.

And on and on, as if her time weren't precious right now. She didn't like to keep her mother and the Englishman waiting. She didn't want to show up late and feel that Sunday had been a waste of time.

How infuriatingly slow he poured! It seemed to her as if he could stop time and make the wine trickle out oleaginously just to drive her mad.

Pour it and drink it, goddamn you, she thought.

But even this she did not say.

He was standing and she was still seated on a kitchen chair when he finally offered her the glass. His torso was so close to her face that she could smell his cologne and his sweat and the rankness of his breath.

She took the glass, and they clinked.

"How goes this investigation? This strange death on our miracle land?" he said.

"How should I know?"

"Well, you seem to have become great friends with this interloper, this marshal who is no true marshal at all."

"He is no marshal?"

"Oh, come, you mean to tell me that you don't know? Have I taught you children nothing about our fine army? What a terrible father I am!"

That's right—you are, you prick. You did nothing for me. Nothing, all those years—

"A marshal is a low rank indeed. A puppet controlled by masters. His rank exists solely as a way to cheaply staff the outer provinces with lesser men. But in *this* case they sent a captain to take the marshal's position. Which is strange, do you not think so? I looked into it extensively. All I can say is that he is an exile, *carina*. An outcast from Rome. That he should come here and lord around our town, putting on airs, is completely absurd. His superiors have no use for him. Why should we?"

She shrugged. "What does it matter?"

He is a good man, she wanted to say. A good man. She could feel it. There was a gentleness to him. A strength. Even a kind of showy, naive folly about him too, judging from their conversation at Charlie's vineyard yesterday.

"If you intend to go strolling with him more often, as you did last night, then you ought to know. That's why I call your attention to it."

"So you're having me watched, is that it?"

He fluttered his fingers in a dovelike gesture of innocence. "Who me? You make it sound so malevolent. Why wouldn't I take an interest in you? One, you're my daughter. Two, we are business partners, yes?"

The wine stuck in her throat. It was dry, tannic, harsh. Had he poisoned her? Jesu—no, it was just the wine. Wine and her nerves.

"Leonardo," she called, "get your things together. We're going to Nonna's."

"Oh, come now," her father whined, tilting his head back as if howling at the ceiling. Nanda's spoon clanked as she spooned fatty juices on the leg of lamb.

"You leave this in here for four more hours," Nanda told the old man. "You don't touch it, you hear? Or else it'll still be kicking you when you eat it."

"Yes, yes," he told the housekeeper.

My God, the kitchen was so warm right now. In late summer the walls of these stone houses warmed up to the point that they felt like ovens. And then you prayed for summer to end and for the return of the cool nights.

"Leo! Did you hear what I said?"

Her father tried again. "Lucia, please. I mean only to reiterate that we have an understanding. That's all. It wouldn't be fair if you came back after having your fun overseas, letting yourself be the plaything to God knows how many men, then robbing me of that which is most precious to me. I won't have it. If you can't handle the business aspect, we can dissolve it. I take back the land. If you have grapes and oil to sell, sell it and pay me my percentage. And let us return simply to the bond of blood."

Which is no bond at all, old man.

The truth was, she could not pay him a thing. She had yet to sell a single bottle of wine. And she wouldn't, not for another year. Her bank account was nearly drained. She had mortgaged the land to renovate the house and the outbuildings, and to install top-of-the-line winemaking equipment in the barn. No, she could not simply hand the land back to her father. The only way she could get out from under it was to sell the land, something her father will undoubtedly block.

The old man knew all these things, but refused to talk about them openly. He would only drop irritating hints.

"You could always ask that husband of yours for the money."

"You know I can never do that."

He stepped closer to her. His torso heading straight for her face. She kicked her chair back to the wall, its legs scraping on tile.

Her father embraced her head. She could feel his hot belly against her face.

Hold still, she told herself, hold still.

"How different our lives would be if he were still alive," he said. "I miss him. I miss my son so much. Can you not see that, Lucia?"

He had tears in his eyes.

She was about to say something vicious, but held her tongue. Much as the old man disgusted her, speaking those words now struck her as impossibly cruel. She was too good a person for that.

"I am sorry for your loss," she said.

The words were mechanical, and the last of the wine which she drained from her glass tasted like chalk.

Ah well, she thought, maybe it had been a bad year after all.

Chapter Twenty-Six

Down at the old chapel, Scarpone ducked when the one-eyed nun pitched a bucket of mop water at his head.

She saw him and shrieked her apologies.

Her dialect was rough. For a second he imagined that she was speaking some relic of the Etruscan tongue. She was saying something about the *istrice,* the fat crested porcupine that was known to live in the neighborhood. That lazy, nocturnal marauder had turned up all the flowers she'd planted earlier this week outside the chapel, and gobbled up their roots.

She swept as she told Scarpone her story. Her broom, fashioned from natural bristles, looked like something Hecate had made.

He asked if he could go inside. She hesitated, then agreed. He wasn't sure if he was supposed to make an offering; she was no longer selling candles. But since his hand was already in his pocket, he simply withdrew some coins and dropped them on the cane seat of the chair outside the door.

Inside, the old smell: spice and wax.

There was no one else there. Everyone was up in the piazza taking their Sunday *passeggiata,* strolling back and forth with their neighbors while dressed to the nines.

He walked to the back alcove.

It was a confined space, just big enough to hold a few wooden chairs and candles. Stained glass windows depicted peasants bowing before a man on a horse. Scarpone tried to read the inscription, but that part of the window was clouded by grime.

The floor was covered with marble slabs. Names chiseled into tombstones.

Patrizio.

Giuliana.

Iacopo.

There were a mix of surnames, but the ones he saw most often were:

Cortese.

Cortese.

Cortese.

He closed his eyes, and tried to recall precisely where Lucia had kneeled.

Here, closest to the door. He was practically standing on it.

He looked at the stone and read the dates.

Quick subtraction: the man who lay below the slab had been about thirty-two years old when he'd died.

Beloved son, beloved brother.

And the name, hidden in the shadows:

Marco Cortese.

Chapter Twenty-Seven

"Here—how about a little piece of pork?"

The fat cop D'Orazio perched on a tiny cafe chair outside a coffee bar in the nearby town of Bagnoregio. He'd bought two sandwiches of roasted pork—*porchetta*—from the food truck in the parking lot. He tore off tiny strips of meat and passed them to his two-year-old grandson. The child reclined in a blue stroller, all knuckles. He grabbed each piece of tender meat and stuffed it in his mouth. His face and fingers were greasy and fragrant with the scent of rosemary and fennel.

"You sure you don't want a sandwich, Captain? They do a good job."

"I'll bet they do, but no."

The garden outside the bar offered one of the most incredible sights in the entire nation. The park ended in a tiny, candle-lit cave that was said to be the prayer grotto of the city's most famous son—Saint Bonaventure. And just beyond the railing was a view of the saint's old city perched on a crumbling hill. The bridge that stretched to the dying town was its only link to the outside world. That afternoon, when they'd first gotten there and the mist had not yet burned off, my captain thought he was looking at a town riding on clouds.

"I don't know what to tell you," D'Orazio said. "They're a strange family. The only nobles I've ever known. They've certainly had their share of tragedy. The son, Marco, died in a car accident. Terrible thing. You know those cliffs you hit on the highway on the way in from Orvieto? Right there. Went off the road one night, drunk as a priest. He died when Lucia was in America or wherever she was. He was slated to take over the azienda, but as usual he didn't show much interest in anything but cars and women. It was only after the customary period of mourning that the talk started."

"What was the talk?"

"Oh. I thought you knew."

"I don't know anything about these people. I ask because I *don't* know."

The big cop chuckled. "Different from those who speak with authority when they know nothing."

Of all the men on the force, D'Orazio was the one who was most likely to hold a grudge against my captain. He was fifty-four years old. In two years he'd retire from the service. By rights, he should have been permanently appointed marshal upon the departure of the previous marshal, Vitalo Vitellone, who'd been itching to retire to his son's place a few towns over.

Scarpone had never met Vitellone; D'Orazio had taken over as interim marshal before Scarpone's appointment. However much he may have enjoyed the boost in pay, D'Orazio never desired the title. He was a cheerfully unambitious man who regarded responsibility as an irritating burden. He was the force's most jolly member, and looked forward to collecting his pension and perhaps feeding pork to all his grandchildren.

"So be it," said D'Orazio. "The count was wise enough to invest in properties in Rome years ago as a way of providing stability outside of agriculture. Apartments, I hear. The wife had already left him and moved to Bolsena. The two children were living at home."

"They didn't move with the mother?"

"That kind always knows where the money is. But what do men know about raising children? He left them to their own devices when he was out of town. The son was reaching the age of majority then. The daughter was just a few years younger. But no matter. I was on patrol one Saturday night when I came upon a barefoot girl walking down the Orvietana in the dark. Dangerous, as you know. That stretch of road has no light.

"I pull over to investigate. The girl's in her teens—a young woman from one of the small towns to the south. She's walking with two hands holding her shirt top together, where it had been ripped. I get her into my vehicle and that's when I see her swollen face. 'Who did this to you?' I say. No answer. Then I see the lights of another vehicle heading up the road slowly. That car stops when it sees me and makes a U-turn and shoots off in the other direction. I ask the girl, 'Is that him?' She plays dumb.

"I lock the doors and give chase. Sure enough, he leads me into town, right to the door of his father's villa. The young man is the count's son, Marco Cortese. I tell the girl to stay put and go ask him a few questions. An arrogant kid if ever I met one. He says she ripped her shirt on his car door. I don't even know how that's possible. He was going to take her home but she wouldn't listen to reason. The two of them had obviously been drinking. But as he was home now, I didn't see the point of writing him up. I radioed the station and took the girl home south all the way to Attigliano. She refused to talk about it.

"I mentioned it to the marshal the next day. I mention her ripped shirt and he said, 'Let me guess. Marco was out at the clubs again.' It wasn't the first time. It wouldn't be the last. I visited the girl a couple of times that week but she wouldn't press charges. Wanted it to go away."

He paused a moment, rooted in his pocket for a handkerchief, which he used to wipe the baby's face clean. Then commenced breaking off more pieces of the pork.

"Divorce is terrible thing, but it seemed to us that the old man was out of his league. Had no idea how to raise kids."

"How'd the contessa live? She had money of her own?"

"Who knows with these people? My impression was she wasn't averse to getting her hands dirty. Worked in some hotels in Bolsena till the settlement. That's how her father made his money. Hospitality. Hotels in Orvieto and Bolsena. Some land here and there. She probably had a sack of money she kept to herself. Funny—I remember when she left him, the count was mewling around town. He's an odd man. Strangely sentimental. My grandfather used to hang out at the social club in the lower borgo. When I was younger I used to serve the men there on weekends to pick up tips and watch the matches. Now I'm old enough to be one of those old farts.

"Anyway, I remember the count coming in one day and it was like Christ himself had come for a drink. Men all scattering to get him a chair. His eyes were red. 'She's left us,' he told my grandfather. 'Left me and the two children like we're dirt.' My grandfather had worked the railroads and the highways. He'd been a foreman at many of the cantinas in town. Everyone looked up to him. He was wise. And here the wealthiest man in the village was crying to him. 'I should have known what I was getting into when I married her. You have to watch certain women. They play like kittens but strike like hawks. Years ago, when her father drowned, I should have seen the truth. It was right there in front of my eyes. I saw, but did not comprehend.'"

"Wait," Scarpone said. "What's this now?"

"It's a sad old story. When they were first married, the count and his new contessa were out at her father's property in Bolsena. The old man was swimming in the lake and went under. The daughter jumped in to rescue him. She got the father to shore, but by then it was too late. 'I should have seen it then,' the count told my grandfather. 'She'd worked in his kitchens and had such powerful arms. That should have been a sign.' Strange story, isn't it, Captain? Where do children get these tendencies if not from the parents?"

Chapter Twenty-Eight

Nanda said he was to leave the lamb in the oven at least four hours. He was fine on salad. It was waiting in the ice box. The chicory and garlic she'd sautéed that morning sat on the counter covered by a kitchen towel.

You know how to reheat that, yes?

The count merely brushed her off. Yes, yes, yes, it was all fine.

By then he was angry at his daughter's sudden departure and the increasing silence he heard from his windows. His windows were all he had now.

Yes, he had land, hectares of it. At least three times a week he walked the land with his foreman, planning the work that needed to be done and glad-handing the workers. And he had men and trucks and plenty of work for anyone who wanted it. He had money and idiot businessmen at his beck and call.

But what he treasured were his windows. There were four of them. They were situated on the second level of his house, and looked out onto different views. The south window presented him with a glimpse of the courtyard of the azienda. He could watch workmen coming and going. This was most important now, during the harvest season. The western and northern windows looked out into the streets and allowed him to gauge the busyness of traffic and how well the shops were doing today.

The western window gave him a view to Umbria and the mountains and his own sorry garden patch, long overgrown with wild blackberry bushes.

The streets were getting quieter as families headed to the piazza. He couldn't see that far from his office balcony. The count himself was left to pace in increasingly louder circles around his upstairs apartment. His feet clomped along the tile as if trying to break the silence drifting in the windows.

He was bored.

Bored off his ass.

Look at all he'd given her. Given her the land. Yes, she'd been forced to liquidate some of her patrimony to set herself up in business, but that had taught her a lesson, had it not? He'd given her access to his people. Given her advice on which vines to plant, though she had certainly ignored him there and gone with the flashy varietals, thinking she could make boutique wines.

Which was absurd. The smart thing to plant these days were simple whites and reds, nothing fancy. Anything that you could sell to the co-op to make their swill. Take your money, hand over the grapes, and let them take the risks of bottling and selling it. That was the only way. The smart way. His father had lost his shirt continuing to bottle wines when the market began to change.

Yes, the count had given his daughter everything, and somehow it was not enough. What more was she looking for? Free and clear use of the land, unencumbered by his insistence on a percentage of her profits? His stipulation was merely good business, a way to make sure that she kept up her end of the bargain. Otherwise, there was no guarantee that she would make any use of the land at all.

Did she want the azienda itself? *That* was out of the question. Not while he breathed. And even then, when he passed, the titles would pass to the boy.

Not to his daughter, who had returned home with a child and a forever absent husband when the outside world had proved inconvenient.

Not to the ungrateful wretch of a wife who had abandoned him.

Damn them all. They had no sense of how difficult life was. If he had one job at all, it was to show them that life could indeed be cruel.

He stalked into the kitchen, intending to pour himself an *aperitivo*. He could sit on the balcony and—what? Stare at nothing?

He was not supposed to eat until five. And yet—the scent was too much. The meat seasoned with rosemary and fennel.

His lips tasted his drink but it was the meat he craved.

Damn them. Damn them.

You did this, bitch. *You* taught your daughter to hate her own father and she has continued to do so, even in your absence.

He used oven mitts to withdraw the roasting pan. He was about to lay it on the kitchen counter, but thought better of it.

He carried it into his office, and dropped the pan on his desk blotter. The pan was burning a mark into his blotter when he returned with the fork and carving knife. He made a quick incision. Pried back the meat to judge its doneness. It was red. Bloody red. The flesh still raw. He cut off a sliver of the crispy outside layer and popped it into his mouth.

Greasy, moist, and hot hot hot.

He greedily gulped it down. He shook his head like a dog trying to swallow a not-quite-dead bee. Thrashed his head. His hair became unkempt. The gray locks rose like fur around his ears.

He dug in. Carved great chunks of raw meat and popped each of them into his mouth. The flesh inside was still cool, but delicious. He laughed, thinking what a sight he made. Blood ran down his lips. He laughed and shook his head and whooped a bit, like a wolf calling to another across a field: *Time to eat.*

Chapter Twenty-Nine

Aurelio Zenobia did not have much in this world but he did have this: a parking space just steps from the back entrance to the Orvieto train station.

In the old days, when he was just a young man, he used to walk down the street from his apartment in the lower part of town. But marriage, children, and a new apartment outside town necessitated the use of his dilapidated Cinquecento a few days a week, when his wife wasn't taking it to do their shopping. When he did drive, he liked to park in the spot he'd called his own for nearly twenty years.

The tunnel led directly to the train platforms, one line heading north to Siena and Florence, the other leading south to the vile cesspool that was Rome. And if one walked straight ahead through the tunnel, one arrived at the staircase which led up to the vomitous green station where Aurelio had spent those two decades.

On one side of the stairs, the newspaper vendor sold his tabloids, sexy magazines, cheap paperbacks, toys, and puzzles. And on the other side of the staircase, the cafe man sold coffee, bad pizza, tourist trinkets, and dried panini to the hordes who traipsed through daily. Together, he and they comprised a triumvirate who had watched each other grow old: the ticket clerk, the newsman, and the coffee slinger.

By rights, because Aurelio was an employee of the state, he was supposed to park in the far reaches of the parking lot. Such was the directive from Milan, but since no one from Milan had ever shown his pale snooty face in this station, the triumvirate had long assigned themselves spaces of their own choosing.

And now, for a whole week straight, someone had had the effrontery to park an Audi—bright, shiny, and reeking of money—in a critical space just outside the station. The car was there last Thursday morning when Aurelio had arrived for work. He'd been forced to park farther afoot and suffer the smirks of the newsman and coffee slinger. He supposed that he could bear one day's displacement. He could use the exercise, frankly, but the car was still there days later, parked under the plane tree which had shaded Aurelio's car from the hot summer sun for decades.

Had someone gone away for the holiday? Would he have to endure the unknown length of this person's vacation?

It galled him. This was all he asked of his job at this point. He was fifty-three years old, expecting to retire in another year or so and collect his munificent pension. My God, did he not have the right to park where he wanted? Had he not earned that right?

At night he obsessed about this in bed as Assunta lay beside him, her snores and breath filling the room with their exhalations.

Just today, aggravated beyond belief, he had gone to the parking lot though he was still on holiday. The car was still there. He'd cupped his eyes and peered inside. A shopping bag in the back crawled with maggots.

The image was too terrible.

It sickened him even as it gave him hope.

The police should know about such a car.

Chapter Thirty

The first to hit the table was a basket of tiny fried fish, *lattarini,* smelt fried to the point of crispiness. And a bottle of white wine and some mineral water.

"Help yourself," Cimini said, popping a few of the fish in his mouth.

Scarpone stared at the fish. They were pale gray under their greasy fried shells. Dark spots indicated their eyes and the tiny speck of excrement still left in their bodies. Years ago, he would have munched them without a thought. Today, the smell of them disgusted him.

"I'm delicate in the morning," he told Cimini.

Cimini shot one of his cuffs out from under his uniform. He looked at his watch. "It's eleven thirty. Not afternoon, but surely not morning. Have one—they're not going to kill you."

He inspected the bottle and let the waiter pop it.

They were sitting in the flagstoned patio of a trattoria in the old city of Montefiascone. The white wall of the patio was bleached by the sun behind them. Beyond the wall was a road and a sheer drop to an expanse of blueness. Lago di Bolsena, Europe's largest volcanic lake. The scenery was breathtaking, the air fresh, the sunlight so overpowering that Scarpone wished he'd brought his glasses.

"I heard you met the commandante. Fun guy if your idea of fun is being dressed down every fifteen minutes. What a cockhead. Most of us try to avoid him. He's part of the old club who think the job is meant to provide stability for us men and little else. He ignores the central truth."

"Which is?"

"We've got some real problems here that need to be dealt with. Oh—I'm sorry, wine?"

Scarpone didn't bother protesting. If he wasn't going to eat the man's fried fish, he had to drink the wine, regardless of what it would do to his insides.

And to be honest, he was frankly curious. Est! Est!! Est!!! was *the* official wine of Montefiascone. He'd had it before, of course, but never here in its birthplace.

"This is the dry, by the way. If you like, we can get the sweet." A smile crawled onto Cimini's face. "Or both."

They weren't supposed to be drinking at all, but so be it.

"Dry will be fine."

Scarpone picked a few fish off the basket with his spoon and fork. Cimini used his hands—tossed them into his mouth like salty snacks. He was a hearty man with a red face and thinning black hair. Striking blue eyes. About a decade older than Scarpone.

"Here, the biggest issues are just what you'd think. The usual domestic shit, but I don't even count that. We have forty-three kilometers of coastline and that's tough to police, especially this time of year when people are crawling the beaches and killing each other with speedboats. And we have second-story men. They use mountain-climbing equipment, if you can believe it, to break into houses. Upstairs windows are so much more vulnerable. The city's especially attractive because we have so many second homes here. Foreigners, mostly. This has been the playground of the Germans for centuries. But you probably know that."

"I didn't."

"Oh, no? You never heard the story of the wine?"

Heard the story? Sure—it was depicted on every bottle of Est! Est!! Est!!! A medieval clergyman on pilgrimage sends his footman ahead to sample and locate the best vintages. On the walls of every suitable tavern the footman writes, in Latin: "Here it is!" Hence the name of the wine.

Yes, Scarpone had heard versions of the story a million times before.

"But I didn't know the clergyman was a German."

"Oh yes!"

"Is the story true?"

Cimini shrugged, fish crunching away. "There's a German clergyman buried at the church here in town. It's an old tomb. It's supposedly him, but who the hell knows? But it makes for a good story and sells wine and keeps the tourists happy. Once upon a time, the popes vacationed here. Barbarossa marched through here on his way to Rome. The Nazis retreated here and took a stand when the Americans invaded. We've still got the war dead in the cemetery outside town to prove it. It's as if, through every war, we were bombed and rebuilt. But none of that matters. Our claim to fame is we're the city of wine. Do you like it?"

"It's wonderful."

"But back to the point: we have drugs here, more than we can deal with. Hashish typically, though a lot of kids are playing with E now. So that's an issue. Believe it or not, we even have Mexicans bringing in marijuana via Dallas."

"That's happening in Rome, too, now."

"Hey, why not? The economic downturn worldwide means all of these pricks have to look for new territory, right? Heroin's the big issue, of course, the one cockheads like the commandante aren't truly addressing. Why here, why now, we don't know. If I had to guess, I'd say it has something to do with the forming of the EU. The borders disappeared and our own are porous as hell. We're surrounded by water, for heaven's sake. It's just so easy for them to sweep the shit off Anatolia in Turkey and have it land on our doorsteps. The problem is rife. We bust one gang up, and a new regime replaces it within months. We'll never get the Calabrian bosses, so we don't even try. We're just trying to get it off the streets."

"Where do they hole up?"

He drew himself up and set down his glass. "No offense, but I'd rather not say. We're working on something right now and I'm not at liberty to discuss it."

"Fair enough. But what I don't understand is why it isn't noticed on the borgo level."

"You'd be surprised. If it was your son or daughter and they were bringing home money to put food on the table, or they stopped asking *you* to put money in their pockets, would you ask too closely?"

"No, but my neighbors would."

"Exactly. Which is why we must try to ask. But there we encounter the curse of every carabiniere."

He didn't have to spell it out. In most towns and cities, carabinieri came and went; your neighbors were with you for life. Why would you rat out someone you had to face till the day you died?

"You. You're not eating."

Embarrassed, Scarpone stuffed something in this mouth just to be seen doing it.

"Will you excuse me?" Cimini said. He stood to take a call.

Scarpone chewed—

Scarpone's walking through the forest. The ground so chilly he's cold up to his knees. A man drives down a hill not unlike this one, with a view of mountains beyond the passenger side window, and the rock wall of a mountain out to the left. The car speeding like crazy. The man sitting at a cafe like this one. His finger raised to the waiter, ordering another round. The car speeding. A blur of scenery. A truck appears on the roadway below. Scarpone's once again in the woods. He hears the sound of steel on steel.

—until his stomach flopped and he was forced to spit the fish into a napkin and stuff the napkin between his knees. He glanced nervously at Cimini, who was still chatting amiably. Cimini eyeing his visitor, then turning his back to him.

I have to stop eating, Scarpone told himself. It's always the same. Food does it. But how will you live if you cannot eat? How will you live if you cannot sleep? I'll find a way, he thought. I must. Damn.

Scarpone sipped the wine. It was cool, crisp, bracing.

The taste of Montefiascone filled—

A woman on a balcony turns and smiles at him. She wears red eyeglasses and pushes her hair behind one of her ears.

—his mouth and floated to the top of his brain.

Cimini clapped his phone shut. And eyed him. "Ah, you like the wine, am I right?"

Scarpone did not realize he'd been smiling.

THE CHURCH WAS EIGHT HUNDRED YEARS OLD AND looked it. Gape-mouthed creatures stared down from the columns. Patches of stucco had broken away to reveal powdery bricks. Bizarrely, the smell of mold mingled with the faint scent of urine and wine.

"It's toward the back," Cimini said. He extracted keys from his pockets as he walked, shaking them out.

"Are you deacon here or something?"

Cimini shot him a look that told him the question was ridiculous. "They had to lock up the poor bastard," he said. "He's been the recipient of bad attention over the years. Vandals and drunks. The first time tourists come to town, they always want to see the grave of the famous bishop who gave the world Est! Est!! Est!!! We encouraged it for a long time. Once a year, we used to dump a tub of wine on his grave."

"Really?"

"The new priest is fighting us on that. He says it breeds fruit flies. But now they get idiots coming in here all the time, baptizing the guy anyway they see fit."

"It kind of stinks."

"Yeah, well, it used to smell like a bus depot. It's presentable now, but they had to make some concessions."

Scarpone saw a crude plywood enclosure covering one of the chapels. The unfinished wood clashed strongly with the nobility of the old church. It looked like something workmen erected during renovations.

"Is this never coming down?"

"Not in the near future."

Cimini unlocked the door and ushered Scarpone into the darkness. As soon as they were inside, Cimini pulled the door shut after them.

A click, then a 15-watt bulb threw its meek light into the chapel.

Scarpone saw a sarcophagus tablet embedded in the floor. It

depicted the worn image of a man in ceremonial robes, a bishop's miter on his head.

A heavily Gothic text ran across the bottom of his feet.

"This is the famous inscription," Cimini said. *"'Here lies my master, Johann DeFuk, who died of too much Est! Est!! Est!!!'"*

Scarpone bent to look.

But Cimini grabbed him by the front of his shirt and flung him against the stone wall of the crypt.

Scarpone went for his weapon. Cimini swatted his hand away and loomed over him.

In the miserable light he saw the man's lips hovering over him.

What the hell was this?

"I don't know you," Cimini said. "I have chosen to trust you, but I don't want you to get the wrong impression. I don't give my friendship lightly. I have never been a trusting man. Some say I'm jolly, but that comes at a price. I have been burned before and I won't let it happen again. Do you understand?"

"What are you talking about?"

His meaty paw pressed against Scarpone's weak chest.

"I have made inquiries. Men in Rome whom I trust. They speak highly of you, for the most part. Others say you chase ghosts. But your closed cases speak for themselves."

"What have I done to offend you?"

"Nothing. Yet. I have no choice but to make you my friend. I want that. But I enter the bargain reluctantly because we're not of long acquaintance."

He rooted in his pockets and came up with a minuscule bag filled with a light brown powder.

"Heroin. You see?"

"I see."

"Very high purity. Better than street. For years now, there has always been a standing order to set aside a high-strength cut destined for one borgo in the region. I don't know why. None of the idiots we bust know why. They just do it and collect their pay. Do you know the name of that borgo?"

"Castelpietra?" Scarpone croaked.

"Exactly. As near as we can figure, they like your shithole because it's close to the A1. A short ride north and they're in Florence. A short ride south and they're in Rome. They can even take the train and eat bad croissants all the way down."

"Who is the contact in the borgo?"

"Who *was* the contact, you mean?"

"Demaci?"

"Your dead Albanian, yes."

"We found him naked, stung to death by snakes. Or so we think."

"Asps. Vicious creatures. See? That interests me. Doesn't it smack of torture to you? Doesn't it smack of vengeance?"

"How can you possibly know all this? If you know this much, you must be close to shutting them down."

Cimini stepped back. He dropped his palm from Scarpone's chest. He stood under the light and removed his cap. His forehead was dotted with beads of sweat. "I have a man inside," he said. "A young soldier who is dear to me. One whose family I love as my own. I give you this information as a courtesy to you, as a gesture of my faith. There will no doubt be more, but that will take time. When I know something, you'll know it too—if you do me two favors."

"Which are?"

"Somehow they're getting a free pass in Castelpietra. Someone's sheltering them. They amass a shipment or pieces of a shipment, then route it north or south. I need to know how. That's one. Two, you and your men stay out of my territory. Stay off the lake. I can't have you here. Your methods are not welcome in Montefiascone. *Mi capisci?* If all goes well and you don't cross us, then I will know you are worthy of being called brother. Do we understand each other?"

"But...you said that they keep sending new crews. So what difference does one more bust make?"

"It does to me. Because the violence keeps escalating. Dismemberings, beatings, shootings. Oh yes—it happens. Every year, they get warier. And the last man I sent in was nearly killed before we shut them down. You will not mess it up. You investigate your Albanian. I'll deal with the heroin. Understand me, capitano?"

"Yes, certainly."

Cimini mopped his brow. Then he patted Scarpone's shoulder

apologetically. His paw felt like lead. Scarpone felt an immediate crick in his lower back.

I need exercise, he thought.

They walked out of the church in silence. The sun blinded Scarpone. Each man went to his own vehicle.

"Go," Cimini said. "And be well. They tell me you are a good man. I sincerely hope you are. I long to call you my brother."

Chapter Thirty-One

The restaurant was one of those spotless roadside automats that sold premade panini, salads, and a couple of hot entrees. The place gleamed so much that it reminded him of some of the galleries in Rome that sold modern office furniture. Chairs made of orange and light-green plastic. Matching lights around the refrigerated cases that held twenty brands of mineral water alone.

Behind the cafeteria line, workers in orange aprons fired up the warming trays for a line of motorists. The sickly sweet scent of industrial pasta sauce wafted through the air.

They needed to keep this conference brief. They were due at the Orvieto train station.

"I have answered two central questions," said Claudia Cavalcanti, the pathologist.

"That was fast."

"I used a friend's lab in Perugia."

"So these would be unofficial results."

"They're certified, so they'd hold up in court."

If the prosecutor gets them through, Scarpone thought. But they could deal with that later. Since he had never worked with the Viterbo lab, he had no idea what to expect. Judging from the commandante's attitude, Scarpone expected lab results to be merely tardy. He had no way of knowing if they would be accurate.

"The preliminary tox screen does indicate venom, as from a serpent. Those marks on the body are indeed snakebites."

"What species? Gismonda didn't know."

Cavalcanti shifted awkwardly in her seat at the mention of Horseface's name. "He is not an expert, is he? We should hold off on making assumptions. I have a friend in herpetology who now has a sample of the man's blood. We'll hear from her department within the week. But it's safe to surmise that it was extremely deadly. Demaci was injected with an incredible dosage, I must say. If it was a viper, one strike is enough to hospitalize a grown man for three days. He received about a dozen bites and no medical attention. He could have easily absorbed enough venom to kill a dozen men."

"From the same snake?"

"I don't think the experts can tell you that, frankly. But when I mentioned it to my colleague, she said it was bizarre that someone should be bit that many times—not unless he'd been tossed into a snake pit. Which is what got me thinking about the lotion that was smeared, you recall, all over his body."

"In what sense?"

She shrugged. "Let's wait on the experts, shall we? But here's what I found: the lotion is unremarkable. It's just a homemade body lotion: coconut oil, water, beeswax, and a hint of some other fragrant oil. On some parts of the victim's body, lavender is present. On others, bergamot. Still others, the oil of blood orange. They squeeze the peels to extract the oil."

Scarpone leaned forward and looked at her documents upside down. "I can't picture this guy smearing this stuff on himself. What would be the point? Those are not fragrances a man would use."

"No, but a woman might apply it to him, during, uh"—her tongue peeked nervously out of the corner of her mouth—"during lovemaking."

"Is that a thing?"

Her face flushed.

"Okay," he said, "so we're looking for a woman who bought some body lotion. It should take us the rest of our lives to find such a person."

"Well, see, this is what I find intriguing. Did you hear the list of ingredients? What's missing?"

"They all sounded natural."

"Exactly. There are no industrial ingredients. Nothing that you'd find in a strictly commercial preparation."

He leaned back and searched the ceiling. His face hardened in thought.

"You seem angry," she said.

He took a deep breath and let it out slowly. "That might be because I'm realizing it's just an ordinary case of snakebite. Two young lovers are accustomed to meeting in the grotto. He stumbles into a snake pit and gets himself bit. End of story."

"And that upsets you?"

He didn't respond, preferring to stare into the light emanating from the drinks case. She looked at the time on her mobile phone, and began packing her things, taking pains to avoid his eyes. "Oh, I thought you were mad at me."

"Why? *Oh.*"

"I should apologize for that phone call."

"Don't bother, please."

"I haven't been happy here. My job, my work situation, *tutto*. But none of it has any bearing on you or this investigation. I'm prepared to be professional."

Which is why you're telling me this, he thought.

Chapter Thirty-Two

"Who found it?"

Enzo scanned his notebook. "The stationmaster. Says he saw the contents of the vehicle and was concerned."

"Concerned?"

"Concerned, sir."

Scarpone smiled. People's concern amused him. What was often expressed as concern was veiled self-interest.

Dottoressa Cavalcanti, again dressed in her shapely suit of Tyvek, pulled herself away from the Audi to allow Scarpone a peek inside.

The interior of the car stunk.

Under a sweater in the rear footwell was a shopping bag containing a couple of pieces of putrefying, store-bought meat which crawled with maggots.

The man's clothing—his pants, shoes, socks, underwear, shirt, jacket—were stuffed in a pile in the trunk. The wallet in the slacks had clearly belonged to Arbend Demaci.

"That's the food he was supposed to pick up at the market for his mother?"

"It would seem so, yes," Enzo said.

"Fingerprints?"

Claudia shrugged. "Maybe, yes. Cars are difficult—"

"Please spare me. Are we going to find anything or not?"

"The steering wheel. The door. The mirror. Yes. It appears that there are a mix of small and large prints."

"Small as in not a man's."

She shrugged. "I'd prefer not to speculate."

He asked her to step aside and bent low so that he could stick his upper torso into the vehicle. Enzo prattled on. The stationmaster had called the Orvieto cops, who told him to call a tow truck. The stationmaster said he would, but he was *concerned* that there was something dangerous in the vehicle. The cops had sent a carabiniere who inspected it and reiterated that the stationmaster should have the vehicle towed if it offended him so. Aurelio Zenobia insisted they file a report of some kind. What if the maggot-infested object in the backseat were a pet? Or a child?

"Zenobia is a *remarkably* concerned citizen," Scarpone said.

"He thought that he should swear out a complaint."

"Right. For meat gone off."

Scarpone borrowed a long stick from Claudia and poked around the coffee cup well and other nooks and crannies.

"It's clean. The kind of car someone cleaned on a regular basis."

The responding carabiniere had called the insurance company indicated in the car's documents, Enzo said. The Falmarra insurance company was in a nearby city called Capalba. No answer.

"But Demaci can't be the owner, of course," Scarpone said. "He doesn't have residency. Just the work permit. Do we have the name of the owner?"

"All efforts to reach the insurance company have failed. Documentation in the car says it's registered to Dentare, a farmer's co-op in Viterbo. I'm checking with the auto club. In any case, the carabiniere remembered that we were looking for such a car and called us."

"Let me guess: his superiors were delighted to punt this to us."

"With the chief's blessing, sir."

Scarpone looked at Claudia and Enzo.

"Which of you is shorter?"

Enzo self-consciously drew himself up to his full height.

"You then. How tall are you?"

Claudia told him.

"Put down your tools for a second. Do you mind sitting in the vehicle?"

"I would rather not disturb anything in the vehicle just yet."

"You won't be touching anything."

"I'd rather not."

"Please don't annoy me. I need to make a decision about this right now and I can't wait three hours for you to conclude your processing. Please."

She complied. Held her arms across her chest, placed her rump on the seat and then drew her bootied feet after her, gingerly resting them on the immaculate carpet.

"Are you comfortable enough to drive, do you think?"

"Certainly."

"Get out."

She stepped out carefully, her eyes bouncing between Enzo and the captain.

"Damn it," Scarpone said. "Damn it, damn it. How fast does it take to run DNA tests in this area if I got you samples to compare?"

"If you let me put it on my budget, and we do it in Perugia, less than a week if I ask nicely. Maybe sooner. If we go with Viterbo, it's a minimum of fourteen days, maybe longer, if we ask for the Captain Scarpone special. Why do you ask?"

He ignored her comment. He checked the time. Then swore. The ride to Montefiascone had killed his day.

He asked Enzo, "Is D'Orazio in town right now?"

"He should be."

"Good. Tell the magistrate I must speak with him *tonight*. Tell D'Orazio to find her and get her down to the station tomorrow morning."

"Find who, sir?"

"Isn't it obvious?"

Chapter Thirty-Three

The borgo's only gymnasium was located on the top floor of the same building that housed the local theater. A tall exterior staircase led from the street up to the business. Scarpone was halfway up when he paused to rest.

Just these steps alone could be my exercise, he thought. But he pushed himself up to find himself in a spacious room that smelled of new carpet. Gleaming machines. A few small flat-screen televisions blaring away.

A short, tubby man was wiping down the equipment with a spray bottle and some old undershirt rags. He paused in his work to smile at Scarpone, who perceived instantly that the fellow had Down syndrome.

Another man with thighs like tree trunks was sweating away on a treadmill while he simultaneously played with his phone and watched TV.

The place smelled of cool, conditioned air, spray-can air fresheners, and the faint stink of cigarettes. A few newspapers littered the machines. Either they had been left behind by previous clients or they were set out for the enjoyment of fresh arrivals.

The Down man signaled the proprietor, who muted the TV, slowed his machine, and came over. His head was nearly bald and shaved thin. He wore bicycle pants and a new Lycra shirt. Muscles rippled under his arms, so much so that his head seemed smaller than anything else on his body. He was about thirty.

"Sbuccio?"

"You must be Scarpone?"

Scarpone's lungs were still protesting the climb.

"Enzo sent you?" the gym man said, his eyes narrowing as he watched Scarpone try to get a word out.

"Water..." Scarpone said.

The two men watched him drink. They were about the same height and coloring, obviously brothers. At last the captain coughed out one sentence:

"I need to be stronger."

Then he sank into one of the chairs inside the doors.

He thought he would die.

A GOOD HALF HOUR LATER, A SHIRTLESS SCARPONE STOOD in front of the man, who was looking over the results of an exhausting physical fitness test.

"I took exercise frequently in the old days, but not lately," Scarpone said.

The man's eyes looked over Scarpone's torso.

"What happened here," Sbuccio said, "if you don't mind my asking?"

My captain's body was dotted with three puckered scars. One at his shoulder, just below the nerves whose destruction would have meant the loss of the use of that arm. One under a bottom rib, which had missed his right lung. The final wound was lower, where the last of his attackers had hit him before dying himself. It was that last shot —the one that had ripped through Scarpone's abdomen—that had done the most damage to his appetite and psyche. The physicians had been in there for hours, rooting for the bullet and stitching his intestines together.

"Jesu Cristo. What happened to the other guy?"

"Three of them. Tragically, they did not survive."

"You were invalided for a while, then?"

"You can tell?"

"The legs suffer atrophy right away but they catch up once you start moving again. Your lung capacity, though, doesn't improve much if you don't push them to do work. And from the outline of your ribs I'd say you have been neglecting good nutrition."

Scarpone shrugged. "I don't have a taste for it."

"I can't help you if you don't eat."

Scarpone was silent. His eyes drifted to a newspaper that had fallen under the treads of one of the machines. He could use that newspaper. Tonight, perhaps, he could try to build this very building. It would be a challenge: the theater marquee, the exterior staircase, and this small air-conditioned room that probably didn't get much use from the vast majority of people in town.

"Is this your place?"

The muscle-bound man launched into a lovely story of how he'd used a bit of his patrimony to open a bike touring and rock-climbing company in Orvieto. "People don't want to exercise," he admitted. "But bike excursions are popular with foreigners."

"Good money?"

"I made a sack of it. But in the end I sold it. I couldn't take the stress."

Scarpone nearly laughed aloud, but the man was completely serious. "Can you help me?"

"Yes. I'll work out a program for you. The physical therapy program at the hospital? I designed it. But that's intended for injured farm workers. You—I prescribe the weights, the treadmill, and some swimming or cycling. I can get you a deal on a bike. Enzo just upgraded. If you two get along, you might consider going with him on his circuit."

"Sounds good."

"And you will eat. You must. My program can be punishing. I must have total compliance."

No response.

"How can you not eat?" Sbuccio said. "We have the best food in the world."

Indeed, Scarpone thought.

Out of the corner of his eye, he spied the man's brother bend to retrieve the errant newspaper and stuff it into a plastic bag.

Damn it.

Chapter Thirty-Four

"May I ask when you last saw him?"

"Who?"

"Your boyfriend, of course. Arbend Demaci."

"He was no longer my boyfriend at the time...at the time of his..."

"His death," Scarpone said.

"That's right. We went together for a while. A year maybe. But then we stopped. He wasn't serious. We never should have been together."

"Did the occasion of your split have something to do with your condition?"

"My condition?" the girl said, sipping from her cup of water.

"Please don't waste my time."

Caterina Chiostro was a sullen girl of about nineteen, with dull, flat eyes, a doughy complexion, and stringy black hair. She had a job as a clerk at a perfume and ladies' notions shop owned by her aunt and uncle.

She sat across from Scarpone at a table on the ground floor of the carabinieri station. The top floor held the barracks, where all the unmarried soldiers bunked. The middle floor held the admin offices. This floor held, among other things, their recreation room, which was outfitted with a cheap television, some sofas, racing posters, and a long bar where they were able to brew espressos while watching the matches.

One of the men—Puzio, the blond northerner—was theoretically watching TV in the corner now. Though, strangely, the TV was muted and the young soldier seemed to be doing nothing more than scrolling through the screen of his *telefonino*. A steel door leading to the outdoors was propped open with a brick, allowing a slight breeze into the otherwise damp, cinderblocked cavern.

"You're wasting *my* time, aren't you?" the girl said. "Asking me these stupid questions. All right, then. He was the last person I wanted to see. I was certainly not spending any time with him."

"It's strange that you let him off so easily. If it were me, I'd keep an eye on him. I'd want to know that he was around to provide in some way for our child. I wouldn't be able to stomach the thought of him keeping company with any other girls. Or leaving town. Or taking a job in another borgo. All of these things would be on my mind, if it were me."

She sneered, laid a hand on her swollen belly and turned uncomfortably in her seat so she was now looking more at the Peroni beer sign over the bar than him.

"Oh—are you a woman, Signore?" she said. "I'm sure your experience with pregnancies entitles you to make such comments. Can I go now?"

Scarpone said calmly: "I'm sure your experience with an unwanted pregnancy and the shame of the entire borgo entitles you—"

Caterina Chiostro swiped at her water tumbler. It flew off the table. Water everywhere. The plastic glass rolled harmlessly across the floor.

The girl hung her head and pouted. "I can't sit in uncomfortable places, talking. It's not good for the baby."

Scarpone leaned forward, keeping his eyes focused on hers. "Just a few more questions, okay?"

Puzio, over in the corner, now roused himself from his phone and came over to retrieve the cup and whisk it out of the room. He muttered something about getting a mop, but Scarpone barely acknowledged him.

Clever of them.

If the girl had been watching, she would have seen how gingerly Puzio had retrieved the cup, with a gloved hand.

"I'm not even sure I'm supposed to talk to you like this. What are the laws? My parents—"

"The law of the republic is pretty clear on this, Signorina. Nothing you say right now could ever be held against you. Believe me —if this were serious, you'd know it. Magistrates and lawyers would be present. There would be video cameras and statements. This? This is just you and me talking. Can I get you an espresso?"

He wasn't even sure he knew how to work the machine.

She shook her head.

"Well, I'm going to have one."

He went behind the bar. He made a show of adding water and coffee to the machine and pressing buttons. It was nonsense. He was merely buying time until Puzio's return.

The TV played silently in the background. Some talking heads were discussing the recent conviction of a member of Parliament. The newscaster seemed shocked, shocked by this.

After a bit, Scarpone turned away from the machine with a cup of dirty water. Puzio was there with a mop. Their eyes met. The young cop nodded curtly, dabbed at the floor with the mop, and left.

Scarpone sipped his coffee. It tasted terrible.

"Now," he said from the bar. "Your doctor says that you are near seven months along. Assuming you stopped seeing him when your condition was made known, you have not dated him for six or seven months."

She nodded.

"I'm sorry, I didn't hear you."

"Yes," she said, rolling her eyes.

"So when did you last see him?"

"I see him every day. We live in the same stupid borgo. It's not possible to avoid him."

"But you haven't seen him privately at any time?"

She stared at him, seemingly incapable of speech.

"Did you hear me?" Scarpone tried again.

"Yes?"

"Well, did you?"

"No," she said.

He set down the coffee cup, and returned to his seat.

"You claim you haven't seen him for months. But your fingerprints match the ones found on his vehicle, which was parked at the train station in Orvieto last week."

Silence.

"Oh, okay," Scarpone said. "So *now* you shut up. You're trying to think your way out of this."

She looked at him, eyes terrified. "I don't understand what I said."

"As long as you're thinking, think about this: If you keep lying to me, that only raises my suspicions. Based on your statements, I already have enough to turn this over to the magistrate."

The girl looked terrified. "What on earth are you saying? What statement? I've said nothing."

Scarpone held up a hand. "Please, let's not go this route."

"What did I just say? What did I say wrong?"

"Signorina, think carefully. The most likely thing to say is, 'Well, but I did date him for so long and it only follows that my fingerprints would be in the vehicle.' But he appears to have kept his vehicle immaculate. Fingerprints would not survive the current length of your pregnancy. So you have to try much, much harder—"

"Shut up!" the girl snapped.

Her fingers tugged at her chin.

"You saw him," Scarpone said. "You spoke, perhaps you even slept together. He died. You moved the vehicle. This seems without question."

"No! That's not true! That's not true!"

"Then what possible explanation can there be?"

"Just wait, okay, wait. I don't know. I don't know. I'm not the one who knows..."

"Knows what?"

"I don't know how to talk about...things." She pressed her hands to her belly. Then looked up. "Do I have to keep talking? I don't know how...Can I stop?"

He knew he should stop. But what did he have? Not much.

"Caterina, listen to me. What you said just now? 'I'm not the one who knows'? And earlier, you said, 'What did I say wrong?' Explain that. Are you following some kind of script here?"

"No."

"Then what can that possibly mean? Who is the one who knows how to talk about such things, Signorina?"

Her jaw was set. She stared at him the way a cow stares at passing cars.

Their interview was over.

Chapter Thirty-Five

They went out the basement door, into the light of day, where the rest of the girl's family were waiting by a small delivery van.

Two parents, and the girl's sister.

The father was speaking in quiet tones with D'Orazio, the fat marshal.

The younger sister was about eighteen, with short blond hair that hung a bit over her eyes. She wore a faux leather jacket, a man's undershirt, and work boots. She was fiddling with her mobile phone.

The parents, who were barely into their forties, nevertheless looked a decade older. They stood with their arms so entwined that Scarpone didn't see how it was possible for them to breathe.

Scarpone already had the magistrate on his mobile.

"What do you want me to do, Matteo? You know the law. Until we confirm a crime's been committed, I can't even get involved."

"We have physical evidence."

"That she drove a car."

"If you call it tampering, it's enough to hold her under the law, pending a full investigation."

"No. I won't do it. Not in her condition. Her lawyer will say she's ignorant and pregnant and thus unreliable. If you take her in, she'll have to go to Viterbo. I won't do that to one of our children. Confinement to the borgo is enough."

"She's nineteen. Our only hope of getting her to talk is to lock her up."

Saviano laughed. "Listen to you. Where are you, Rome? These are not thugs. These are simple people. Her father was a grape grower. Her mother works at a perfume store. Just do your job. Give me something I can hang on. Otherwise, I can't do this to our people. I can't do this to her family. They've suffered enough. Excuse me."

Suffered enough?

Saviano rang off.

Of course. It was not them who were in the wrong. It was Scarpone. *He* was the outsider here. *He* was the straniero.

That was plainly obvious. It chilled Scarpone to watch the exquisite deference D'Orazio displayed as he helped the mother into the van, and then stood speaking with her through the open door. The two girls had already piled in back.

Scarpone squinted.

This was a game he played sometimes.

Squint and see what you see.

With one eye, he saw the family and D'Orazio as they were, talking about a dead man, and a girl in bad circumstances with a swollen belly.

But close the other eye. What did you see?

The younger sister comforting the older.

A mother looking dead on her feet. Running to fat, with thick, uncomfortable ankles.

The father shambling along, his fingers fretting with the van keys. The father gaunt. As gaunt, Scarpone thought, as I am.

Starving themselves or else gorging themselves. Their eyes bloodshot.

Something else was at work here.

They've suffered enough.

The mother shook D'Orazio's hand with both of hers. "Grazie, Signore," the mother said. "I can't lose another."

Chapter Thirty-Six

That night, he found that the plants he'd bought at the gasoline distributor on Sunday were already dead on the balcony. He poked his finger into the soil of each. Still damp.

It was late summer. Nighttime temperatures had been warm. There was no earthly reason why the plants should be dead, except that he asked them to be.

He had brushed his fingers along the length of their leaves and whispered the words.

And now, a day or so later, they were dry as husks.

It was impossible—unless it *was* possible.

Below the balcony, he heard the animals stirring in the barn. The train coursing on the tracks toward Florence.

He came inside and locked the glass doors.

He had no stomach for the paper houses tonight. In the bedroom, he climbed on the bed, put on the red reading glasses, and took the files in his hands again.

Dead young men.

Their deaths beginning three years back.

Egidio Tubecchi.

Gabrielle Santello.

Luca Dancione.

Domenico DelCillie.

He counted the files. One, two, three, four. But didn't Saviano say there had been as many as five deaths?

Scarpone paged through the files again, carefully, turning each sheet of paper at a time. And there, in the Santello file, he found another file tucked into the back. Somehow, they had become enmeshed.

Allora—

He opened the file, and flipped to the first page.

Here was the last boy, about two years gone:

Fabrizio Chiostro, 18, deceased, heroin overdose. Son of Gioia and Corrado, brother of Caterina, 17, and Allegra, 16.

Three children in that family.

Fabrizio.

Caterina.

Allegra.

He flipped through the file, excited. This was something significant—a link between the dead Albanian and the dead boys.

Today he had interviewed Caterina, the pregnant girl.

Her brother had died of heroin.

She had dated the Albanian.

Demaci, the Albanian, was suspected of *dealing* heroin. Or so the Montefiascone marshal had said.

But there was something else. Something else eating at him that he could put into words.

One by one now, he took the files and paged through them again.

I know there's something here, he thought. I just don't know what. Something about the dates. The ages. The names.

He dropped the case files. Part of him wanted to sleep. Craved it, demanded it. The other part of him wanted to stay up all night to look for the truth.

It is right there in front of me. It *must* be. He knew this feeling well. It was the mark of closeness, something at the tip of his tongue, his fingers, his mind.

He looked up and stared at the corner closest to his window.

For a moment I worried that he would see me.

But he did not. Was it possible he never would?

Chapter Thirty-Seven

Scarpone doubted seriously that anyone could miss the presence of the police vehicle parked up the block from the Chiostro home on the eastern side of the borgo.

The family lived in a two-family house on the outer ring, just above the cliffs. The house was pink stucco with aluminum awnings. A picture window on the top and bottom floors.

Both Gismonda and D'Orazio seemed surprised to see Scarpone roll up on a bike. He leaned it against the front of their car and sat in the backseat. "You rang?"

Gismonda dropped his racing magazine in an effort to look like he was doing his job.

"That's right. We just put something together that we thought you ought to know about," D'Orazio said.

"You know the family long?"

D'Orazio shrugged again. "No more than any other. Father's a grape grower, or was, anyway. Now he works for the daughter."

"The *daughter*?" Scarpone said. "How is that possible?"

"Not the pregnant one. The other one."

"The dyke," Gismonda snapped.

D'Orazio smiled awkwardly. "Anyway, Gismonda and I got to talking. He happened to mention that they found a strange lotion or cream on the dead man's body."

"How did you hear that?" Scarpone asked.

Gismonda looked away. "Claudia happened to mention it."

"Claudia?"

"The pathologist."

"Oh, the 'bitch,' you mean? Since when are you on a first-name basis with her?"

"We've reconciled. Anyway, she mentioned this and it got us—D'Orazio and me—talking. Tell him."

"Look at the house, sir. It's rather nice, isn't it? Built-in garage. You see the plants out front?"

D'Orazio pointed to an ugly roll-up garage door of corrugated steel. A couple of potted trees on casters were stationed out front.

"What are those?"

"Lemon trees," D'Orazio said.

"No—that one's an orange," Gismonda said.

"Whatever. The point is, every morning the older signora, Eufemia, the *nonna*, pulls them outside to get their sun. I don't wish to make a fuss, sir, but look."

D'Orazio nodded at the garage.

Scarpone saw a long table set up inside the space. He saw boxes. He saw a tower of empty glass jars and lids wrapped in plastic. "What are we looking at?"

"I was telling Gismonda here all about it. The younger girl has a business. A profitable one at that, I take it. Lotions and creams and things. It started as a hobby, something she could do for fun and sell at her uncle's perfume store. But I gather it's spread to Orvieto now and there's talk of selling on the Internet."

"Screw the Internet," Gismonda said. "It's such a fad."

"The lotions are handmade?"

"Well, they're doing it in their garage. That's about as handmade as you're going to get. The father helps her with the distribution to Orvieto and some of the other tourist towns in the region. I think it was intended as a way to help him through his grief when the son died. I gather she does all right for herself and her family."

My captain felt something akin to anger well up in his chest. How many other things did D'Orazio and his men know about this piece of shit town? How many other things were they going to fail to mention?

"Did you know the son who died?"

"No. But his death was like the others. An utter tragedy. A waste."

My captain was thinking. The car was silent for a second. The men could feel the air grow warm and stuffy.

"Hey," Gismonda said. "Is that Enzo's bike you're riding?"

"This lotion," Scarpone said, "does it have a brand name? Can you draw the logo for me?"

"You don't have to have me draw it. You can just go buy it at their store."

"That's exactly what I *don't* want to do."

"I might be able to draw it, then."

D'Orazio rooted around in his jacket for a pen and his notebook.

"I don't want either of you to breathe a word of this. What can you tell me about the younger girl?"

Gismonda uttered one word: "*Strega.*"

Commonly meant to indicate that a woman was a raging bitch. Or a hag.

"She seemed nice when I saw her," Scarpone said. "Kind and solicitous to her mother and sister."

"That kind wears the pants, if you know what I mean," Gismonda said.

"No, sir," D'Orazio said. "He means that literally. She fancies herself a witch. I told you: a strange girl."

"A dyke, *and* a freak," Gismonda said.

Scarpone slapped the hat off Gismonda's head.

Chapter Thirty-Eight

"I have things to discuss with you," Scarpone told Lucia Cortese over the phone later that morning. "Things of a personal matter. I can come out to the house, if you like."

"No," she'd told him.

"Here at the station, then? Or I can arrange a nice office at the city hall."

"What is this about again?"

"It's about Marco."

Silence. Dead silence.

"I meet my designers once a week in Orvieto. We'll do it there. I'll pick you up."

She hung up.

They'd driven out in silence in her BMW convertible, her hair braced against the wind with a bright yellow scarf. She parked at the top of the hill, where tourists disembarked from the funicular.

I thought it was nice to see the two of them walking together in the freshness of the day, their feet slowly coming into sync on the cobblestones.

My captain seemed more preoccupied with getting his bearings. Walking in Orvieto was like navigating a maze. The tall stone tower was one landmark, the piazza and the chocolate-shop-cum-Internet-cafe was another. The duomo was in the other direction, due south, in the direction of the borgo.

The shops and the people and their stylish clothes told him he was a world away from the simple people of the borgo.

She led him away from the piazza, under a stone archway. They pressed themselves to the sides of the buildings as they walked to let a government vehicle pass by.

The air smelled of burning wood.

"I've never known anyone who did what you do," Lucia asked him. "Do you like it?"

The truth is, he had never thought of doing anything else.

By now I knew my captain well enough to know that he didn't like talking about himself. But I could tell he was softening on that score. He probably felt he had to. Considering the purpose of their outing, he felt he ought to pave the way toward trust by revealing something of himself.

So he told her that he could have gone into his father's trade. It was not a lucrative business, to be sure, but if one was clever, one could figure out how to turn it into something. His father's brother had segued neatly from chair weaving to buying, refinishing, and selling old chairs. This had blossomed for him into a fine business selling antiques to tourists and upscale Romans in the vicinity of the Spanish Steps. But his uncle was a singular man: odd, fastidious, clear-headed, socially nimble, and flamboyant. Not at all the man Scarpone's father had been.

His mother had urged Scarpone to be practical, to choose a career path leading ultimately to *sistemazione*—a good setup, preferably with benefits and a pension. If he worked for the state, he'd never know the travails and uncertainties of the self-employed life.

What no one had not counted on was that he'd *like* the job, be good at it, and give a damn about it.

"*Are* you good at it?" she asked, blithely unaware that she might be giving offense. "I suppose you must be, if you have made it all the way to marshal. But you're not a marshal, are you? Your rank is actually higher." She gestured toward a restaurant. "We're over here."

The place was small but inviting. Plain, wood-paneled walls were covered with a mismatched collection of paintings and drawings.

I will have to eat something, he thought.

He thought he would play it safe with a plate of prosciutto and a side of spinach. Sbuccio, his trainer, had insisted he begin including vegetables at every meal.

She ordered a dish he'd heard about but had never seen, let alone tasted: *umbrichelli*. Strands of pasta twists coated in a golden sheen of oil. The proprietor set it down in front of Lucia and went to work shaving black truffles over them.

Black flakes on a dish of gold.

"Try it," she said.

"I couldn't possibly. This is enough."

"This is what you eat, Captain? Spinach? My son is four and eats more than you. Try this. You'll love it. It's the dish of the region, typically Umbrian."

She proffered a forkful across the table, her hand under it as if to catch the oil. It was the same gesture she'd used the first day they'd met. Now, for some reason, neither of them thought it uncomfortable.

He had no choice.

He leaned across the table and gulped the pasta off the fork.

The pasta was dense and chewy, the oil nothing but slippery goodness, the truffle shavings—

He is walking in the woods again. Sunlight filters through the trees. He smells woodsmoke, and sees his boots striding across the leaves. His fingers and arms are cold. He beats his hands against his arms. He hears the screech of brakes. The sound of steel on steel. He runs. The woods end and he is standing at the side of a road. A car has been crushed against the side of a hill by a giant food truck. He sees a woman in the passenger seat, equally crushed, blood spattered across her forehead. She looks at him. She is about to say something when her eyes glaze over. He takes another step and peers into the backseat of the vehicle. What have I done? he asks himself. What have I done?

—a breath of the earth.

A chill came over me as the captain shook the vision from his head. The walls of the restaurant felt as cold as a meat locker. But my captain did not feel this way at all. Instead, his forehead was instantly hot. Sweat squeezed from every pore of his face. He reached for his napkin. A thought occurred to him: spit out the pasta. But he couldn't. Not here. Not in front of all these people. Not in front of her.

Look at her—head to toe, put together so beautifully. Do you want her to see you're nothing but a dirty, food-spewing cop?

He gulped down water.

The pounding in his head receded.

The walls around me grew warmer, but my heart was not pleased. Every part of me wanted to grab the captain and shake him. *No, no—go back to the woods. Go back and see what needs to be seen!*

"Are you okay? Do you not like truffles?"

Scarpone's heart thumped. *What have I done?* he thought. *What have I done?*

"They're delicious. But it's been so long I have forgotten—"

"Ah! *Capito.* I forget sometimes. Some people find truffles to be too strong, but I think they're irresistible."

He dove into his spinach—comforting, delicious, steamy, fragrant, the heavy odor of garlic rising with every forkful.

She reached in her bag and produced the wine labels. She'd come to pick these up in the pretentious office on the main drag in Orvieto that was full of young men and women parading around a bunch of slick modern furniture.

She lay the designs on the table.

He saw a stylized illustration of a woman in a crimson dress, standing on the crest of a hill. Wind in her hair. The label, in English, read: *SCARLET WOMAN VINEYARDS. Get to know our mysterious reds.*

"So," she said. "Did you like these? You haven't said."

"Why English?"

"It's the trend. It'll sell better where we need to go. And pictures are better than just the name on the bottle or a boring image of a villa or grapes. People remember your wine better and ask for it by the picture."

"Is this your husband's advice?"

"In a sense. It represents the new way of thinking about an old problem."

"Which is what?"

"How to be discovered. How to make an impact. How to stand out in a crowded market. It's about marketing."

"Will your wine be part of his brand?"

She shook her head. "I can't deny that being married to Charlie has brought with it certain...advantages. But I'm determined to do this myself. He has his business. I have mine. He's introduced me to certain importers. When the time comes..." Her voice trailed off. "What do you think of the labels? I was looking for a feeling of mystery. Of scandal. Do you like them? I think it's *carina*. Very cute."

He set the label aside. "Why didn't you tell me you're one of the Corteses? That your father owns the biggest azienda in town?"

"What does it matter?"

"It was such a simple question. But you dodged it. That only gets cops more interested in you."

"You're new here, Captain. I was a different woman five years ago. I hated myself. I couldn't wait to get out of this town. Charlie's California program didn't start until March. I left in December, right after the Christmas pageant. I wanted to get as far away from this borgo as I possibly could. And I did. My mother left home when we were in our teens. I didn't see why I had to stick around. I fled. I found a man I could trust. I changed my life."

"So what's changed?" he asked her. "Five years have passed, or thereabouts, and you're still ashamed of the Cortese name. Nothing's changed."

"It has!"

"How?"

"I shun the name but I intend to make something of the land."

"The land matters, then?"

"It's the only thing that does."

He sipped a glass of mineral water, letting the bubbles scour the olive oil from the back of his throat. The spinach had been cooked well; he was getting it down his throat without problems. But still, that chalky taste...

The plate of prosciutto now seemed unappetizing. The thin pink veils looked like what they were: fatty, greasy flesh on a plate.

"This probably has no bearing on my case, but as long as we're talking, what was so bad about your life here? One has to wonder why you ever came back at all. What brought you back? Sentiment?"

"I would have run to the end of the world. I practically did. My mother got out early. It was just me in that house with my father and brother. Two animals. You don't know my father, and you can never know my brother. He was a fool. A cretin. There's something in the blood, I think, that makes certain families, noble ones, think that they are born to possess everything. Marco contributed nothing. He was a taker. He had a notion that he could make a splash for himself by hiring an enologist to help him concoct the perfect vanity wine."

"So what? Many people do it. It's an accepted practice."

"Yeah—but they don't ignore the man's advice after they're paid good money to hear it. He could only hear his own voice. That was God's punishment to my father—to give him a son who was the perfect reflection of himself. I left. I wasn't coming back. I had some money, and I was willing to work. But then, after a while in California, I found myself pregnant. I could have ended it. It's so easy there. But to his credit, Charlie did the right thing.

"The point is, I was as far as a girl could go on this planet from home. And then I heard that my brother had died. My father was alone. My mother was brokenhearted. And the land my brother had hoped to turn into a vineyard again was just sitting here, waiting. Call me crazy—I thought it was a wonderful place to raise a son. That's it, Captain. I came for my son, and because it's home. *There.* Are you happy? What earthly good is knowing this? I have no idea what this has to do with your dead man. I have to think that putting such questions to me is irrelevant and intrusive."

He reached over as if to pat her hand as it rested by her plate. Which was strange for him. He didn't often touch others. Not anymore. He snatched the hand back before it touched her skin.

"I was hoping we could have a buon rapporto. I'm a stranger here. I need the help of people in the know. I can't do that if we start off lying to each other. So, as long as we're speaking frankly, there's another question which *does* have bearing on my case. Are you aware that you have eight vehicles registered in your name with the automobile club?"

"What do you—oh..."

"Oh, indeed. Are the illegals driving them?"

"Everyone I have working for me has at least a work permit. That allows them to drive a rental car, but they can't own a vehicle outright. That creates problems for employers like me."

"I just don't understand how you can bear the cost."

"I don't. *They* buy the vehicles with their own money. Beat-up Fiats. Dilapidated Fords. The occasional farm vehicle. *They* pay the insurance. And my name goes on the insurance and registration documents. I'd be happy to have Magda run you over copies if you want to be a stickler about the whole thing. Everyone does it. Baldini does it too. He's even tried to help some of his people get residency and it's proved more hassle than it's worth. As soon as they get residency, they leave for greener pastures and you lose the time and money you invested training them."

"God forbid the poor immigrants should move on to living their lives."

"You joke, but it's no laughing matter. I can't afford to make the same mistake. On a crude level, it's best for me if they remain somehow dependent on me. I don't like lending my name out to all these people, but it's the only way we can help them get a decent life around here. Otherwise, they're a bigger burden. We have to shuttle them all over the place."

He rooted in his pocket for a sheet of paper. Then lay it on the table.

"You know this?"

"Stregabella? Sure, that's Allegra Chiostro's company. I don't know her personally. She's young. Half my age." She smiled. "Maybe a bit more than that. I was living abroad when she started the cosmetics. It was just a harmless schoolgirl's whim. I think she wanted to make some money to go to concerts. The parents wouldn't give her the money, so she started making the stuff and selling it at the art school she attended. She designed the packaging, printed the labels, an industrious girl indeed." She paused, tapping the logo. "It strikes me that we have a lot in common, she and I."

"You know she pretends to be one? A strega."

"I only know what people say."

"From a business standpoint—marketing—is hers a good business?"

"I don't know anything about the money behind it. She can't be making *that* much. I don't know how many cities they can possibly be in. But a lot of the shops here carry the brand."

"Here, meaning Orvieto?"

She nodded toward the street. Toward passersby. "Look anywhere. Any woman's shop. The product's beautiful. All natural. I've tried it, but it's always too overpowering for me. I think she does soap and other things. The funny thing is, I doubt anyone knows how seriously she takes herself."

"Which brings me to the other favor I was going to ask of you. You see, I don't know anything about this stuff. Nothing about women's...things."

He stammered. Stopped and busied himself with his drink.

"What I'm trying to say is..."

"Yes, Captain?" She seemed on the verge of giggling.

"Would you like to go shopping?"

Chapter Thirty-Nine

A week or so later, they were back in the basement of the carabinieri station. This time, Gismonda and Puzio had their backs to Scarpone and the girl, watching television while playing with their phones.

Allegra Chiostro was a handsome young woman with short-cropped blond hair and lovely brown skin. Her hair was dyed, but her dark roots only added to her beauty. When she shrugged off her denim jacket, even in the chill of the station's rec room, Scarpone was struck by the denseness of muscle under the skin of her shoulders and upper arms. They poked out of what looked like a man's white undershirt.

"I presume you have heard details of the statement your sister made the other day concerning her relationship with the Albanian?"

Her eyes were green, wide, and blankly innocent. He saw nothing in them that suggested she knew where this was going—but that was preposterous. "I know she had a relationship with him that ended badly. That it ended at all I regard as fortunate."

"You were not fond of the young man?"

She shrugged and looked around the room, her eyes roving the ceiling in an effort to appear bored. Her eyes were too focused, Scarpone thought, for that to be the truth. "Did you know him well at all?"

"He wasn't bright, and didn't apply himself to much of anything.

He was a good-looking guy. A big stupid lug. That's about it. He was typical."

"Typical of what?"

"Typical of the guys you see around today." Her voice sounded drearily exhausted. Scarpone felt as if he were talking to the old winemaker, Baldini. "He embodies the old adage, 'Eat, drink, sleep, and don't do a damn thing.'"

"You don't approve of that?"

She stood up straight and wagged her head with mock earnestness. "Good work makes for good young people, Marshal."

"There are few jobs to be had, Signorina," Scarpone said. "For adults, let alone teenagers. I'd argue that the charge you level at Demaci could be said of nearly every young person in town."

Her mouth went straight. Her nostrils flared. "I've had a job since I was fourteen. I worked in the fields with my father and brother. And even when my brother started thinking that work was beneath him, I *still* worked with my father. I worked too in the perfume shop with my uncle and our family. And then…later—"

"Later? You mean when your brother…"

The word was unspoken but they both knew it was there.

When your brother died…

"My father gave it all up. Sold our land. Then I started my other business. My separate, personal business."

"How would you describe this business?"

"None of yours."

"Did you have a separate, personal relationship with the Albanian?"

"Why would I? He was my sister's boyfriend. May I go?"

"No. None whatsoever?"

"None. I'll say it again: May I go?"

Scarpone stood and went behind the bar. He returned with a gaily colored shopping bag made of thick, ridged paper and tied with a ribbon. He pointed to the brand printed on the bag. "You know this establishment?"

"It's in Orvieto."

"I was there a while ago. Would you like to see what I bought?"

He withdrew them. A bar of soap. Shampoo. The lotion. And blue bottles containing tinctures of lavender and valerian and St. John's wort. He set them all out on the table facing her, logos facing her.

"Do you recognize these?"

"Yes, of course."

"They all bear the same logo. Stregabella. And see, there are symbols here which resemble stars. And the woman's hair is designed to resemble the *mano cornuto*—the horned hand intended as a gesture to ward off evil. These are all yours, yes or no?"

"It started as hobby of mine. It's become a nice business. But so what?"

"I would argue, according to the income statement your father provided to the school over the last three years, that this is no mere hobby. It has provided a handsome income for your family."

"What is this about? Is this about the business license issue? Because if that is the case, that matter is still being adjudicated and the statutes continue to change. My feeling is this: our neighbors make wine and cheese and oil in their homes and sometimes they even sell those products without the benefit of a license. I don't see why I alone should be hassled about this."

"Signorina, I could not care less about your business license."

"If you're being honest about that, you're in the minority. There are many in this town who are threatened by free, independent women."

"If you're unhappy here, why not move somewhere else? One of the big cities, perhaps?"

"I can't leave them."

"Who, your sister?"

Her gaze darkened. A shrug.

"Your father and mother, then."

"They need me. They need us, Caterina and me. It hasn't been the same since...since...you know what I mean, so what is the point?"

"One of my men knows your family. He says the Chiostro land was fertile, flat, rich, and planted with all kinds of vines for a number of years. Trebbiano. Grechetto. Malvasia. Classic Orvieto wine grapes. Your father gave that all up?"

"He expected his son to take it over. His dead son. His foolish dead son."

"And now things have changed, haven't they? Think how unusual that is: Your father works for *you*. That puts an enormous amount of pressure on your ventures to succeed. You can't have obstacles in the way. You can't have men who embarrassed your family flaunting themselves in the piazza every time you run an errand."

"You're talking about Arbend."

"Have you ever had intercourse with him?"

Her face blanched. Her ears crawled back against her head. "You make me sick to suggest such a thing."

"I'm told that a number of young women in town found him attractive, but he doted on your sister when he first came to live here. But she threw him over, embarrassed by the pregnancy. My men have spoken to some girls who say that they've seen the two of you chatting at one of the bars, and also at the discotheque along the southern highway, south of where they're building the bridge. Are you going to deny that he would find you perhaps more attractive than your sister?"

"Why would I say such a thing? She's a pretty girl."

"Maybe, but uninteresting in comparison to you."

She paused to consider his remark. I thought I saw a bloom come to her cheeks. A flush of embarrassment. "I frighten men. They want nothing to do with me. I speak my mind too much."

"Then speak it now, why don't you? Why don't you admit you slept with him in the grotto on the night of his death?"

"Why would I say such a thing?"

"Because the proof is here." He withdrew some pages from the paper bag and lay them on the table. "Do you know anything about DNA? Yes, a little? We have some results of the, ah, evidence we took from a mattress in the grotto. It *doesn't* match the DNA we took from your sister's saliva some time ago. But it's a classic fifty percent match to Caterina, with an identical X chromosome."

"I have no idea what this means. Are you intentionally speaking obliquely?"

"Siblings have more in common genetically with each other than with their parents. I don't even have to ask you for your DNA. The science incriminates you."

"What do I care about your science, cop?" She appeared to be making up her mind about something. "Okay, enough—you know what?" she told Scarpone. "I had sex with him. He wanted me. He wanted me to run off with him to Rome, to America, anywhere to get out of here. He was a joke. A stupid joke of a man."

"Why do you speak of him so angrily?" Scarpone said. "You didn't love him?"

"He performed a satisfying service, nothing more. It was not intended to last. He found me attractive for the reason all men despise me and cast aspersions on my name and my products: because I have the power they so ardently desire."

"What power is that?"

"Power over nature. Over the air, wind, water, and the plants and beasts of the field."

"You sincerely expect me to believe that?"

"Men never do. But my grandmother had this power, and so do I."

"The lotion you rubbed on him? What was that?"

"My own concoction. Just for him. I smeared it on his body, yes. On his back and his ass and his fat stupid gross cock. I lubed everything, even his chest and balls."

Scarpone looked over to the sofa. Gismonda and Puzio hung on her every word.

"I wondered about something," Scarpone said. "How on earth did you get him to go into the field without shoes or pants?"

"That was the best part. It was near dawn by then. He was pulling on his clothes and I stopped him."

"What could you possibly say to convince him?"

She reached across the table and gripped Scarpone's arm. She threw back her head and batted her eyes theatrically. "'Oh no, *bellezzo*. Don't get dressed. Run out the way you are. You're beautiful. I want to watch your beautiful body run across the field. Go. It'll be fast. Get us a drink and we can screw again till morning. Go, *amore*, go!'"

She bit her bottom lip and grinned.

"There, Captain. Wouldn't *you* do exactly as you were instructed after such a performance? You would, wouldn't you?" She turned to Puzio and Gismonda. "And *you*?"

Gismonda looked as if he were about to hop the sofa and take her.

Scarpone massaged a temple. "You seem to be taking great pleasure in this, but I'm afraid we're going to have to stop this, unfortunately."

"Why? I want to get it off my chest."

"She wants to talk," Gismonda said.

Scarpone glared at him.

"You made an admission of guilt. Under the law, that means we have to stop and we need to bring in the magistrate."

But she would not be stopped.

"I used an incantation, Signore. Very powerful. I conjured forth the serpents of the field to suck his body dry and fill him with their venom. It was the only way he would pay the price."

Over his shoulder, the captain heard Puzio say, "Captain, with all respect—this is absurd."

The girl had slouched back in her seat. One knee leaned up against the top of the table, her fingers laced across it. In her undershirt and jeans and belt, she looked like a feminine version of James Dean, from the American movies.

Scarpone looked amused. "May I ask *why* you did it? What price did he have to pay, exactly?"

"He had to pay. And he did. I'll say no more."

Chapter Forty

Glass terrariums. And snakes. That's all the basement room of the academic building in Perugia seemed to contain. Some of the snakes were sidling along branches of desiccated wood in their glass prisons. Most could barely be seen, huddled as they were under layers of curled cedar shavings.

The magistrate looked fascinated. Perhaps he was.

Claudia Cavalcanti's herpetologist friend, Antonia Pallai, was a short, heavy woman whose cushion of flesh strained against her starched white jacket. Exquisite shoes poked out from under her jeans.

She too seemed fascinated. How often did law enforcement officials—*a magistrate!*—come to consult with her?

She showed them around the lab before finding them benchtop seats.

"Do you know much about them, vipers?" she asked them.

They shook their heads no.

"What I know," Scarpone said, "is that you never want to be near one."

Indeed, he'd been hearing this all his life. Even as boy, visiting the Frascati area where his father's family had their place, he was told that if he saw a serpent with a triangular head, he was to run in the other direction.

And any other snake, he wondered, *I should cozy up to?*

He didn't like the things at all. He had none of the country boy's fascination with wild creatures. Once, he'd seen two snakes mating in the field. Two glistening bodies rose from the sod, bodies entwined, tails undulating. Together, they were two or three feet tall, a living caduceus. Young Matteo watched them, transfixed, until they simmered down like a pot left to cool, dropping to the earth and disappearing into the grass.

Beautiful and horrible all at once.

"A lot of snakes are oviparous. They give birth by laying eggs. But vipers are ovi*vivi*parous. In other words, the mother retains the eggs within her body. When the time comes, usually in September in this region, the eggs hatch inside the mother and the babies drop free."

The magistrate was nodding, his notebook and cane at the ready. He was the only one of them not sitting. He merely leaned against his stool, his hip cocked at an uncomfortable angle.

"At the time of birth, typically the mother climbs a tree and gives birth by dropping the young from the tree limb, one after another."

"Raining snakes," the magistrate said.

"Exactly!"

"Disgusting," the magistrate said.

On the ride up to Perugia, as they'd tried to share cornetti without getting greasy bread flakes all over Claudia's Alfa, Saviano had treated them to a long discourse on all the features of the case which he'd found disgusting.

Young people fornicating in unclean grottoes disgusted him.

Filthy, unwashed mattresses used for this purpose were also disgusting.

Lubricating one's lover with lotions and then salaciously telling the world about it was disgusting.

Sleeping with the former lover of one's pregnant sister? Also disgusting.

Pretending one was a witch? Reprehensible. Childish. Not to mention disgusting.

But judging from his sneer, being pelted to death by a rainstorm of live baby snakes was the height of disgust.

"That depends on your point of view," Pallai said. She gestured to the tanks in front of her. A brown viper. A red-brown viper. Both apparently sleeping. "They are not naturally offensive creatures. I think the tight scales give them a rugged beauty. The shape of their heads satisfies the child-like geometer inside me."

As this geek was speaking, Scarpone noticed that the snakes didn't have *truly* triangular heads. Not at all. In fact, Scarpone realized that if he had followed that one piece of advice as a kid, knowing the sort of literalist he was, he would have probably gotten himself killed.

"The beauty lies in the reason they do this."

"Can we hear about your tests?" Claudia said. There was an exasperated tone to her voice. Maybe, Scarpone thought, Cavalcanti couldn't bear to hear another scientist pontificate at length. "We'd like you to comment on the alleged means of murder."

"Please," the magistrate said, "let her finish. What is the beauty, Dottoressa?"

"The mother drops her young from trees," the shaggy-headed woman said, "in what we think is an act of self-preservation. The venom is so concentrated in the young that if she were to give birth on the ground, the babies would probably kill her with their strikes! This way, they drop *away* from her!"

"Disgusting!" Scarpone groaned. (He couldn't help himself.) "But please, tell us: Do we think this is what happened in the case of our victim?"

"Yes, undoubtedly. Most people who work the fields this time of year know to take precautions. Typically, September is the birthing season, but we had a warm year this year and last, and births are happening sooner. If you took someone who knows nothing about field work and sent him out under a tree this time of year, he'd be taking a risk."

"She didn't just send him under a tree," Cavalcanti said. "She smeared him with a lotion designed to *attract* snakes."

The scientist tucked in her chin and peered at them over her glasses.

"This I find dubious."

"You do?" the magistrate said.

"Absolutely. We ran a couple of tests using this so-called lotion of yours. Smeared it on a couple of heated toy animals that we use.

Dropped them in the tanks with a couple of these rascals. My teaching assistant will be writing this up for one of his papers. But it will be bullshit, exactly the sort of thing you give a graduate student. He did it about fifty or sixty times so far, and you know what? He hasn't gotten a more robust response to the lotion-smeared toy than the toys that are merely heated. Sometimes the snakes strike, sometimes they ignore them. There's no significant statistical difference. I would pay attention to this," she said, nodding at the magistrate. "Because if this ever came to trial, that's exactly what we would say in our testimony."

"There's no such thing, then?"

"There is nothing I can think of in nature that would act as an attractant. But just for the sake of argument, I ran a search on the scientific literature of this topic yesterday. Bear in mind: anyone who invents such a thing will make a sack of money for himself, without a doubt. Who wouldn't want to round up all the snakes in their field and kill them off? But it can't be done predictably. One study got interesting results from a collagen excreted by earthworms—"

"You people are sick!" Saviano moaned.

"Oh, perhaps! It was a clever study, but it only worked on certain species of snake. No one knows if it would work on vipers or other species. Others have baited traps with food or chemicals or dead rodents. The results are all debatable. The problem is, these snakes have a highly developed sense of smell. They're attracted to live or freshly killed prey. The second that prey starts to decay, they lose interest. With humans, they're responding out of fear. Self-defense caused them to bite that poor bastard more than any attractant this girl could have concocted. And what is she, anyway? A layman with no training in science? Please, I find the idea ludicrous. Insulting, even!"

She crooked a finger at them and pointed into one of her tanks.

"Look. You see there? See that indentation between their eyes? It's a heat sensor, a most remarkable gift which nature gives these creatures. They spend their lives craving heat. And they use heat to home in on their prey, ideally mammals. Mice, rats, small creatures. That dip, if you will, tells them they are in the vicinity of something that is the right body temperature. Then they flick out their tongues to smell their way toward the prey. Their vision is okay, but not great."

"Would the lotion increase or decrease the chance of a strike?"

Pallai shrugged. "Who knows? It might do the opposite of what is intended, and *disguise* our natural human odor for a while. But don't forget: our body heat would still tell the viper that something's there. He knows there's a living creature in front of his face even if all he's smelling is lavender."

"Lavender," Cavalcanti intoned. "Bergamot. And citrus."

"Yeah, those would do nothing."

"What about the beeswax?" Scarpone said.

"No."

"Or the oil in the lotion?" said the magistrate.

"No."

They went on this like for a long while. Had she considered this or that or the other thing? All these queries evoked the same response from the scientist.

"If you were to put me on the stand to weigh in on this, my answer would be the same. And I can think of at least three other scientists like me, all at the top in their field—in Milan, Naples, and La Sapienza in Rome who would back me up. And they *hate* me and my work. I'll say it again: if this girl, whoever she is, has figured out a way to attract snakes, I want to meet her. The right backer, some seed money, and we'd make a killing."

She meant it as a joke, but no one was laughing.

Chapter Forty-One

They were silent now, the three of them, not so much walking down Corso Vannucci as drifting through it. They were lost amid the tourists and the street musicians and mimes. It was still early in the day, but the pizzeria at the top of the hill already smelled fragrant. Saviano peered into the window of Sandri, the famous pastry shop, peeking at the adorable baked goods in the window emblazoned with the face of the city's son, the medieval artist Perugino.

Saviano squinted into the sun. "Coffee?"

Of course they would have coffee. But neither of them made for the door. Inside, they could see the shop's waiters hurrying about in their red jackets and bowties.

"Aw, don't berate yourself, Matteo," the magistrate said. "It was a good case. A good case. Solid work by your men. Solid work by you, Dottoressa. But we knew from the start that it looked more like a case of accidental death than anything else."

"You're dismissing it?" Cavalcanti said. "I don't see how you can. The little bitch confessed."

She was dressed like the magistrate in a heavy coat, her neck swaddled in a winter scarf though temperatures were as warm as a summer day. As everyone knew, the temperature had nothing to do with how one dressed; nor did one's comfort. The summer holiday was over, and one had to dress accordingly.

The magistrate looked at Scarpone. "Tell her."

"He can't act," my captain said. "He can't intercede unless we find proof that a crime has been committed."

"But the confession—"

"The confession is delusional. And the medical examiner in Viterbo says it's an accidental death. Death by viper."

"Now, I *could* petition on the grounds that evidence contradicts that finding," said Saviano, "but I don't find the confession credible. She's an oversexed girl taking credit for an act which nature alone performed."

"I would argue that there *was* premeditation," Cavalcanti said. "She brought the lotion to their assignation and had every reason to believe that it would work."

"Listen to yourself," the magistrate said. "Would you for a second accept such a charge if it were your client or your child? *Premeditation?* So what? The lotion doesn't work. It's one thing to douse a man with kerosene and then toss a match on him. It's another to spray him with water you *think* is kerosene and then ignite him."

"Right, but in this case the man died."

"All she did was ask her lover to fetch her water. She sent him on his merry way and the vipers got him. End of story. If we proceed with this case, it'll get thrown out. Good for headlines and little else."

"She confessed," Cavalcanti persisted.

"She's deranged. The whole town knows this. Just because she is under the delusion that she has powers or mystical visions doesn't mean we should embarrass ourselves in a legal setting."

Scarpone chimed in: "Wait a second. We *can* prove that the two sisters colluded to tamper with the evidence. The older sister clearly moved the Albanian's vehicle. And they callously abandoned a dead or dying man. For all we know, he might have survived if they had called *Pronto Soccorso.*"

The magistrate considered it. "Yes—you're right, Matteo. We may be able to get them on the tampering, and I will speak to the preliminary investigations judge on that point. Reckless endangerment, negligence—that will be difficult. They can easily argue that they're not doctors or experts. They assumed he was dead and then acted to prevent further embarrassment to Allegra and the family. But we can try. If the judge agrees, we'll all get our day in court, the judge will levy a fine and I'll owe the judge another favor."

"And then?"

"We move on. Your strange case is dead. Make your peace with it. The two sisters must go free." He flung the stub of his cigarette to the cobblestones and crushed it with his cane. "Coffee?"

Chapter Forty-Two

Mornings cooled in the borgo. Farmers tugged on light jackets each morning to attend to the seasonal chores. One by one, the fields of the borgo gave up their precious bounty.

The migrants employed by my Lucia piled fruit from the two- and three-year-old vines onto rented trucks and ran them down to the fermentation rooms in the barn. Juice ran from the presses and were tucked away to await their fate.

At the azienda, the count took to the fields in the company Fiat driven by his foreman Adriano. Cortese cut a strange figure each afternoon, standing at the end of the grape rows, waving his white hat at the workers who dripped with sweat. Grapes were plucked and sent as quickly as possible to the co-ops or other vineyards that needed fruit. In some cases, the grapes were crushed and the juice sold as well. Each night, the bookkeeper Damiano inspected the numbers on his aging computer and felt wonderful, as if he had harvested each digit himself.

My poor captain returned to his newspapers and morning coffees, and the gym, its machines, and his bike. Under the tutelage of the muscle-bound Sbuccio, my captain gained weight and muscle, and his skin turned a pleasant brown in what was left of the sun.

Some afternoons he rode west with Enzo to return him to his wife and home. They drove past fields where threshers were shearing wheat low. They watched as sunflower heads drooped to snooze and were lopped off to be pressed into oil and euros.

The captain rode back alone to the borgo and headed to the *pizza al taglio* place next to the bakery. In anticipation of shorter days, the baker's brother opened his pizza place an hour earlier. The captain, dressed now in his spanking new helmet and bicycle pants, would line up among the children with their skateboards and motorini and choose from the various pies. Potato pizza. Red onion pizza. White onion and pepper. Spinach pizza. Pizza Margherita. His favorite was the cauliflower-potato slice, which was satisfying, dense and chewy on the tongue—enough to sate a man like him for most of the evening.

For a few days he ate while leaning against the bike racks outside the tourist office. But when he realized that his presence scared off the teenagers, he began asking for his slices to be wrapped in waxed paper. He'd tuck them into his basket and pedal out to the overlook on the east side of town.

A strangely desolate shopping center was home to a couple of odd shops that could have easily fit in on the main street but had somehow opted for oblivion. A shop that sold computer supplies and repairs. A babies' clothing store. A linen shop. And another of those ubiquitous ladies' undergarment shops. These all occupied the first level under an apartment house. The shops faced east toward Umbria. The parking lot at this time of day was deserted, except for a few boys on skateboards who scattered as soon as Scarpone wheeled up.

I felt sorry for him. It was sad to see him bereft of anything of importance to hold his life together. He would study the fields below the cliffs and crunch through his crispy, lukewarm pizza slices.

How can it be? he wondered. *How can it be that so much life is out there? How can it be? How can it be?*

One afternoon, when he wheeled his bike to the edge of the parking lot, he spotted a *motorino* parked close to the edge. But no one around.

He left his bike and stretched. The afternoon train from Rome was gliding into Orvieto. Cars buzzed up and down the A1.

He laced his fingers and lifted his palms to the sky. Muscles flexed in his legs. Oh Jesu. Wonderful.

He drank in the chill of the autumn day.

The edge of the cliffs sprouted a spray of green, fuzzy vegetation. He stepped to the end of the parking lot and peeked. He felt the breeze sweeping up at him from the rocks. He bent now, taking care not to throw too much of his body's weight forward, and squinted at the greenery. Wild asparagus.

He was a boy the first time his aunt taught him to forage. Asparagus was always a special treat. You picked it out of the landscape by looking for its fuzzy brush. One had to look sharp to find the green-purple stalks growing within the shrub. You found only a few stalks at a time, but they were always so tender and delicious that you'd eat them on your walk home, before they ever hit the pot. It was late in the season now. Anything he found now would surely be too bitter or woody. But still—he couldn't resist reaching for the stalks.

Something moved below him.

He leapt back.

Something was crawling along the rocks, just a few feet below him. What? A boar? A goat, maybe? What else would be surefooted enough to be out on such an incline?

But then he caught a flash of color, and realized that it was no animal at all.

It was a girl dressed in camouflage pants and a bright orange hooded jacket. She picked her way along a rough path cut into stone with a pack strapped to her back. He heard her grunting as she pulled herself up the hill, hand over foot. Finally, he caught a glimpse of her face.

Allegra.

He felt like leaving. There was no point to seeing her. But still—she was climbing up a dangerous incline. It seemed only right to stick around in case she needed help.

When she appeared over the top of the cliff face, he could see that her face was dripping wet. A V of sweat marked the front of her shirt. Her hair was spiky and damp. When she took the top, she sighed heavily and carefully placed her pack on the ground. She said nothing to him as she withdrew a water bottle.

Then came over to sit next to him.

She drank deeply before speaking.

"The great marshal," she said. "Funny to see you taking exercise. That's a foolish outfit, I must say. Why do men think it's okay to inflict their sexuality on the rest of the world? Women who do the same are branded whores."

"Isn't this a dangerous place to be playing?"

"You speak as if I'm a child out for fun."

"Well, aren't you? If you fell, how would anyone ever know you were here?"

"I'd never fall."

"Who's being foolish now?"

"I know these rocks like I know my mother."

"Why come here at all?"

She reached inside her pack and withdrew what looked like handfuls of weeds.

"You're foraging?"

"I'm working."

"So what is that? Mullein?"

"It's wonderful for making earache medication. I do a nice business with ladies who grew up with it but don't know how to make it themselves. Isn't that sad? Every day, the old ways are being lost."

Her hand dug into a front pocket of her pack, and slowly came out with a handful of dried seed.

The scent of it was powerful—I could smell it from where I stood behind my captain.

"Fennel seed," he said.

"Yeah. I'm working on a dentifrice. Should be fun once I get the mix right. And there are spells you can do with it. Here, Marshal—you might want a few of them—"

Damn you, witch, I thought. *Don't you dare give that to my captain.*

She held out her hand.

My eyes locked on the seeds. *Wind,* I thought. *I must have wind.*

"What am I supposed to do with that?" he said.

"The stregas of old used to say that if you put a seed in the crack of your door—or even the lock itself—that you'll stop evil spirits from entering."

"I don't have any evil spirits."

Get it away from him, strega! Get it out of here, bitch! Blow, winds, blow.

But nothing blew.

Instead, I had to watch her smile at my captain.

"And mallow, of course. Nice medicine here. But this is almost the end of the season."

"I don't understand why you'd risk these rocks. You can forage this stuff by the side of the road. Fennel you can get at the supermercato."

She looked at him as if he were insane.

"This way, I know it's fresh. And I *like* coming up here. I see things I'd never see anywhere else. It's the best spot in all the borgo. Shall I show you?" She pointed north and west. "Look there. Do you see? That's Lucia's hill. You know her, of course. Lucia Cortese."

"Lucia Anderson."

"Yeah, right. You can see her property from here. And that's the hill where she comes to stand in the mornings when she wants to be alone. I know because I've seen her. She interests me, I must say. I don't know why; she's not my type. If I were the kind of woman who truly liked men, I would want to have hair like hers. Skin like hers. It's interesting, don't you think, to be so desirable but not caring for it? To care for something bigger?"

"What do you think she cares for?"

"Shouldn't you know already, Marshal?"

Sly smile. One of her hands reached again for the pocket containing the fennel seeds. She grabbed a few of them and rubbed them in her fingers.

"Why would I know?"

"Those bicycle pants are making it hard for you to think. And there, just to the right there, you can see a newly planted patch of land. You know who owns that property? Massimo Baldini. Wonderful old man, *carino* and *autentico*. You see that olive grove? How old would you judge it to be? Go on—guess."

"I have no idea. I know nothing about olives."

"Everyone knows something about olives. Guess. How old?"

"I don't know," he told her.

She raised the fennel seeds to her lips and popped them in her mouth.

What are you doing, strega? I thought.

"Truly? What a spoilsport. I'll tell you, then. They're one year old. They only look older because he babies them. Goes out there once a week to spread manure out to their dripline and hoe out the weeds. He's amazing. I hope I have that dedication when I'm his age. No one else would do that. People are lazy. They plant the olive trees and leave nature to take its course. But Signor Baldini doesn't fool around. He makes nature work for him. And then...oh, you'll like this, as it's in your line of work." She pointed due north, to the road leading out of the borgo. "You see that car way off there, on the old Orvietana?"

"That red speck? Is that a car?"

"Yes, yes, do you know the driver? She's always there by the side of the road. Tell me you haven't seen her there."

Scarpone said a word his mother would have swatted him across the mouth for. *Putana*. Whore. But the girl wasn't offended. She bit her lip.

I could feel her tongue moistening the seeds in her mouth.

The scent was powerful.

Intoxicating.

Enfeebling...

"That's right. She's the lady who waits by the side of the road for men. She's been there as long as I've been alive. When I was little I asked my mother, 'Why does that lady sit in a parked car all day?' And she said, 'Why, she's waiting for the bus, Allegra.' Isn't that a cute answer? The woman is Bulgarian, I've heard. Married one of *our* men, who works in a hair salon in Orvieto. I used to think he didn't know the truth, but now I get the feeling he does. He *must*. She probably makes more money than he does. If I had a job like that—not that I would want it—I would make good use of it. I'd read every book in the library in between spreading my legs."

"That's enough."

"Ooh, you're sensitive! A prude, our marshal is. And you know—it's weird. She used to be parked over here."

She stood now, pointing in a different direction—to the east. "You see that bend in the road on the way to Orvieto, almost as if you're heading right to Lake Corbara? She used to be parked there for as long as I can remember. But then a few years back, she moved west to where you see her now. The off road. I always wondered why. Isn't that strange? Did your beloved carabinieri run her off, do you think?"

"I doubt it highly. Common practice is to look the other way."

"It's not a crime when a woman is exploited, then? Only when a man is hurt or ripped off or has his property taken—"

"That's enough."

He was standing now. His eyes glaring. His cheeks red.

"You like messing with me," he said. "That seems to be your only purpose in life. Well, tell me this: *Why* did you kill the Albanian?"

She was silent.

"What's the big deal telling the truth at this point?" he said. "I can't arrest you. The magistrate doesn't believe a word you say. I can't say as I do, either."

"Then what does it matter?"

"I want to hear it from your lips. Tell me why."

"You know why. You tell me."

He made a face. Wiped the dirt off his butt, clomped over to his bike on his cleated shoes, and rode away.

SOMEHOW I DID NOT LEAVE.

I could not leave.

The girl sat looking at the view. After a bit, she glanced at me.

She looked me right in the eyes.

She opened her mouth and showed me the fennel seeds. Four of them. One for each of the winds. One for each direction of the compass. She uttered a word I had never heard before. I felt the wind rush around me. I was pinned to the earth. Unable to move.

I could not look away from her.

"He's a good man," she told me. "That's obvious. He has no knowledge of your existence at all. So that can't possibly be fun or productive for you. Why not give it up?"

She was lovely, not Lucia-lovely, but lovely in a different way, one of the oldest ways of the earth. The sun struck her skin and gave it back to the land.

"You *think* you understand," she told me, "but you don't. God knows, you know things I'll never know. I envy you that. I do. I wish I could go where you go, see what you see. But you've got it all wrong if you think your purpose here is to help him remember. He has never forgotten. *You have.* I'm sorry, but that is the truth."

Release me, witch! I thought.

She smiled.

"I love that you stand by him. I love that you care for him, that you inveigle yourself into all of his woes, but the truth is, the time has come."

I had no idea what she was saying. She was speaking utter madness. I tell you what I have always known: My purpose here is not clear, not even to me. No one has ever given me my orders. I have had to figure them for myself. I dwell among men, but I am not man. I am a thing wiser than men.

To hear this sweat-coated adolescent speak to me this way—

Oh, it was too much.

Release me, strega!

Allegra took a sip of water from her bottle and swallowed the seeds in her mouth. *"Vattene!"* she said. Get out of here!

I let the wind take me.

Chapter Forty-Three

Scarpone had to imagine that the arrival of two men anywhere near the vehicle parked on the gravel road would have been greeted warmly by its occupant. But instead, the middle-aged woman dropped the magazine she was reading and bolted upright. Her eyes widened with a look every cop knows. To lessen the chance that she would bolt, he and Enzo leaned their bicycles gently across the front of her old Fiat. Enzo hung back, dressed in his bike pants. It was the end of his day; he was heading home.

Scarpone rapped on the glass.

The woman started the car and lowered the window.

"Can you kill the engine, please?"

He dug for his ID in the back of his bike shirt, but she waved him off.

"No need to show it," she said, her voice tinged with an accent. "I know who you are. Can we just get to it?"

Interesting, thought Scarpone. While the townspeople were still trying to take his measure after three months, those on the fringes hadn't wasted time making assumptions about him. He was a cop—and a cop was a cop was a cop.

"I'm not hassling people," she said. "All I do is wait. Same as ever. It's not like I'm doing anything I haven't done for years."

"So I hear. And I could not care less."

She was a chesty woman in her fifties, a little on the worn side, circles under her eyes. Hair a tad too stiff. But her clothes were nice. A skirt, of course, and a nice top and scarf. About all she needed.

"Then what's the problem? I'm not parked on anyone's land. Every borgo has a right of way of about six feet onto any road property."

"Well," Scarpone said, looking at Enzo, "she certainly knows her zoning laws, doesn't she?"

"I've been doing this longer than you, *caro*. And no one has ever had problem with my services. I keep a clean ship."

Enzo looked as if he were about to vomit.

"Much business at this location?" Scarpone said.

She shrugged, nervously. "What's this about?"

"I'm wondering how we can help each other."

"Your predecessor didn't have a problem as long as I didn't *make* problems. What else is there to say?"

"I'm interested in your relocation. If local lore is to be trusted, you used to be parked on the main road. A straight shot down to the bridge east to Baschi, or north to Orvieto. Now you're here on a *strada bianca*, the gravel road. That can't be good for business."

"What can you possibly care about my business?"

"Deviations from habit interest me."

"Please, just go," she said, waving a meaty palm. "I don't have the patience for this. You're encroaching upon my time."

"No—you're encroaching on *mine*. Is that the tack you want to take? Your whole existence depends on my good graces. Correct? You either make me happy or you don't exist."

He was conscious of Enzo shifting awkwardly behind him. Until now he had never seen my captain behaving this way.

"Shakedown, then, is that it? Want me to give you both a blow? I'm willing to do that for the sake of good relations. What do you say? A good, hard *pompino* for the two of you to end your day? More than that, and you'll have to start paying like everyone else."

Scarpone smiled at the younger man. "How about it, Enzo?"

Enzo turned away.

Scarpone leaned in and lay a hand across the hood of the car. "Why close up shop? Why walk away from the main traffic?"

"It's nothing. Girl's got to change sometime."

"In my experience human beings *don't* change. It's against our nature. We change only when we are forced to. Which makes me wonder: who forced you?"

Silence.

"Signora, now you're thinking whether it's worth telling me or not. Or how you can spin it so I don't think it's a lie. Save your breath. Enzo—do you see her eyes? You do? Well, Signora, it's confirmed. Someone maltreated you. The question is who? Enzo, do we know whose land it was that she was always parked on?"

Enzo spoke through his grimace of disgust. "The family is Amaldi, but I don't know how long it's been since they used the property. That's why she'd been able to get by unhassled for so long."

The woman raised a hand through the window, brushing Scarpone's sleeve, trying to get him to look at her again. "Please, for the love of God, why don't you take your pompino and go your merry way? I haven't gotten this much attention in more than a decade. A decade. Leave me be. If you want me to find another place, I'll do it. Okay? Just stop with the questions."

"See, Enzo? Again she reveals herself."

"In what sense, damn you? Who the hell are you, you stupid clown?"

"I think we're done here. Have a nice day, Signora."

THEY RODE SOUTH TO THE END OF THE ROAD AND HUNG A right toward Lubriano, toward Enzo's home. It would be dark soon and Scarpone didn't want to keep Enzo long, or else his wife would have to come pick him up.

They drove just past the auto body shop that lies along that road and parked in the shade of the garages. The owner waved once, looked curious, and then went back to his undercarriage clanging.

Enzo futzed with his bike.

"I don't know why you're so nice to her, sir. If it were my station, I'd run them all out of town. Their work is disgusting."

"At least she's doing it voluntarily. There are others who are forced into it. Slaves."

"That's why they sacked you, isn't it? In Rome?"

Of course Enzo had heard something about it. It pleased my captain to know that Enzo felt close enough to him to bring it up. The others had not presumed such a relationship. "Among other things, yes. This woman's a woman, but that's as far as the similarities go between her case and the one in Rome. The profession continues because the demand is there."

I cannot believe I am discussing this with an adult, my captain thought.

Scarpone withdrew some sheets of paper from his bike bag and unfolded them on his thigh. They were the size of legal documents, all taped together. Enzo saw a map of the region, outlining each individual parcel of land, and its owners.

"A cadastral map," Enzo said. "Why are you carrying that? They only issue them when you buy a piece of property."

"Or you're an engineer about to survey a property. Or a guy trying to hassle prostitutes. I'm sorry to say this is all leading to more work for you. Paperwork. I hate to throw it in your lap, but you're the only one I can trust to do the research properly."

"I am honored, sir!"

Anything to stick close to a desk, my captain thought.

"Look at this. Where on this map would you say she used to park her vehicle?"

Enzo pointed to the Amaldi property.

Scarpone put his finger on the spot. He rooted in his bag and produced a stubby, dull-tipped pencil. He drew a line from the point marked by his finger directly *across* from the Amaldi property. He marked an X on the map in the vicinity of a couple of rectangular shapes.

"What are these shapes, houses?"

"If memory serves, sir, that stretch is abandoned. Nice land but no one's planted there for years."

"And the structures?"

"Abandoned, I'd guess."

"Who owns it?"

Enzo hunched in closer. "They usually print the names right there."

The name was foreign. German by the look of it: *Schultheiss.*

"Regardless, I need you to pull the records. I want to know who owns this parcel."

"The parcel that would have been visible to the whore?"

"That's right."

"Do you think she saw something? Why not come out and ask her straightaway?"

"Because if it's what I think, I'd rather not get her in trouble. She deserves our protection in this matter."

"She's a whore, sir!"

"You saw her face, didn't you? The thought of talking about her relocation was enough to frighten her. So much so that she was willing to move yet again. She'd rather trade a lousy location for a still lousier one than be forced to talk about her change of scenery."

"Your logic here is interesting, sir."

"Look. I need a man watching these structures. The Schultheiss property for sure. The Amaldi one, too, if possible."

"For what case?"

"I'm not sure."

"The dead Albanian again, sir?"

"Maybe. I don't know."

"We're tight as it is. Do you want one man tied up looking at abandoned houses? If there is something to see, wouldn't his presence scare off any activity?"

"Not if he were hidden."

"Where could he hide? The road's wide open."

"I know just the spot. He wouldn't even have to leave the borgo."

Chapter Forty-Four

What if I've missed something?

He was thinking this one night as he was finishing up at the gym. He happened to ask the younger Sbuccio brother what he did with all the newspapers he collected in the course of his cleaning.

The young man's eyes were momentarily vacant as he considered the question. He stood with a damp rag and some spray cleaner, newspapers under his arm.

"Why? Do you like papers? I like papers. I like origami."

"Really? Have you made some nice things?"

"I'm teaching myself. It's hard. I have a book. Why? Do you like papers?"

"I save some of the articles," Scarpone told him. "And...I'm working on a special project."

"Your project is special?" the young man said. He always seemed to dress in clothing that was coordinated with his brother's. But while the older Sbuccio's things were always skin-tight across his muscular form, the younger man's garb only highlighted his pale skin and paunch.

My captain was seized with an awkward sense of sympathy. Why did I bring this up? How can I possibly explain?

And yet—

And yet, this fellow might be the only one who'd appreciate it.

"Would you like to see?"

Which is how Scarpone ended up driving the fellow back to his place in the October gloom.

Scarpone's landlord was still sitting outside, sipping one of his favorite concoctions—Budweiser and 7-Up. He didn't think the American beer was sweet enough.

"Scar-poooooone!" the old drunk hissed when they appeared in the drive. "Who is it you have with you? Who is it? Ah—the town retard! What could you possibly want with him?"

Scarpone's neck hunched.

Thankfully, young Sbuccio appeared not to be listening. He was preoccupied with climbing the stairs with his plastic bags filled with newspapers. When he reached the top of the stairs, he became transfixed with the view of the night sky.

"Scarpoooooone!" the old man cried again.

Scarpone stepped under the light of the old man's porch. "What is it?"

"What are you doing with this mongoloid? It's best not to pity them. In fact, it's best not to encourage them. If you have an odd job that must be performed, you let me know, okay? They will only screw it up, these people."

"Is that so?"

"Oh yes. Not to be trusted. You might as well hire a goat. A goat would have more brains."

Scarpone raised a finger. "I'll keep that in mind."

He turned on his heels and walked across the foreyard to the staircase. As he crossed the yard, Scarpone allowed his fingers to graze the tips of the old man's beloved artichoke plants.

His lips moved as if in prayer.

I condemn you.

And you.

And you.

I condemn you all, you prickly bastards.

And then he rushed up the staircase to unlock his apartment door. He realized with some surprise that he was giddy to have someone over. Was the place in good condition to have someone visit? It hadn't mattered with Rolando. They were brothers. They were used to each other's filth. But this was different. Surely the fellow wouldn't stay long. But was Scarpone expected to provide an espresso, or some sweets, or biscotti?

Sbuccio was still outside, staring at the purple outline of the Apennines.

"We live in a pretty place," Sbuccio said.

"Excuse me?"

"We live in a pretty place."

Yes, it was beautiful. It just didn't *feel* that way.

Sbuccio broke his glance and hurried into the apartment, entering ahead of Scarpone. The marshal quickly followed, hit the lights and commenced fussing.

"You can lay your things *here*, and perhaps you'd like some refreshment? I may have some mineral water, but I can't make many promises. I'm a terrible host and housekeeper."

Sbuccio moved farther into the apartment, as if drawn by the light coming from the eastern windows. He was saying things like, lovely place, very nice, oh—you have pictures on the wall, oh, you are lucky to have nice carpets...

Scarpone wasn't sure how to reply.

Scarpone hit the lights in the lounge, and Sbuccio exhaled with delight.

By now my captain's creation—the newspaper borgo—occupied the entire wall under the far windows. Paper structures perched on card tables and coffee tables and the window ledge, mimicking the terraced levels of the borgo itself.

"It's stupendous! How wonderful! How marvelous."

Sbuccio dropped his bags and squatted awkwardly to inspect the diorama.

"There is the church. And there is the city hall. And there is the piazza. Oh, surely, those are all the shops. There's the *small* piazza. There's the coffee shop. And there's the theater and the schools and the fountain."

"That took a while to figure out," Scarpone admitted.

The fountain's spout was a tight spindle of newspaper that had been torn nearly to shreds, simulating a cascade of water.

"Well handled, I should say."

"Thank you."

Sbuccio knelt on the carpet now to get a better look, his ample rump pointing toward the ceiling as he peered at the lowest tier of buildings.

"When I was a boy they used to put up the nativity scene in front of the church every Christmas," he said.

"Don't they still?"

"No. Now they moved it inside. But it's not the same. In the old days we used the real sky and the real mountains. And they planted real grass, or real moss, rather. It was pretty." His eyes shifted. "Hey—you're missing the important part."

"What's that?" Scarpone said.

Sbuccio patted the carpet with both hands.

"The carpet, you goose. But that will be the hardest. Oh yes, that is the trickiest part to do, isn't it? People always forget it's the reason the borgo is here. The reason any of us are here in the first place."

"I'm sorry—I don't understand," Scarpone said.

Sbuccio had a weird look in his eyes.

"Oh, I want a little paper city, too. I should do this. I have the newspapers."

"Please," Scarpone said. "What is the most important part of the borgo?"

Chapter Forty-Five

His new bike had thick tires, which were supposed to help him navigate country roads. But the next morning, as he headed down the hill, heading for the flat farmland surrounding the borgo, he felt every bump. Going downhill was easy; coming back up would be a pain in the ass.

His lungs protested, his face dripped with sweat, and his gut tightened with cramps, but he pushed through it.

At the bottom of the cliffs, he took the gravel road northwest until he reached a farmhouse at the back of an apricot orchard. A black and white dog hounded him as he rolled up to the house, but he simply ignored it. His legs were stiff coming off the bike, and he felt as if he'd punctured his balls.

It stank here. Some rabbit hutches closer to the house smelled as if they needed some attention.

The side door of the house was already open. An old man standing there in a stained T-shirt.

"Sorry to trouble you. I'm the new marshal. I came to ask about your grandson. My apologies, about his...passing."

I was shocked to hear him speak of such things. You must understand: Talk of death does not come easily in this land. You do not ask about a neighbor's loss. You do not inquire. To lose a family member —especially in rural areas where such a loss has a direct economic impact—is a terrible thing. A horror. You do not discuss such matters without grave apologies. And then you had better have a reason.

The man looked terrified. "My grandson? What has happened to my grandson? Have you come to give me bad news again?"

"No," Scarpone said. "I speak of Domenico, Signore. Domenico DelCillie. The boy who passed some time ago."

The man sighed with relief. "Grazie Dio! Come in, come in."

The confusion had lifted. The man turned and limped away. Scarpone entered a messy kitchen. A fan was running over the stove. The room seemed filled with aerosolized grease and the smell of frying.

The man loped into another room to turn down the TV. He hobbled back to the kitchen and opened the fridge.

"Sit, Marshal, sit. I'll get some drinks."

Two glasses and a bottle of mineral water came to the table. Next came a small bottle of beer, and more glasses. The man stumbled off to the stove one last time to spear clusters of fried dough from the crackling oil. Scarpone watched him drop them onto a plate covered with a paper towel.

He lurched back to the table with his plate, his face glowing with quiet pride.

"Thirty years, Signore," he said, moving as if his back and hip and leg were fused together and painful. "Thirty years, I worked the fields and never learned to cook. My wife did it all, but all this time I thought, why wait for her to make these delicacies that I enjoy so much? Why not simply make them for myself, so I can take my pleasure when I want and not when it strikes her fancy? She is at my daughter's, or she would be here to tell you herself that she is proud of my independence."

He placed the plate in front of Scarpone. A fried squash blossom, seeping grease into a paper doily.

The man raised a fork and gestured with it. "Signore, first you will taste the fried dough. Always delicious, yes? But then the taste of the flower. And inside *that*, a bit of fresh mozzarella, refrigerated so it holds its shape. And then, deep in the center, an anchovy in the old style. Good, eh? I don't know how I would have made it through all this sorrow without my fondness for the culinary arts. Eat, eat!"

Scarpone could not say no. He accepted the water, a sip of the beer, a sliver of the dough. The taste was so—

He is walking in the woods. Cold. So cold. The damp creeping up his legs. His uncle's voice in his ears: "You will get through this." His mother's face flashes before him as he walks. She is crying. Her eyes rimmed red.

—tempting.

His teeth chewed. He tasted—

Light up ahead. A road. Traffic. Voices. He steps out of the wood and onto the road.

—vegetable, cheese, fish, dough.

He laid down his fork and washed away the taste with the beer.

"I'm sorry to bother you with this," Scarpone croaked.

"So—is something wrong? You scared me, Marshal," the man said, "But it's a simple misunderstanding. You see, we married late in life. So I was a father older than most. Two children. The boy and the girl."

"Domenico was your son?"

"Yes."

"I'm sure that my predecessor knew this well. I'm coming on, and I have the notes and papers and I thought it would be appropriate to introduce myself, to ask after whatever details you can remember at this late date."

The man stared at him. Anger, or what looked like it, crept onto his face.

"What do they want with these drugs, these children? Why do they find it even a temptation, I wonder? Education, which is something I believe in, destroyed him."

"In what sense?"

"What do they learn at school? To read, to write? To make their numbers, all well and good. But beyond that, what else do they need? I think it takes too much of their day. My wife cannot speak of it, I tell you. But from time to time, she will remark, 'Maybe we gave him too much?' The motorino. Nice clothes. Nice shoes. The mobile phone he wanted. We had none of these things when I was a boy. I had only what my father and grandfather left me. Some of those fields we had were planted with vines my father put in. That's what kills you: the questions you keep asking yourself. Was I too indulgent? Was I too strict? Did I pay him no mind? On and on. That's what hurts."

He paused. "Do you like the fried flowers, Marshal?"

Scarpone said yes, though the oiliness was perhaps a bit much. He nibbled slowly. The man speared another fried blossom onto Scarpone's plate.

"Today I picked the last of them, I'm afraid. The season is over. So sad to see the summer go." He paused. "Why do you ask about my boy, I wonder? Are you here to tell me that the trade has ceased, or has gone off to break the hearts of parents in another country? When we grew, we grew to feed ourselves and others. We grew grapes to make joy. Nothing else. What kind of farmers are they, who grow such things?"

"I can't say. But I imagine it's done because it's a reliable cash crop, same as anything else. Who found him, may I ask?"

"His mother did. She has never forgiven me. Never forgiven herself."

His voice choked. He bowed his head over his plate and chewed solemnly. Sipped beer. Sipped water. Then munched some more. When he looked up, flecks of dough clung to his lips. His eyes were red.

"I am told the children do it because their lives are unhappy. Because they want to relieve the tedium. To this I can only ask: Why is there tedium? If I were this lucky, if I were this free, I would be elated. My soul would soar. When we were children, we dreamed of having nice possessions like the city children. But no—our sons today tire of TV and sports and cars and even girls."

"I've been meaning to ask," Scarpone said. "Do you still work the land? No offense, but I see the leg gives you trouble."

"This?" He smiled. "This injury and I are old friends. It gives me the most trouble in the winter or when the fog comes, which here is every morning. Hah. I run a tractor for hire when there is work. We had much more land, nice flat land just south of the borgo, but we gave it up. Now I'm down just to this parcel you see. My apricots. The chickens. The rabbits."

"Excuse me, did you say you *had* the land?"

"We sold it. After. Didn't see the point of it. Why should it sit without a future? My daughter wasn't interested. She's married now and they live outside Orvieto. My son might have worked it. I don't know. He might have, once he got out of school, and realized that the free ride wasn't going to last forever. If he wanted money for his pocket, he would have *had* to help out around here. I'm sure he would have. He would have worked with us and he would have come to like it."

"You held it for him, then?"

"By local law we must. Well, until they come of age and decide if they want it or not. We don't have much, Luisa and I. We needed a *stipendio*. Our bank helped us with that when the money came through. Now we have a little money every month. Not much, but enough."

"Who bought it?"

He shrugged. "Who knows? Croatian, Albanian, Hungarian—one of those crazy nationalities. Moroccan, maybe? Good people, I'm told. I've been by to see them since the closing. Can't speak a word of our language. But they work the land together *as a family*, the way we used to in this country. Cousins or brothers and their families. That's the way to do it, if you're going to do it at all."

He paused.

"Not a day goes by when I don't think of my boy, Signore. It kills you. Do you want another fried blossom, by the way? They aren't bad, are they?"

Chapter Forty-Six

The road was called Via del Lago because it supposedly led to a lake, but that was puffery, because that body of water was not much more than a pond at the edge of an uncultivated field. The owner had not kept up the fence for years, so it had become a favorite watering hole for shepherds in the area.

The address to the former DelCillie property was somewhere along that stretch. The house was situated on a rise set back from the road. A long dirt drive to the left looked rough, but the vineyards in front looked clean and well tended.

According to the engineering department at city hall, the electricity had been off for years but someone had recently applied for a water permit. And here was a store-bought hose running from a hole in the dirt up to the house.

Scarpone walked his bike up the rutted drive. There was no point trying to pedal on this terrain. Rain had washed the drive in spots down to the bare rocks. At the top of the drive, he lay his bike to the ground and looked around.

A field of mature grapevines behind the house. Each vine looked as thick as his arm. Old, and thus good.

A three-wheeled Piaggio farm vehicle was parked there, its windows coated with clay dust.

Some of the windows of the house were open. Fabric stretched across them, probably to reduce the flies. Footprints here and there, indicating the presence of people.

He thought about going around the back.

"Hello?" he called.

Heard nothing but the drone of some insects crawling along a patch of rocks under the window. Probably a hornet's nest in there behind the mortar. The insects were sluggish and confused, dropping off the rocks and then trying to climb them again. It was the time of year when the world of insects was cruelly shutting down.

On the books, the house was listed as uninhabitable. How could someone be living in an unrestored farmhouse, without electricity, without heat, with only a water hose snaking up the drive from the aqueduct in the street?

He took the steps two at a time.

It pleased me to see his body working so well.

He knocked on the door. Nothing.

The door was hardly that. Something you'd find on a woodshed, with a chain passed through a splintered hole to lock up come nightfall.

"Hello?"

Still nothing.

He pushed in the door.

Inside, a crude camp kitchen. Paint peeling from plaster walls.

A pot hung in the old stone hearth. A wooden table crowded with foodstuffs—flour, dried beans in plastic bags, bottles of olive oil.

From another part of the house, he heard a drone not unlike the hornets outside. Voices speaking low.

He rapped his knuckles on the table. "Hello?"

The voices continued.

He stepped across the main room and headed for one of the old bedrooms.

But even as he did this, his mind was thinking, *No, this is not correct. You are intruding here.*

But by then, he was already in the room.

By then he was already seeing four or five adults and some children, their heads and hands pressed forward on prayer mats.

Everyone looked up.

Scarpone threw up both hands: *"Excuse me! Excuse me! I'm sorry!"*

And away he ran, back outside, back down the steps, his weapon thwapping against his side.

Another twenty minutes passed before the door opened. The family was there, watching him.

He muttered his apologies again.

The men and women were dark skinned, more from sun than anything else. The children with beautiful thick eyelashes.

One of the men, dressed in a tattered wool jacket and a scarf at his neck, came down the stairs, extending his hand, and trying to speak.

"Problema?" he said. *"Problema?"*

"There is no problem," Scarpone said. "I mistakenly intruded. I'm deeply sorry."

Blank stares.

The man was old, with a head of thick, dark hair, surprising for his age.

"Documenti?" the man said, digging in his jacket pockets.

Scarpone kept saying, "I'm sorry. I'm sorry I interrupted you. I was concerned. I was concerned. Do you understand me?"

The man was showing him things now: his work permit, his passport, his green-and-white fiscal code card. And there was a longer pause while he unfolded a legal-sized document.

During this whole time, none of the others left the house. All of them were crowded in the doorway of the crumbling farmhouse, watching their patriarch deal with what must have seemed like a bizarre intrusion of the state.

The man handed him the legal document, gesturing.

"Proprietari!" he said. *"Proprietari!"*

Owners, owners.

Scarpone felt obligated to inspect the document. It was a photocopy of one of the pages from a recent real estate transaction.

The implication couldn't be clearer: We have a right to be here. We own this place. We call it home.

Chapter Forty-Seven

He waited on the park bench between the church and city hall, sipping a chilled bottle of mineral water. Enzo came down once to hand him a thick folder, then dashed into the municipal building to snag more of his research.

My captain seemed agitated. It was another of those moments when I could feel the heat wafting off his body. What it was, I couldn't say. Anger? Frustration? Disillusionment? I know only that his eyes were fixed across the parking lot piazza, staring off into the distance at nothing.

"I don't know what it means," Enzo said upon his return. "The clerks are copying the pages for me now, but I can confirm that that family of Moroccans have taken up residence at the old DelCillie farm. I don't understand why you're upset, though. It seems perfectly straightforward."

My captain struggled to put what he was feeling into words. He felt shy when he considered the work he was putting Enzo through. Every second the young man spent with his nose in paperwork was a second he wasn't pulling his weight down at the station.

Scarpone nodded his chin at the municipal building.

"How do they treat you when you come on these wild goose chases?

"Well, they're not the *friendliest* people, especially to out-of-towners like me. It's primitive. If they would only allow me to take everything back to the station, I'd be able to photocopy everything there and return it. But no—that's out of the question, even for a soldier like me. There's only one copier in the building and things tend to be slow."

"Fine, then, I guess. Because you're going to be here a while."

"I'm happy to do it, for as long as you need me to. I just wish I understood *why*, sir. I hate to think we're wasting manpower. Can you tell me what it means?"

"They're screwing with us."

"Who is?"

"I don't know. But listen: The DelCillies, you'll recall, lost a son almost two years ago. One of the drug ODs. They still live at the bottom of the hill, right where the flat land of the borgo begins."

"Yes," Enzo said. "So far as I know, they've never left. They have that house behind the apricots. And they worked a second parcel of land which consisted of several hectares of grapes, olives, and a dilapidated farmhouse."

"They never lived in the house out on Via del Lago?"

"No—it's a wreck. DelCillie's grandparents built it."

"But these Moroccans I met live there now. *Own* it now, in fact."

"So it seems," Enzo said. "Technically, their family business owns it. 'The Harrak Corsorzio' is the name on the deed."

"These migrant families you're turning up in your research—are they all on the level?"

"They all have work permits, if that's what you mean."

Enzo opened the first file, which was lying next to my captain's hip. "Let's see. The Vajdas are from Hungary. The Harraks are from Morocco. Muslims, I gather. The Iordanescus, Romania. The Dlugos family, Slovenia. And the others are from Albania."

"And they all own their places?"

"Well, it's a little complicated. There are leases on file with city hall. Technically, each family rents from themselves. The homes are owned by family trusts or businesses."

"Is that normal when groups of relatives buy houses?"

Enzo made a face. "I don't know. I've never bought a house. My wife's parents offered to buy us an apartment in Turin, but we decided to wait until my service takes us back there."

"Are there mortgages on file for these farmhouses?"

"No. They own them outright."

"Hmm," Scarpone said. "You—you rent now?"

"Of course."

"So do I. Is your lease on file at town hall? Have you ever heard of anyone actually filing that paperwork?"

"Well, no."

"Of course, because no one wants to pay the stamp tax. So these foreigners are exceptionally law abiding."

"It's different with stranieri, sir. Foreign renters are supposed to register—"

"I know. I also know that very few do so. Landlords don't want a record of that rent. Okay. So. That's quite a list. Serves us right for thinking everyone's Albanian or Russian. Not a single one of these people has residency?"

"That's right."

"Over the next couple of days, I need one or two of the men to go around and introduce themselves to each of these families. Maybe Puzio? He probably speaks all these languages."

"Oh, I doubt he's that proficient, sir. Why make him go, though?"

"He should just be polite. Say hello, give them the phone number of the station in case they ever need help. That sort of thing."

"Is that all?"

"Of course not. I want him to see how these families are getting along in these houses. Can we manage that?"

"Sure."

"Don't send Gismonda. Oh, and you said you had something for me about their auto insurance?"

"Ah yes—the vital records office only asks for basic documentation when people move here and register. They want a copy of your passport, your local address, your fiscal code, and the work permit. If you have all that, you can register for the national health service, and pay the garbage tax. That's all city hall cares about, frankly. You can, if you wish, hand over any supporting documents but it's not necessary. One of these couples handed over their marriage certificate. One family, for some reason, gave a copy of their auto documents."

"Let me see those." He took and flipped through them. "The car's registered to a company in Viterbo: Consorzio Agrario Dentare, S.R.L."

"That's a farmer's co-op, sir. They can pool their money, buy feed, equipment, livestock—"

"I'm aware of that. And the insurance company is Assicurazioni Falmarra, Capalba. Do you know this town, Capalba?"

"It's far. Close to Viterbo but off the road. I haven't been there."

A smile came to the captain's face. "Do these two businesses ring a bell, Enzo?"

"Should they?"

"One problem in our work is that we cultivate short-term memory. It's out of our heads the second we file the paperwork. You don't remember these businesses? *You're* the one who noted them in the first place."

"I was?"

"Yes. More than a month ago, when we found Arbend Demaci's car at the Orvieto train station. *His* car was registered and insured by the same two companies."

"Huh. Is that so? I suppose that's interesting, isn't it? The Albanian shared a connection to a family that bought land from one of the grieving families. That shouldn't be too hard to check out. I *could* just ring the insurance company."

Scarpone went for his bike. "Now why would you do that?"

Fifteen minutes later, Scarpone had locked his bike in his apartment, changed into a fresh regulation shirt, and retrieved his car. As he started the engine, he glanced at the foreyard of his landlord's place and smiled.

The artichoke plants were dead.

Chapter Forty-Eight

He drove hard and fast to Capalba, but still arrived as siesta was starting. A strong sun shower had just ended, and steam rolled off the tops of buildings and along the cobbles. It was a one-fart borgo, one of those places that would look deserted even in the busiest times of day.

The centerpiece of town was an old Farnese villa that had played host to some papal dignitaries in one of the long-gone centuries. It was significant because a famous architect—whose name excited only other architects—had designed part of it. The structure was in the guidebooks; that's all that mattered. Tourists who took such books as gospel zipped into town, took one look at its crumbling exterior, shot a pic, and zipped back out. The front of the palace was left to teenagers, who rode in circles around the courtyard, stinking it up with the exhaust of their motorini and skateboards.

The address led him toward the end of town, around a couple of corners, down a path which ended in a stone wall. A bar cleverly used the dead end to spread out some tables and umbrellas, but no one was sitting in them. A couple of small children played foosball under the front awning. A young woman in her twenties, overdressed with makeup and jewelry, glared at Scarpone as he arrived, then disappeared into the apartment building beside the coffee bar.

Scarpone expected the insurance company to be on the upper floor of the building. But it was a storefront. Or was trying to be.

The window was smeared with white plaster dust. He peered inside. The floor looked as if it had never been laid, just ripped up as a prelude to run plumbing and electrical work. There were stacks of tiles, tall canisters of joint compound, wires and tubes and not much else.

Yes—it looked *exactly* like a place that was writing insurance policies for vehicles driven by migrant workers who'd just bought farmhouses and land worth hundreds of thousands of euros.

Someone had shoved menu circulars through the mail slot. But nothing else seemed to be piled on the floor inside.

The proprietor of the coffee bar across the alley seemed delighted to see him.

"I was just going to shut up. Coffee?"

"Yes. And a soda, I think. If you have ice, all the better. I have a ride ahead of me to Viterbo."

Most customers here plucked their drinks from the frigo in the back, paid, and bolted. The barman was pleased to see one lingering, even if he was a carabiniere in uniform.

The fall day had turned out to be warm, and sticky, now that the rain had come. The kids outside were making a racket. The barman cranked out the coffee, set it on the bar, and produced a glass and a small dish of ice. Scarpone leaned against the counter where the lottery ticket machine stood, next to a rack of gaudy magazines that offered a free romance novel if you bought this week's issue.

"I may join you in a bit," the barman told Scarpone, "if you don't mind."

"Not at all."

Scarpone dug out his notebook and jotted some notes. He drained his coffee in one gulp, sans sugar.

While he was mulling things over, the barman came around the bar with a white tablecloth, which he flipped over one of the indoors tables with a flourish. He dusted off some chairs and gestured for Scarpone to sit.

My captain did.

The man grabbed a lemon soda out of the fridge for himself. He wiped his forehead and left the towel at his neck. He looked too old to be the father of the children outside. But then again, the signora

Scarpone had seen disappear upstairs had been absurdly young, thin, and prancing awkwardly on spiky heels.

"You come for the villa?" the barman said.

"No, the insurance."

He stared at Scarpone blankly. "Oh," he said with a chuckle. "Yeah, *that*."

The barman raised the glass bottle to his forehead before sipping. Rolled it across his flesh till the condensation rubbed off.

"It's been there as long as I've been here. Which is to say, six or seven years." He lowered his voice. "This is my father-in-law's place. I'm not from here. But my wife won't leave. The town's dead. All day I look out this window and *see* a dead end. It's claustrophobic. I don't care for it." He lifted his eyes to the business across the alley. "Them—they never got around to finishing."

"But mail. They must get some."

"The postman leaves it with me or the furniture shop."

Scarpone ducked his head slightly to peer out the window and over the heads of the children. Yes, he'd thought the smell was familiar. The smell of shellac, lacquer, and sawdust.

"But who comes to take it?"

"Young boys, mostly. Who knows? You try to talk to them, but they're all foreigners."

Scarpone nodded. He spooned ice into his orange drink, and paused to think mid-drink.

His mind raced. In all the time I have watched him, I have rarely heard him think about *why* he does the work he does. But today, in the back of this bar in the sticks, I feel his outrage. He knows something is at work here, deep and internecine, but he cannot put his finger on it. He knows only that he is in the grip of rage.

These thieves. *Ladroni.* Mafiosi. Who the hell did they think they were?

He hated the thought of driving farther, but he knew he must. He knew *exactly* what he was going to find in Viterbo.

Another dead end, that's what.

The farmer's co-op in that city had been listed as the *owner* of Arbend Demaci's Audi. It had also been listed as the owner of a vehicle driven by one of the foreign families on his list.

Which was absurd.

This investigation had officially closed a month ago. Yet he knew he had to press on, if only to make himself more angry.

"Would you like another?"

"No," Scarpone said, digging for coins. "I need to get going if I'm going to make it to Viterbo and back before dark."

"Where's home?"

Scarpone told him.

"I've never heard of it. But I'm sure it's better than here."

Chapter Forty-Nine

That night he found it impossible to sleep. The apartment house was still and I could smell the anxiety on him as he reviewed a new chart he had drawn up.

A list of names.

It meant something.

At least he thought it did.

Carefully now, he dressed by the light of the bedside lamp, pulled on his shoes and his weapon, and headed for the door.

Too late now to ride the bike to the station. But the moon was so bright he could see all the way to the office without turning on his headlights.

But he took care. The air was chilly, the fog had not yet descended.

He heard the animals rustling in the barn below.

His engine sounded like a monster come to claim the darkness.

He made the quick hop to town, turned left past the gasoline distributor, past the supermercato, and pulled into the parking lot of the cinderblock structure covered in pink stucco.

Inside, the carabinieri station looked as bright as day but you could still tell it was night.

A lone soldier sat at the phone and radio, his TV turned on low.

"Iucci?"

The pale-haired young man looked up.

"Yes, Captain?"

"Anything tonight?"

His face said it all: *nothing, nothing, nothing.*

"Who's on patrol?"

"Puzio."

"Anything from him?"

"He's patrolling the *frazioni*, now, sir."

The frazioni were hamlets on the outskirts that did not qualify politically as borgos. They were tiny—a few clusters of houses on the plains or nearby hills, mostly populated by seniors who refused to leave their dying cities. Since the towns were so little, they had been lumped into the jurisdiction of the borgo and the station.

"There's an agriturismo out that way," Iucci told him. "Some tourists came in last night. A busload of Dutchmen, Puzio thinks. The bridge workers, you remember, were on strike, but it looks like they're working again. Puzio says the structure looks pretty nice, all lit up at night. Four lanes. Won't be long now, I guess."

Scarpone smiled. This information was hardly worth mentioning. The longer he and his men were stationed here, the more significant such tidbits would become. The mention of such news made them all sound remarkably observant. *Puzio is on the job, noting things!*

"Can I show you something?"

"Is it a case, sir?"

"Yes. Just look at this and tell me what you notice."

Iucci looked over the handwritten document:

- *Egidio Tubecchi, 16, deceased, heroin overdose. Son of Maddalena and Eusebio, brother of Lorenzo, 12 years.*
- *Gabrielle Santello, 17, deceased, heroin overdose. Son of Arianna and Fulvio, brother of Gisella, 8.*
- *Luca Dancione, 17, deceased, alcohol/heroin overdose. Only son of Gianna and Carmine.*
- *Domenico DelCillie, 17, deceased, heroin overdose. Son of Luisa and Antonio, twin brother of Patrizia, 17 years.*
- *Fabrizio Chiostro, 18, deceased, heroin overdose. Son of Gioia and Corrado, brother of Caterina, 17, and Allegra, 16.*

"It's just a list of names, sir."

"You don't notice something odd about the list?"

"These are the boys who died? Enzo said you were looking into that."

The captain knew he was close. It was right at the tip of his tongue. So apparent, yet so slight that he wondered if he wasn't just imagining things.

He took the sheet back.

"Would you like a coffee, Iucci?"

The young man brightened. His face flushed. He was flattered that his captain would offer.

He gestured at the opened soft drink can on his desk. "I have a Coca-Cola, sir."

His Florentine accent glanced off the hard Cs: *Hoha-hola.*

"I'll go down and make some for you." *I should have the hang of that machine by now.*

Scarpone stripped off his jacket and hat. He left the sheet on the desk.

The young soldier was solicitous. "Do you want me to look at it, sir, while you're gone? Maybe something will occur to me."

Scarpone nodded yes as he headed for the stairs. At night, using a stone staircase in a stone building was like descending into a tomb.

He already knew Iucci would not see it. This worried him.

Once again I am chasing ghosts, he thought.

And if Iucci didn't notice it, chances were Enzo or D'Orazio or even Scarpone's predecessor Vitellone would not have, either. If they had, they would have thrown themselves at this case with everything they had.

If they had seen what I now see, Scarpone thought, they would have known.

Yes—they would have known that a terrible, intelligent evil was at work here.

Chapter Fifty

"Nonna, can I have another bowl of gelato?"

I have never cared for Lucia's boy. He has always struck me as the type that will grow up to be an indolent man. But I will allow that the boy is adorable, with the luxurious lashes and succulent cheeks that grandmothers crave to touch.

"But caro," the contessa said, "you had a bowl with lunch. You'll ruin your appetite for dinner. How about a nice piece of cheese instead?"

This logic escaped me and my captain, but of course the boy said yes.

The contessa gave Scarpone a conspiratorial glance as she headed over to one of her three refrigerators. The one she opened was the size of a walk-in closet. Everything about the contessa's kitchen was larger than it had any reason to be. One side of the room was outfitted with commercial dishwashers. There were four stainless steel benchtops and two gas cooktops. It could have been the kitchen of a caterer or one of the upscale restaurants in Rome, with one significant difference: the people preparing the food here had no idea what they were doing. They were foreigners mostly. I could tell from the way they stared vacantly each time the contessa spoke. Their eyes immediately bounced to Lucia, awaiting her English translation.

Today they were supposed to be making something that involved slicing pork tenderloins and pounding them within an inch of their lives. Only four of the students were doing this. The rest were trying to navigate the intricacies of today's baking assignments.

Lucia's harvest was in for the season. And mother and daughter were taking advantage of Lucia's free time to make a killing on these classes.

The contessa set a wheel of hard cheese on the counter. She peeled back a bit of the rind and cut a perfect wedge for the boy. She wrapped it delicately in wax paper and presented it to him with a kiss. The boy was chomping on it even before he wandered off.

Lucia glared at her mother.

Or perhaps she was glaring at the captain. Usually I could tell. The fact that I couldn't today may have meant that the brunt of her anger was directed at both. I knew Lucia's heart well: This was supposed to be her time away from the farm. Yet she was reminded of her life in Castelpietra by the intrusion of my captain, who only wanted to ask her mother a few questions.

"You see that face, Marshal?" the contessa said as the boy walked away. "I live for it. That is all I need in this world. Can I tell you something? If I could round up all the hungry children of the world, every one of them, and feed them until they were all nice and chubby, I would consider my life's work completed." She was an attractive woman, but somewhat scattered. "What's that, Lucia?"

"The class is waiting. Maybe the marshal can come back another time?"

She cocked her head and smiled wickedly at Scarpone.

His throat clenched.

"Is this true, Marshal? Can you come back another time?"

"I'll be brief," Scarpone said.

"*Va bene,*" said the older woman, patting his arm with a touch that seemed as earnest as the one she had given the boy.

The contessa gave the class a few more bits of instruction, then led Scarpone to a corner of the kitchen where she was assembling a tray of food. Two bowls of soup. Slices of prosciutto, speck, salami. A selection of hard cheeses. Artfully drizzled spoonfuls of honey and marmalade.

"Go on, Marshal, you were saying."

"We're looking into the provenance of a property in Castelpietra.

It's on the Orvieto highway. Impossible to miss. Right across the road from the Amaldi land. And in the course of the search, my man found out that the property was once owned by your father."

"Oh, that one."

"You know it?"

"Yes, of course. My father had no business buying that property in the first place. We were hotel people. But it shows you that at the time, right before things got bad before the war, he thought it might be wise to grow some crops on the side. I don't know that he ever did. He always said that he bought that parcel for me. It was to be an estate that we could turn into something one day. It had all these outbuildings. Barns. A tower for drying tobacco. The house. But my God, Signore—you know how long ago that was?"

She raised her hand beside her ear and waved the years away.

"You sold it?"

"Yes. To an Austrian. A German. A Swiss. I tell you, I can never tell the difference."

"Schultheiss."

"Yes! That's the name!"

"Excuse me for saying this, because I frankly don't know how to address this delicately. Did the count handle the transaction when you were still married?"

Her face glowered. She was like Lucia in a lot of ways. Overdressed for the kitchen, prone to melodramatic moodiness, spoiled, but pretty and integritous in a way you don't see often. She seemed incapable of standing still. Her eyes looked away from my captain to the cooking students. Her arms and fingers darted nimbly over the tray of food. My captain found her restlessness irritating but did his best to hide it.

"Contessa?"

"I'm not a contessa anymore," she informed him coldly. "He took even that from me, I'm afraid. That property you speak of? For some reason it was placed in a trust of my father's that didn't migrate with me when I married. Good thing too. I was able to sell it to get the money for this place. I tell you—I was *happy* to let it go. That place was so strange. *Altibuono,* it was called. The high, good place." She shuddered. "I never thought it was so. Just the opposite. Like a place for the dead, God forgive me."

She lifted her right hand to her forehead and did a quick sign of the cross.

"How so?"

"Have you seen it?"

He shook his head.

"But you say you are investigating it?"

"It has come up in an investigation we're currently conducting, yes."

"You can go look at it now. The German or whatever who owns it is nice. But he doesn't use it. He was going to fix it up and have a place to come in the summers and winters. But I don't think he liked the architects he first hired. Or maybe he was disputing the permit tax city hall levied on him. I don't remember which. All I know is, he washed his hands of it and is trying to wait them all out. I think they expect him to put it back on the market again and try to get his money out of it. I don't know how these foreigners have the patience to buy properties in foreign countries. I could never be away from home too long; the food isn't any good anywhere else. And the weather is miserable."

"Why didn't you like the property?"

"I didn't like the tunnel."

"Tunnel?"

"Yes, my cousin used to take me when I was little. A tunnel leads from the animal stalls in the main house to the road *below* the house. Not the Orvietana, you understand. The gravel road. My father bought it thinking that those grottoes would be valuable if we ever needed to hide anything. It stayed fairly warm even in winter, and it was a nice place to park tractors and other tools."

My captain tried to envision the road she was speaking about.

"Do you like white or red, Marshal?"

"Excuse me?"

She pointed through the glass panel of a well-stocked wine fridge.

He looked from the wine to the food on her tray.

"Are you making this for *me?*"

"But of course. You said you didn't have lunch!"

He had foolishly admitted as much.

"And if you don't eat now, you'll be starving by the time you get back. Please. Come with me. Lucia, will you be okay?"

Lucia glared at them anxiously as they left. Scarpone carried a bottle of dry Est! Est!! Est!!! The contessa lugged the tray of food.

She led them into the late fall day, across a stone terrace and toward the lake.

"You're just like Bertie. He *never* takes lunch at the right time and then he wants to know why he's so hungry. Some men are like babies, Signore. They too need to be fed until they are nice and chubby. But he's English. I don't know what your excuse is, Marshal."

The rear of her villa overlooked Bolsena, the volcanic lake he'd seen the day he visited Montefiascone. That city was somewhere on the distant shore. Where, Scarpone had no idea.

The contessa headed to a dock on the shore of her property. At the end of the wooden planks was a bizarre structure that could only be the product of a British mind.

"You like it?" the contessa said. "Bertie calls it his folly. But I don't know what it means in our language. *Follia?* Something stupid, in other words? You probably know more than me, Marshal. You know, I never went to school the way the children do today—"

Her face changed now. The skin around her lips practically twitched.

"Listen, Marshal, please. Can you take this now?"

She meant the tray. She was thrusting it at him, almost forcefully. Her feet had reached the end of the dock, where the planks of wood met land. "Please, Signore," she said, her voice sounding wounded.

He took it.

A look of relief came across the woman's face. Scarpone headed down the dock with food and wine, though he had neither hunger nor thirst.

Chapter Fifty-One

The occupant of the folly wore an absurdly unmasculine hat which Scarpone associated with English gardeners. *Female* English gardeners. The sixtyish, bald man also wore glasses, an ascot, a gingham shirt, and chino pants that were stained with newspaper ink.

"Hello, hello," the Brit said, *"Buon pomeriggio."* Scarpone assumed he was trotting out both tongues in an effort to see which language Scarpone wished to use.

"Ah, I see Andreina saw fit to burden you down with all that. So sorry. So sorry." Bertie took the tray and set it on a table between them, and set about wrenching the cork out of the bottle. Scarpone couldn't bear to tell him he couldn't stay to eat. "She's deathly afraid of coming out here and always sticks me with the honor. I tell her that her fear would not be so magnified if she would only learn to swim. Let's see—it's just the Est! Est!! Est!!! Nothing fancy, but nice. I like the dry myself. Nice of you to come out. Lucia has spoken of you, and what a great friend you've become."

Bullshit, Scarpone thought.

Bertie poured the wine, and dug into his minestrone without waiting for my captain. Scarpone hesitated. The truth was, he was hungry. But he didn't have time for lunch. He selected one of the triangles of cheese and dipped it tentatively into a puddle of honey. Washed it down with some wine.

"Do you know the lake, Marshal?"

Scarpone had learned his English in the course of overseas training programs at New Scotland Yard. "Not really," he said self-consciously. "I've been out once."

"You speak English well. My compliments." Bertie waved his spoon at the view. "I fell in love with the place when I first visited. I'm a lucky man, to be able to have all this."

Cast-off foreign newspapers lay at his feet. A man after my captain's heart.

"I take it you're Roman, so perhaps you're not easily impressed. But if you're the sort of Roman who enjoys his history, the lake and city will not disappoint you. Both are legendary for religious miracles. Perhaps you've heard of the host that bled with the blood of Christ? You can see some bloodstains if you visit the church in town. And this lake is where the pagans apparently tried to do in Saint Christina. The basilica is named after her."

"I don't know Christina."

"Oh, it's a your typical horror show, good fellow. There wasn't anything that they could do to kill the poor virgin. They tried to grill her alive, tear her apart with hooks, break her on the rack, and toss her in a pit of serpents. Nothing worked. Finally, they tossed her into our beloved lake with a stone tied around her neck. And she bobbed back up with the aid of an angel."

"Of course. How'd they finally do her in?"

"Arrows."

"Who would have thought?"

Bertie chuckled. "Of course, there's little you can *confirm* about saints, you know. I myself find it difficult to study their stories, much as I'd like to, because there's so little real history to them. Take, for instance, the stories of the two islands here. See? The island on the left is Bisentina, where they once locked up heretics. Priests who'd gone bad. And the other, Martana—"

"Oh, right. Where they killed the queen, or somesuch."

"Her name was Amalasuntha. You know the story? She died out there."

He pointed to Martana. It was hard to see right now, thanks to the mist rising from the blue water. Still, the view was gorgeous,

gorgeous, gorgeous. You could spend a month here easily, Scarpone thought. Lounging on the beach, cobbling together meals from the sidewalk kiosks or the waterfront restaurants. Discotheques, of course, to entertain the kids at night.

In a different life, Scarpone thought, maybe it would be nice to live in such a place.

"The history there is fascinating," Bertie prattled on. "Amalasuntha was a Visigoth, one of the race of people who had crushed the Romans. Her son inherited the throne of Theodoric, greatest of the Goth kings. But her son was just a child, so they appointed Amalasuntha his regent. She could have bided her time until her son ascended the throne, but instead, she tried to usher in a new Roman order. She loved Roman culture, you see. She spoke Latin and the common tongue, and had been marvelously tutored in Ravenna. So she was partial to the Roman way of life. But she could be brutal too. Procopius tells us that she rubbed out three Gothic nobles who objected to her rule. Then, to solidify her power, offered to share the regency with her cousin, Theodahad. Well, of course he turned on her and locked her up on Martana. It's private now, by the way. You couldn't land your boat there if you tried. Private owners, I think. Probably exiled nobles. The country is rife with them, but don't tell Andreina I said such a thing."

"So Amalasuntha was murdered by her cousin?"

"Oh yes—I forgot the best part. She was only imprisoned a few days when her cousin or her other enemies had her strangled in her bath. Fascinating case. I have some books if you're interested. You could argue that her murder touched off the Goth wars. Theodahad took over and began minting coins bearing his idiotic visage. He died too, murdered by his enemies."

"I heard it differently, somehow. You make it sound so...accurate."

"Thank you! Well, if you want romance, there are no end of stories. I've heard so many variations that it pains me to think about it as an amateur historian. Some say Theodahad was her husband. That's not true. He was married, and his wife was still alive. Others say he was her lover or cousin or brother, who killed her for unrequited love. I don't know why they always toss in the specter of incest; I suppose it makes good copy. I have a book upstairs if you like parsing out such things."

All the while Bertie spoke, Scarpone sipped—

He is walking through the forest. His hands beat his arms for warmth. This time, he comes to the edge of the forest and sees the road empty except for a man and woman. They are standing naked, embracing each other. They are young. The man turns to him. His face is made of stone.

—the crisp white wine.

Scarpone's wine glass fell. The glass bounced and clattered. Wine everywhere. "I'm so sorry. So sorry. Did I drench you?"

"Not at all," the Brit laughed. "And please do relax. This is why I don't allow glass out here. Everything's plastic, you see?"

He tapped his glass.

"I need to go. I'm sorry. Maybe some other time?"

"Indeed, of course. You're the working man here. But is something wrong?"

"No, it's just..."

He struggled, not sure how to say in English that he was needed back at the station, and forgetting that his host spoke both languages equally well.

He was running up the dock before the Brit could say another word.

Chapter Fifty-Two

Fig trees lined the drive behind the villa. They were planted along grassy mounds so that people could stand on the hummocks while they picked the fruit. A gardener with a gasoline-powered weedeater was mowing the mounds, probably for the last time this season. Another was raking leaves.

Scarpone had his foot to the pedal of his Fiat, hoping to round the circular drive and get on the road as quickly as possible.

And then he saw Lucia coming down the gravel drive, waving after his car. The apron around her waist fluttering as she ran.

Oh, God, he thought. Let's not do this now.

But there was no way out of it without feeling the guilt. She was gesturing for him to stop. He pulled over and rolled down the window. The sound of the weedeater was obnoxious; perhaps that would hurry things along.

"How dare you?" she said.

"Excuse me?"

"How dare you come on police business? *Here,* of all places? This is my family. This is my mother and my child. I come here to get away. Why is it that every time I turn around, you're there snooping and trying to turn something innocent into something sordid?"

"Signora, you're ridiculous right now, do you know that? I treat everyone exactly the same. If you answer the questions I ask the first time, truthfully, I go my merry way and leave you alone. Otherwise, what the hell do you think I'm going to do? I will *never* back down when people start lying to my face."

"Who's lying now? I answered everything you put to me."

He shook his head over his steering wheel. His head felt light and hot from the anger. Okay, he thought, let's do this now. He killed the engine and stepped out.

"I'll bet you anything I can ask you a question right now to which you will respond with a lie."

"What question is that?"

"Was it your father or your brother?"

"Excuse me?"

"It's a simple question. And you know what I mean."

"I don't. You're hardly speaking clearly."

"Let's make it easier, then. How old is your son?"

"My son—" She looked at the ground. "What can he possibly have to do with what you're investigating?"

"Where was he born?"

"The United States. Four years ago."

"No. The United States, *five* years ago. See, you lied about that the day we had lunch in Orvieto, which puzzled me because anyone who looks at Leonardo's fiscal code or identity card or birth certificate at the vital records office in town will know the date. But you've been counting on the fact that people never do the math. But I do. I rather like it. So let's see if I have it straight. He was born in September of 2007, just as your viticulture program was wrapping up. You said it was a seasonal program, didn't you? March to September. And Charlie, the day we met, joked about you being the Class of 2007. So... unless you met and fell into bed with Charlie the *second* you arrived in California in January—"

"Stop it."

"Or you were pregnant *before* you left Castelpietra. Hence my original question."

"Go to hell!"

She started to walk away.

"You don't want to leave this hanging, Lucia. Follow the logic. If your son was *conceived* here, then conception was close to the time you left to study in America. Indeed, so close to your departure that it makes me think you left *because*—"

Her hand caught him on the face.

His flesh stung.

"Charlie isn't the father, is he? He seems like a nice man, and clearly fond of you. But your marriage is one of convenience, not love. I sensed it the day we met you both at the winery. You were talking about why you came back home. You said something like, 'By then *I* had the baby.' That's not something a married woman says, is it? From the moment you are married, without even thinking of it, all your pronouns become first person, plural: *noi, noi, noi.* Charlie's registered at your house, but he doesn't live there. And when he *is* in town, he's at the vineyard on the other side of the river. You married to help him get *his* dual citizenship, with the expectation that he would help you and Leonardo get yours. Perhaps such a thing would be advantageous when either of you began importing or exporting wine, but I don't know much about such things. I'm not a businessman. But I do know your marriage saves Leonardo from being a bastard."

"That's enough, *Marshal.*"

"No, it's not. So, again I ask: Which was it, your father or your brother?"

"Neither. I had a boyfriend."

"Oh really? And why would this Castelpietra boyfriend not be involved in the child's life upon your return?"

"He moved."

"And his relations? Did they all up and move too? Tell me: Does your mother know?"

Her head shook. "She can never know."

"Was it voluntary?"

She shook again.

"Say the word and I'll take him in. *Say it.*"

"I can never say it. It's done. He's dead."

"Your brother, then. And when he died, you felt it was safe to come home?"

"How did you know?"

"I told you. The dates. And from the moment I met the boy, he looked familiar to me. Everyone probably assumes it's just a family resemblance. But he looks like the photo of your brother that sits on your father's desk. Little boys tend to look like their fathers, not their uncles. When you put that together with the dates, you running away, and your brother's history of battering women, it all comes together nicely."

"It wasn't just once. It went on a long time. It was happening in that house before I even knew what *it* was, and continued when I was older and he was stronger. He practiced on me before taking it to the girls outside the house. You don't know what it's like, having that on your conscience. After a while, I thought I could keep him from others if I let him. It made it...more...bearable."

"Couldn't you have said something to your parents?"

"Oh, come now. Which of them could I have turned to in my misery? You've seen my mother. She knows food and hospitality. She cannot comprehend such a thing. She was dealing with her own abusive relationship. Trying to navigate her own survival. And my father revered Marco. I was alone."

"There was always the priest. Or the carabinieri."

Even as he was saying this, he knew they were hollow, bullshit suggestions. What girl in her position would have turned to any authority figure—least of all ones accustomed to taking the man's side in everything? No, she would have said nothing, and taken on the *vergogna*—the shame—as her own.

"You must have felt alone. Terribly alone."

"You cannot possibly imagine."

"Is it any better now?"

She was silent. She looked at the ground, at the men working in the orchard, at the lake behind them. Then her hand shot out, caught his chin, and held it.

"I don't care what you're looking into. This cannot ever come out. For once I have something close to peace."

"*Close to?* What good is that?"

"This is all I ever wanted. A son, a mother who loves me, and the land. I bide my time with my father. Nothing more. One day, he'll let my son have the azienda and our wine will have a home."

"Until then, it's worth the lie?"

She pulled back and lashed out at him. Slapped his face once. Twice.

She was crying openly now. My captain didn't flinch. "Look," he said, pointing a finger at the gardeners. "People are looking, Lucia. People are watching."

He turned his cheek.

"Care to try it again?"

Her hands dropped to her apron pocket. She strode off in the direction of the house.

Chapter Fifty-Three

The big cop from Naples, Belluzzi, was not known for being industrious or swift. But under his new orders, he began to shine.

Clearly, he was well suited to the task, which involved sitting on his ass for most of the day. When he came on shift, he parked his vehicle at the edge of the parking lot on the eastern side of the borgo —behind the computer and undergarment and babies' clothing stores —and pointed his binoculars northeast. There was a nice view from these cliffs. And from here he could watch a number of fields, roads, and abandoned houses. Where nothing ever happened.

This did not bother him. The assignment gave him plenty of time to stink up his vehicle with cigarettes, talk with friends back home on his mobile, and wonder why his captain had assigned this task in the first place.

What a freak this captain was! The oddest of all the men Belluzzi had served under. Just one look at him taking his coffee in the morning—reading those papers, cutting them out, folding those articles so deliberately. It was highly bizarre.

And strangely, despite the fact that Belluzzi occasionally became bored and thought about dropping the binocs and napping against the headrest, he fought off this impulse. Scarpone was a lot of things —a twitchy freak, withdrawn, cold, impersonal—but he was not a fool, and he was not tolerant. Belluzzi didn't need the captain raining down on his head. No, if he was going to stay on the job, he ought do it well and figure out a way to make it agreeable.

To stave off boredom, Belluzzi had devised a way to pass the time. Every time a vehicle drove past the point on the road that interested the captain—a spot Belluzzi privately called Whore's Point—Belluzzi jotted down a note about the vehicle.

He set his notebook on the dashboard next to his smoking cigarette. As his car filled with the stench of tobacco, he monitored each vehicle that drove past in the morning rush, and wrote down what he knew of them. If he knew nothing—and Belluzzi was a man who thought it was a wise policy to know little—he simply wrote the make and model as best he could make out from that distance.

Every morning like clockwork came the farm vehicles. Later still came service vehicles: the bread truck, the furniture truck, the meat truck, the supermarket truck. All going into town and later leaving. After lunch, here came the strega's father, delivering his daughter's wares to the shops in Orvieto. Here was the occasional tourist bus. And so on and so on.

After a while, in spite of his laziness, Belluzzi began to see a pattern emerge. When the town was awakening, Whore's Point saw the most traffic. When the town was winding down in the afternoon, more traffic. But not much borgo-bound traffic in the middle of the day. At that time of day, the vehicles seemed to be going straight on through toward the neighboring villages—Lubriano in the west, and from there probably straight on to Viterbo and Montefiascone.

The rest of the time, silence.

Throughout the day, much of the land he surveyed was dead. This was true all over the nation. The land outside Naples, his own city, was equally full of abandoned farmhouses like these in Castelpietra. Belluzzi could hear his own grandfather decrying the trend—it was a national disgrace to have so much land lie fallow. How could this be?

But he was younger than his *nonno* and knew in his heart the truth of the matter. Farm work was bullshit. It was drudgery. Only the old people had a taste for it, only they were sentimental about it —and they were dying off in droves. Sane people bought their food at the supermercato and set their sights on good office jobs with pensions and benefits. Life was safer that way. You wouldn't be wiped out if storms or droughts descended, or a damned posse of wild boar tore through your fields and ran your livelihood to the ground.

Son of a bitch.

He had had some beautiful days in the country. When he was a boy, he'd go to his grandfather's farm and help the old man pick peaches or else apricots on certain weeks of the year. He'd suck down as much fruit as he could, and have the shits for weeks. Mother of God, those peaches tasted like heaven, didn't they? The supermercato peaches, even the ones found at the Saturday farmer's market, didn't come close.

But what did it matter? They were peaches, not gold. They'd never replace a car or bike or a good mobile phone. They were so ephemeral—a juicy commodity today and nothing but a memory tomorrow.

So no—Belluzzi did not fault people like his father for leaving the land and looking for work in the city. Who could fault Belluzzi himself for wanting more security in life than banking on drops of water to fall from the sky?

Ah look—there was another grape truck heading down the road, probably to the co-op. There was another. And heaven knew whose trucks they were.

On his notebook page he wrote: *Time 15:35 Two trucks—grapes.*

Soon the season would be over, and the fields would fall quiet and empty again, like that forlorn farmhouse across from Whore's Point.

Belluzzi leaned forward in his seat to rip an odiferous fart.

Strange, Belluzzi thought.

A vehicle was turning off the main road and heading up the dirt path to the abandoned Schultheiss house.

Stranger still, a man came out of the bottom doors of the farmhouse—from the rooms traditionally used to house animals—to catch the driver's eye. A half-dressed man in pants and undershirt waved angrily, and leaned into the window of the vehicle.

Belluzzi sucked on his cigarette. Then set it delicately on the dash.

I could feel the air change as Belluzzi brightened. It was as if the police vehicle was filled with a single emotion—*orgoglio*. Pride. For once in his desultory career, Belluzzi felt like a cop. See? Here was proof that he hadn't joined the service merely to lock in a meal ticket. He was born to do it. He was man of the streets. He *knew* people.

Right now, Belluzzi *knew* what the man was saying to the driver. Belluzzi could sense it. He could feel it in his bones.

You idiot, wrong way! The other way. Underneath! Underneath!

See—look at his hands, Belluzzi thought. He's giving him directions.

The car started to back up.

Belluzzi's fingers hit speed dial.

The undershirt-clad man headed back to the doors of the farmhouse. Another head peeked out. The two of them conversed. The first man gesturing.

Probably telling him about the idiot driver.

The two men looked left and right. Down to the fields, up to the road.

What are you doing? Belluzzi thought. Checking to see if the coast is clear? Well, it's not, you idiots.

Enzo, the brown-nosing northerner, answered the phone.

"It's Belluzzi. I don't want to make a big deal out of it, but I think we have something."

"Yes?"

"I think people are living in the house at Whore's Point."

"Seriously?"

"They're taking pains to keep it quiet. And they're good, believe me. I haven't seen these shits all week. But if you know what you're doing, you can suss these idiots out. All it takes is good, solid police work. You have a pencil? Take down this license number."

Chapter Fifty-Four

The fog lies thick on the land, and as each of the men comes forward that morning, it seems as if they are one of my own. A head here, a shoulder there, a wisp of mist—and soon the whole man comes together. They've left their vehicles on the lower road and now trudge silently into position. At this time of day the Orvietana is empty and silent. My captain is at the head. Belluzzi and Gismonda follow him with the battering ram, submachine guns at their shoulders. The fat man, D'Orazio, pulls up to the rear with the shotgun.

Each of them is dressed in helmets and vests.

Late last night in the recreation room on the station's ground floor, my captain gave D'Orazio a choice: he doesn't have to be here. He doesn't have to risk himself.

Are you crazy, the "old" man said. It's been so long since we've done such a thing.

That's my point, Scarpone said.

I must be with my brothers.

And so they trudge together up the road.

At the turn in the road which they all now call Whore's Point, the captain halts and whispers into his Bluetooth device.

"Are you there, Enzo?"

He can hear the man's breath.

"Yes, sir. Almost there."

He, Iucci, and Puzio have taken the rear of the property, entering from the lower gravel road. They have more terrain to cover, and in the morning mist it may be hard for them to pick their way across the field under the farmhouse.

My captain waits.

"There's a path between some trees down here, Captain. The grass is worn down to the dirt."

"Tire tracks," Puzio says.

"Puzio sees—"

"I heard him," Scarpone says. "Tell him to lower his voice."

"It's easy, Captain. The path is clear. I can see the house."

So can the captain. The house is a muddle of ocher in a sea of mist. Standing at Whore's Point, he can feel the wetness creeping up his boots.

He thinks about his visions.

Are these the woods he keeps seeing?

He shoves those thoughts from his mind to think about the house. They have talked this over. From the main road, they can see only one door on the top level, and a pair of doors below. These old farmhouses are crudely designed. It's unlikely that the top and bottom floors are connected; to go upstairs you must use an exterior staircase. And since the terra-cotta tile roof appears to have collapsed, anyone who is hiding out at this house *must* be downstairs.

If so, then we have them, the captain thinks. But if they're staying in one of the barns, or the tobacco tower, then there's a chance that we're screwed. They'll surprise us rather than the other way around.

But he doesn't think so. He is a careful man. He has studied the old maps and knows the aqueduct runs along the road closest to the house. If they're staying here and stealing water from the tap, they're staying in the house.

"We see the grottoes, sir," Enzo says. "My God—you have to see this. The opening is huge. They've tried to hide it." His voice breaks off. "What is that?"

Pause.

"Sir, they've hidden the opening with hay bales. Their cars must be here, up ahead. We can see their headlights with our flashlights."

Pause.

Enzo laughs. "Hah. Puzio says it's like the Bat Cave. You know, from Batman?"

"Tell him to shut up."

My captain signals the others, and they angle in from Whore's Point and make their way to the house. D'Orazio takes the staircase leading upstairs, just as they've discussed.

My captain positions Gismonda and Belluzzi in front of the bottom doors.

Then he fans around the side to check the back of the house. No other openings. That's good.

He peeks toward the left, through fields of tall grass. Somewhere underground, Enzo is there with the other men.

My captain doesn't like the mist one bit. On the up side, it hides things. On the down side, it hides things.

In the back of the captain's mind, he worries.

Please don't let them be armed. If they're armed and they get into the fields, we could be looking at a friendly fire situation.

He doesn't want to think of it.

No—most of the busts he's handled, they weren't armed.

That time in Rome, he thinks, we rescued the women without firing a single shot. The shooting came after.

He comes back to the ground-level doors. As Belluzzi gestures, my captain smells the man's aftershave, which is strange; Belluzzi is unshaven. The double doors are heavy, bolted in one spot to a slab of old concrete. A chain passed through holes in the woods tell them everything they need to know.

Locked from the *inside*.

Scarpone texts Enzo: *GOING NOW*.

Gismonda snips the chain.

It clatters just as Belluzzi grunts and beats in the door with the battering ram.

In the field behind them, birds caw and take to the air.

Steel screeches in concrete.

Wood splinters as they kick their way inside.

Already, screams.

My captain runs in first, sweeping the room with his flashlight and his weapon. He punches through a cloud of stale, fragrant air. Nicotine and ass and the sweaty bodies of men.

The room is a dark concrete chamber with wooden slats for animal stalls. The walls crawl with mildew and powdery plaster.

About a half dozen men lay on cots when the carabinieri storm in. And then, quick as that, the men are on their feet, bolting like rats.

Two men scream, see the guns, and throw up their hands.

Another rushes toward them, ignoring the weapons, dressed only his underwear. Gismonda tries to grab him, but merely scrapes the flesh of the man's arm. Belluzzi blocks the man's way, bunts him once with the battering ram. The guy drops and smacks his head on the stone floor.

One of them scampers up a ladder leading to the top floor.

Shit, my captain thinks. The floors *are* connected.

"D'Orazio!" he yells. "Coming for you!"

The fat, older cop is waiting, leaning against the wall of the exterior staircase. He nudges his upper back off the wall. When the idiot in underwear and a T-shirt comes running down, he is too adrenaline-blind to see the cop blocking his way.

D'Orazio swats him across the head and neck with the shotgun.

The man flips over the stone railing.

Splat.

Three men down inside. One down outside.

Inside, the captain trains the flashlight against the back wall.

Rusty farm vehicles. Stacks of wood-bored lumber.

Movement.

"Don't move!"

In the shadows behind the machines, someone is running.

Scarpone raises the weapon but hesitates. He'd rather not send a round ricocheting around those farm machines.

A shot rings out, pocks the wall to his right.

The son of a bitch has a gun.

Scarpone hears a clatter of wood.

Another shot pings metal, up high.

Again the wood. A trapdoor.

Scarpone speaks into his earpiece. "He's armed, Enzo, and he's coming for you."

My captain gestures to Belluzzi and Gismonda—*tie them!*

And then he runs out the door of the stalls.

Running across the grass. Through mist, through dew.

"Enzo!" he screams. "Watch for him."

Below him, he can see the lower field. A car shoots out of the Bat Cave, cutting across the tire tracks in the grass.

He sees his men running—

The tall one, Iucci, drops to a knee. Sights.

A shot rings out.

The car zips crazily but keeps going until it hits a tree.

And then a man dressed only in a pair of tight maroon underwear runs slowly, uncomfortably, across rocky soil down to the road.

"He's got a gun, Enzo. Did you hear me?"

Down in the field, Iucci aims again. This is the first time he's held a gun in roughly two months, since he shot the carrion bird. But judging from the way he took out that tire, he's a remarkably good shot.

Jesu, Scarpone thinks.

"Don't kill him, for God's sake," Scarpone says.

Enzo: "He won't, sir!"

A shot rings out, just past the underwear-clad man's head. He flinches, and throws down his weapon in surrender. But then, realizing that he's several meters away from the carabinieri, he decides to turn and *run*.

By now Enzo and Puzio have arrived behind Iucci. Enzo taps Iucci's arm. The three of them are laughing.

The barefoot man is trying to pick his way across rocks and mud to the *strada bianca,* where more rocks and gravel await him.

"Look at this guy," Scarpone hears Iucci say.

The cops stow their weapons. And Puzio lazily wanders down the path to collect the man.

"When you have him," Scarpone says, "bring the vehicles."

"Yes, sir," Enzo says.

In a while, the van and the Alfa appear on the road across from Whore's Point. Enzo opens the door of the Alfa, which contains a single occupant.

The first thing out of the car is a silver-tipped cane. Then beautiful brown shoes. Saviano is smoking. His hair looks elegant against the pale fields.

Scarpone waves him inside the farmhouse.

Belluzzi is already photographing the scene: the cots, the camp toilet, the makeshift kitchen with empty containers of takeout food. Empty mineral water bottles.

And at another table, a precision scale, boxes of plastic bags, rolls of tape, and an open duffle bag.

The magistrate peers into the duffle bag. Sees one carefully packed block of light brown powder, and the smaller, individually wrapped packets. And another set of slightly larger packets that look filled with dried herbs.

The men lie cuffed, their faces pressed into the stones of the old stall floor.

"Keep it," one of them says.

"Take it!" another repeats. "Take it and let us go!"

Scarpone looks at Belluzzi, who bends and slaps one of the men on the face like a teacher hitting a child.

"Shut up!" Belluzzi says. "I'm not supposed to be working this shift right now. I'm here because of you cockheads. So don't make me mad."

Scarpone has the notebook out. He shows the tally to the magistrate. Saviano drags on his cigarette. His yellowed teeth tug into a grin. "Buono."

Chapter Fifty-Five

"Arrigo Basile?"

The man was just nodding awake from his uncomfortable position in the rec room, where they'd cuffed him, hand and foot, to one of the chairs. Strange that a man so grossly naked could fall at once to sleep. But such behavior was widely acknowledged by law enforcement officers the world over: once brought to the station, the guilty slept while the innocent nervously fretted, protesting their innocence to anyone who'd listen.

Scarpone pulled a chair over to face the man. My captain had set a small cup of coffee on a nearby table. And had brought a blanket to cover the man's nakedness.

The TV was on again in the corner, its sound down. The man on the sofa was not one of the soldiers, but the magistrate himself.

"Arrigo Basile?"

Scarpone slapped him awake.

The heavy lids fluttered. The man shifted, farted, and pulled himself up. He regarded Scarpone warily.

"I brought you water and coffee. I thought we could talk."

"Where are my guys?"

"Everyone's upstairs, in different parts of the station."

A smiled came to Basile's lips. "Separated, eh? That's smart. I suppose I would do that if I were you."

"There's water here if you want it. I can help you drink, if you like."

The man's eyes went to the water. From the way he licked his lips, it was clear he could have used a drink. But he resisted.

"Screw you—I want my lawyer."

"There's no need for a lawyer right now. You're being transferred to Montefiascone. It's their investigation. You can make all your demands there. I just want to know what you can tell me about my borgo."

"Screw you. I don't talk. They don't talk. We all know who we're working for."

"Does anyone really *work* for the Calabrians? Or are they borrowed for a while, then disposed of? You're not idiots. You know the only reason you're here is that others have failed. And now that you're here, someone who thinks they'll do things differently will replace you a month from now. That's how this goes. So why not give us a parting shot before you're retired?"

"Piss off. I always get off. I always come back."

"You lost the product. You ought to cooperate more with us than pin your hopes on their mercy."

Basile pouted a moment in silence. The skin under his eyes was puffy and yellow.

"I'll take the water."

Scarpone helped him.

"Wait till I tell my lawyer how you stripped us naked and left us to freeze in a drafty basement. Wait till I tell them and they bring you up on charges."

"I think the record will show that we were kind to you. I have clothes waiting for you upstairs. I wasn't going to forcibly dress you while you napped. Now: let's talk about how you came to be in the borgo."

Basile spat. A ball of spit hit the captain's shoulder.

I felt the captain's anger surge.

He stood, stripped off the blanket, and knocked the chair back onto the floor. The crash was so alarming that the magistrate swung around.

Basile flailed in the chair, kicking his feet. "You shit!"

Scarpone leaned over and placed his hand squarely on the man's chest.

I couldn't believe what I was seeing. The second the captain's hand touched flesh, Basile thrashed as though an electric shock had coursed through his body. When his body came back down to earth, his lips gulped air like a drowning man. But no sound came out. His eyes trembled.

"Please, no! The pain, the pain!"

"Tell me," Scarpone said. "Who was it who tipped you off about the farmhouse?"

"The Albanian, Demaci!"

"How long have you known him?"

"He was here before."

"He worked for your predecessor, in other words? And what did he do for you?"

"Nothing. He was just a dealer in this piece of shit borgo! He was never inside. I wouldn't trust a foreigner. Please, please...you're burning me!"

The magistrate was behind him now. "Scarpone? What are you *doing?*"

Ignore him, the captain told himself. *Just keep this shit talking.*

"There was a standing order for high-grade product. Why?"

"I don't know! It's always been that way, for three years at least. We were always prepared to deliver it when it was requested."

"Who requested it?"

"Scarpone—you're hurting the man! I can't allow this!"

"Shut up," Scarpone barked at Saviano.

"Some client of the Albanian's. We didn't know who. We didn't need to know. The money was good. They always paid up. Why should we care if someone was getting a bigger dose?"

"Who was the client?"

"Like I would know? I'm nobody. I'm shit! I'm a worm! Oh God, please, Signore, the pain is terrible! Please—you're killing me!"

"Scarpone," the magistrate bellowed, tugging at his shoulder. "Stop at once! I command you!"

"Tell me about the house!"

"Arbend said the owner was in Austria and wouldn't bother us.

Said he would never know, and if we played our cards right, no one would ever see us on the road. But we had to use the grottoes underneath."

"Who roughed up the prostitute?"

"Who? Oh—the woman on the road. Yes, she was always there, always watching. I told her I'd cut her throat if she didn't move. Arbend said she had to be dealt with. She'd been there forever."

"*He* said that?"

"Yes! Please, Signore, please, Signore. It burns! It burns! Oh God, oh God...*porca miseria! Porca miseria! O mamma!*"

His voice broke off into loud, wet sobs that wracked his chest.

Scarpone let the magistrate pull him away. He sat on the floor while the old attorney inspected Basile's skin. Then Saviano raised the chair and murmured words of comfort to the broken man. "There you go... There, there, now." He tucked the blanket in around the man's body.

The smell of piss was overpowering. A large puddle under the chair.

The magistrate glared at Scarpone. Pointed to the exterior door. "Outside!"

SAVIANO FUMBLED FOR A CIGARETTE BUT WAS SO agitated that he threw the entire carton to the ground instead. He pulled himself up to his full height and shoved the captain against the pink wall of the station.

"What in heaven was that? Do you even know? Do you?"

My captain seemed exhausted, his hands clenching the brim of his cap.

"Not really, I just knew that it would work."

"You never told me this. You never told me you possessed this... this...unspeakable thing."

"I didn't hurt him. I knew I wouldn't. I could feel myself holding back."

"Holding *back?* He is *traumatized.* This will go badly for you, Scarpone. Mark my words!"

"He will forget it. You see. He has already forgotten it."

"Jesu Cristo, Jesu Cristo. I have seen such things before, but I thought it was a trick..."

"What was?"

"The *mano diavolo!* You mean...you *did* it, but don't even *know?* What the hell are you? Are you a man of the law? A man of justice? Or are you a demon? Tell me that now, straightaway, or we cannot work together."

"I don't even know what I did. I only knew that it would work."

"Oh Jesu! I was a boy when I first saw someone use the devil's hand. An old woman here in the village caused extreme pain to extract knowledge. But over the years, I had come to think it was a lie. A fiction. A bit of theater old ladies performed to scare children into telling the truth. You say he will forget. What if he does not? How will we be able to guard against a charge of torture? How will we? What an abomination! What an obscenity. The republic does not condone it, and above all, I don't. How could you come to possess such a power?"

My dear captain hung against the wall like a sack of bones. His eyes scanned the ground. "I don't know. I only know one thing: I am cursed."

The two of them panted, waiting for their breaths to calm down.

After a bit, the captain pulled on his cap and headed for his vehicle.

"Where are you going?"

"You're the magistrate. It's your case. I need to go."

Chapter Fifty-Six

I had to work to keep up with him. He gunned the engine of his car to shoot north around the curve of the Orvietana. But then, at the last second, he braked and turned left to head back into the borgo.

By the time he parked at the edge of the parking lot overlooking the precipice, both of his hands were trembling. He slapped the top of his steering wheel once.

"Shit!"

Then he blew the horn loudly and stepped out of the vehicle.

Her motorino was there, parked at the edge.

The sky to the east was dark with thick, gray clouds, and moving fast. He felt a rush of wind come up the side of the hill and chill the tears against his cheeks.

"Allegra!" he called. "Allegra."

He saw her orange jacket down below. She waved. It took her about twenty minutes to reach the top. She went for the water first.

I don't know which of them was covered with more sweat, him or her.

She eyed me, or rather, eyed the air around me. Without a doubt she knew I was there.

"This is real, isn't it?" he asked her.

"In what sense?"

"I had a suspect just now. The one who supplied drugs to Demaci. I put my hand on him..."

Her eyes marveled. "Oh *really?* How did you feel?"

"Terrible, terrible. He made me angry and all I wanted to do was kill him. But all I had to do was—"

"Touch him?"

"Yes. I feel like it's only gotten worse since...since coming here."

"Since the trouble? The shootings in Rome?"

"You know about that?" He smiled grimly. "What am I saying? Everyone must. No one can keep their mouth shut in this town."

"It's what we do. We gossip."

"I'm ready to hear it now. Tell me why you killed the Albanian."

"You know why. You've known for a while."

"I want to hear *you* tell it."

She crossed her arms, the water bottle dangling from her fingers. "I always suspected he was selling drugs. He had no job, yet drove a nice car and wore nice clothes. You *know* his mother wasn't giving him money. She hadn't any to give. That's why I made a point to befriend him. And then, one night when we were together, he confessed it all. 'You know,' he said, 'with your father's van, you could go anywhere to make deliveries.' He was propositioning me, laying it out, blow by blow, how we could make a sack of money delivering to various towns. Like I would wish to profit by that which killed my brother and devastated my parents. But he didn't think of that, did he? He had already forgotten my brother. He was just that dumb. And then I had him. I knew he was part of their machine. For this he had to die."

Silence from my captain.

"I mean—what else can I possibly tell you that I haven't told you before?"

"How did it happen?" Scarpone pressed.

"I rode out on my motorbike to meet him at the grotto. We spent the night, and when it was done, I called Caterina. I hid my bike. She drove his car to Orvieto, and I followed in her car. Then she drove me back to get my motorbike. Simple. She'll deny it, of course. And she should. Why should either of us be punished for the death of a cretin?"

"I didn't...believe the...the...magic was possible."

"But now you do. Only the story's exactly the same. What you don't know is how my brother's passing changed things. You don't know how my parents doted on him. He was everything to them. Their whole future. They almost didn't think of Caterina and me. Two daughters and we meant nothing to them, compared to the promise of this one boy. It was more than he could bear, frankly. You could see he didn't have the brains to deal with that burden. What was he going to do with my father's property, with those grapes and olives? He was not up to the task; he wanted to watch TV and play computer games. This was all. A sweet boy, Captain. Sweet. He should not have died that way."

"Who was the leader? Arrigo Basile?"

"Arbend never told me the names."

"I have a way to find out. Arbend knew too much about local real estate for an outsider. I'm going to check on that. Something I should have checked sooner. Do you have any idea how far this goes?"

"Who knows? I'm not a detective. I took care of what I could. I needed only an ally. A man of logic. Of principle. Of justice. They sent you."

"*Who* sent me?"

She gestured at the sky. "The Lares."

"The ancient Roman gods of the household? You must be joking."

She was dead serious. As she said this, she turned her head to look in my vicinity. I knew the Lares well. They were part of me, part of the things I knew, though I did not know why. I also knew that those Gods were often depicted with snakes, symbols of the fertility of the fields.

But did *she* know this in her bones, as I did, or was she just an adolescent who'd read too much?

"Will I shake this power?" my captain said. "Will it go away?"

She shrugged. "Who can say? Yours is different from mine. That's all I can see. It must have changed for you the night of your pain. If you *let go* of the pain, maybe it will release you. I don't know. All I ask is that when you find the person who orchestrated my brother's murder, you must let me know. That is all you need to do. Point him out to me. He will answer to me."

"No. He will answer to the law."

"God, you're pathetic."

"I'll take care of it. If it goes the right way, he will be arrested. He will answer to the republic, not you."

"Pity."

"For what it's worth, I believe you now. I believe what you did. The vipers...everything. I can see now that such things are possible. But I reject them. Do you hear me? Whatever this power is, it's not me."

"Oh, Captain. I don't know how old you are. You look a million years old to me. But even so, why would you ever want to give up such power?"

He started the engine.

Chapter Fifty-Seven

We drove north out of Orvieto in search of Allerona, a hill town on the edge of the wilderness park. Rain followed us. By the time my captain drove up the side of the old town, it seemed that we were ascending into the clouds.

The notary, a small, thick man dressed in an elegant shirt and tie, demonstrated a gracious manner. He had a secretary usher my captain into a conference room while he cleared up a few things.

The window offered a panorama from the hill town south to Orvieto. Scarpone could make out the spires of the cathedral, and immaculate cultivated fields in between.

It was growing dark. The clouds threatened to drop, obliterating the way home.

We heard the chatter of voices, and the final click of a door, which signaled we were alone. We heard the shushing of the coffee machine and the rattle of china. The man entered, head erect, carrying two cups of coffee. Espresso, dark and tarry from the smell of it.

I wish he had asked, Scarpone thought, but the day had been long, and the drive to this remote town had robbed my captain of his strength. He sipped his coffee gratefully as the notary produced a notepad and an expensive pen.

"You'll have to refresh my memory. I do a lot of these things. And I wish to be of service in any way I possibly can."

This did not sound like bullshit.

"I know foreigners can buy property here," Scarpone said. "I just don't understand the mechanics."

"I'd be happy to explain it. If they didn't, I'd be out of a job. I do more of those types of land transactions than anything else. Every Englishman or German with money wants a villa or a farmhouse or a castle here. It's the way, or it was before the market crashed."

"But if they don't have residency or even a work permit, how is that allowed?"

"The state prefers foreign real estate buyers who don't have a work permit. Typically, they're wealthy foreigners who don't need to derive an income from our labor market. They don't take anything from us; they bring their money in. They buy homes, fix them up, and use them on long weekends and holidays. It's logical for us as a nation to encourage such transactions. Every penny they spend stimulates our economy. All they need to stay in the country is a permit to stay, which is good for a few months."

"But how can they possibly conduct a real estate transaction if they can't speak our language?"

"Oh, well, you're talking about another thing entirely. By law they must understand the details of the transaction. Or else they can't sign the contract. It's a fundamental tenet of law. If they can't speak the language, I'm obligated to determine that ahead of time and arrange for interpreters and translators. Everything is executed in our language, but they read along in theirs."

"The client pays for this service?"

"The buyer pays, because everything is weighted in favor of the buyer. The buyer picks the notary, for example, who is obligated to advise the client in their best interests. What case are we talking about, by the way?"

Scarpone gave him the sheet of paper, slightly amended, which he'd been carrying since his day in the coffee bar in Capalba:

Overdose Seller	Sold to	Origin
Tubecchi	Vajda	Hungary
Santello	Iordenescu	Romania
DelCillie	Harrak	Morocco
Dancione	Dlugos	Slovenia
Chiostro	Berisha	Albania

"Five transactions?"

"That I know of. I know you did one of them. I don't remember if your name was on the others. You have to forgive me. I've had a... difficult day."

"Well," the notary nodded. "If you give me a moment."

"I don't wish to make more work for you."

"It's no trouble, I assure you. We're computerized here. Would you like a biscuit while you wait? My wife's mother makes them. They're delicious but I can't stomach sweets."

"I'm...the same as you."

The notary drained his coffee. Then he went away, cup rattling.

Alone now, my captain slowly sipped the essence of his cup. He tasted blackness. Beans. Earth.

He sees his aunt in her housedress, early on a Saturday morning when the whole family is over. Everyone sits at the table, looking over the cornetti from the bakery, and drinking in the smell of coffee that perfumes the house. His mother brushes a boy's hair with her fingers. When Scarpone looks down at the boy, he is looking into the eyes of a dead child, his face and head battered, covered with blood.

My captain shuddered.

The man was back with a tall, wide paper file.

"In Castelpietra, yes?"

"Yes."

"I've only done one of the ones on your list. The family Vajda. Hungarians. Sorry if I got your hopes up. Now—please understand that the law provides for confidentiality in client matters, but the details of the real estate act itself—the purchase agreement all the way down to the title—are matters of public record."

Scarpone had seen the contract and the deed. They were among the documents Enzo had found at the city hall. Scarpone didn't mention this to the notary.

"Ah yes, I remember this," the notary said. "An appointed family representative attended the closing. He said it was two brothers and a couple of cousins all buying the property together. Good piece of land, too, from what I understand. Planted already with sangiovese and olives. They'd be earning a decent income from the property almost immediately."

"They used an interpreter?"

"Ah, no. We didn't have to go that route because they didn't buy under their names. They bought it under the name of a business, Vajda Consorzio, S.R.L. I just needed to see the power of attorney for their proxy, who was one Giorgio Albirone."

"Was there a mortgage?"

A flip through papers. A shake of the head.

"So they paid cash in full?"

"That's right. A check drawn on a Roman bank. One hundred eighty-three thousand euros. But it's primarily farmland, which is taxed at a lower rate so they pay fewer taxes up front and fewer down the line. I have photos of the property here in the file. I hope I don't sound snobbish when I say that there's not much to it. There's a small house there, but for the purposes of taxation it's listed as uninhabitable. It's quite crude. No hot water. No electricity."

Scarpone silently ticked off each of the names in his head. He had seen the house owned by the Moroccans. And by now, Puzio had visited the remaining properties on the list.

"Every single family on my list lives in tumbled-down wrecks," he said.

"Well," the notary said with a chortle, "let's hope they have all the necessary permits."

"Is that all you have to say? Do you see this kind of thing often? Isn't it strange that a family of migrant workers would have an S.R.L., plunk down 183,000 euros cash, and then move into a home without hot water and lights? My men and I have looked in on every one of these people. They all seem destitute."

The notary clucked warmly. "I have a lot of respect for this class of migrants. They save every penny, and sink it into the land. They'll work themselves to the bone to keep that land and the roof over their heads, shaky as it might be."

"I'm surprised they had the money."

"Did you ever buy a house, Marshal?"

The truth was, Scarpone hadn't. Many of his friends and colleagues hadn't. Every place they'd ever lived had been owned by some family member or another.

"I assure you," the notary continued, "I've seen the strangest things in this line of work."

He laid a forearm on the table, as if reaching across it to reassure Scarpone. It was a remarkably ingratiating gesture. Scarpone liked him more and more.

"This was the first thing I had to make my peace with when I entered into this profession. People will come in these doors looking poor but they have a war chest hidden in the mattress. It is the way. We are still witnessing the fallout from the fall of the Soviet Union. All these Russians showing up in our midst, with millions of rubles to invest. It's not our place to ask where it comes from. Only to make sure that the proper taxes are paid to our government."

He leaned forward. "I'm not one of these people who think all foreigners are criminals. I don't see the evidence for it. Frankly, I applaud people like this. Our people are leaving the land in droves. These farmhouses would go to waste if these foreigners didn't snap them up and fix them up."

He was flipping through the contract and ran his hand along the photocopied maps enclosed in the document. The fragile lines marking off the boundaries of the property were highlighted with a red marker.

Something about the maps made Scarpone think.

Maps.

Distances.

Choices.

"Who is this Giorgio Albirone? He's not Hungarian, I take it?"

"No, of course not. He's an accountant in Rome."

Strange, Scarpone thought. A migrant family in the countryside goes a hundred kilometers out of their way to find someone to act as their proxy at a real estate closing across the river from where they live.

"Why would they come to Umbria to find a notary when the land is in Lazio?" Scarpone asked.

"By law, it doesn't matter."

"But who advised them to come to you?"

"That's a good question. I don't recall how we made the connection."

"Because if they don't speak the language—"

"Exactly! How would they have the resources to find me all the way up here on this hill? Ah, let's see..."

He flipped through some papers.

At the back of the contract, he found some yellow pages ripped from a legal notepad.

"Ah, okay. Vajda Consorzio is a subsidiary of another firm."

"What firm?"

"A farmer's collective in Viterbo."

"Consorzio Agrario Dentare," Scarpone said.

"Ah, you know it!"

What thieves, Scarpone thought.

"Who's the contact?"

"Wait, Signore. This presents a bit of a problem."

"How so?"

"I'm reading now from private notes between me and the client's intermediary. If I were to hand this over to you, and you were to determine later that a crime had been committed...not that you will, you understand? But I have to assume that your presence here is not out of mere curiosity."

"I can get a warrant if you insist."

"I hate to put you through that trouble. I only wish to arrive at a solution that satisfies us both."

Scarpone smiled at the man.

"Is it an important case, Marshal?"

"Murder."

"Oh dear."

"Of young boys."

"My God. You know, I think a mineral water at this juncture might be most refreshing," he said. He leaped up, leaving the file of documents open on the conference table.

Scarpone pounced on the papers as soon as the door closed.

Two names.

The name of a *commercialista,* Giorgio Albirone, a certified accountant, located on Via del Babuino.

The name of yet another corporation on whose behalf he worked. Liberator Holdings, S.p.A., located near Parliament.

Two phone numbers.

Two addresses.

Both in Rome.

Chapter Fifty-Eight

The men sometimes ducked into Il Mulino, the restaurant across from the city pool and tennis courts, to grab a meal or a packaged lunch.

It was rare to have all the station's men together in one place at the same time. Usually, half of them were heading for their shifts, and the ones who had come off might, if the weather was nice, sit out on the veranda of Il Mulino and take their meals before heading home or back to the barracks.

But today was different. It was a day for celebration. The men of the borgo had shown those sons of bitches in Montefiascone and Viterbo what they were made of. Let the crooks and foreigners sling their worst at the borgo. The men of the station would stop them dead in their tracks. They had what it took. They had mettle. They had *palle*—balls.

Scarpone was methodically sawing through a pizza topped with strips of prosciutto, curls of parmesan, and peppery, late-season wild rocket. He sipped mineral water and ignored the fact that some of the men had blithely ordered carafes of wine. His only worry was that someone would wander by and snap a photo of the entire station dining together. There would be hell to pay if this were made known to the bosses.

"In the end," Gismonda was saying. "I think that if a couple has love, it doesn't matter what age the woman is. She could be twenty or fifty."

"Yes, you would deign to be seen with a fifty-year-old woman," Belluzzi said. "You!"

"Many a fifty-year-old woman still has it together. *Molto in gamba.* And much more passionate than these stupid teenagers. Who needs the aggravation of a childish woman, carping and criticizing?"

"Tell me that the next time you're offered a choice between the two," Iucci said. "I know which you would pick."

The breeze was pleasant. Scarpone's fingers had brushed against the rocket so often that they now smelled pungent and peppery. The smell—

His aunt in the garden. Her fingers wet with the juice of that plant. The peppery smell perfuming his scalp when she leads him inside and runs her fingers through his hair. Get washed up, she says, we're going to eat soon.

—assailed his nostrils and lingered there.

He was eating. And it did not hurt.

The phone in his pocket buzzed. He checked it.

His old supervisor, Fausto.

He silenced it.

A few of the men spoke of soccer. Another bunch were listening to the details of a mortadella tasting someone planned to attend in a nearby borgo this weekend.

"I went last year," Puzio said. "I was expecting something more profound, but it was a waste of time. It's held in the tower there. You walk up a dozen flights of stairs, drink copious glasses of wine, eat twenty different slices of mortadella while some fool prattles on about wine pairing for hours. In the end, you pay 25 euros and go home hungry. I say leave it to the tourists and the Orvieto gourmands."

"That's a shame to hear you say that," Enzo said. "I have heard it described as a wonderful night."

"Well, sure. The view is amazing, but it's not worth 25 euros. It's criminal, if you ask me."

"It does, however, sound romantic," Belluzzi said. "The perfect place for Signor Lady-killer here to take his fifty-year-old girlfriend. It'll be dark, so you can't see her."

He clapped a hand on Gismonda, who muttered an obscenity.

Scarpone's phone rang. Fausto again. Insistent buzzing, like a bee dying on the table beside him.

Scarpone clinked his water glass with his fork. The men hushed themselves. They watched as my captain stood. His expression was pained, but he felt compelled to speak. Thank you, he wanted to say. Thank you. You've helped me more than you know. But he did not say such a thing.

"My apologies if I offend some of you, but I think we all know that when we join the service we don't dream of being stationed in a town like this. We dream of beautiful cities. Cosmopolitan places. Excitement. But in the city we're insects clinging to a big hive…what I mean to say is…"

His voice faltered. On the periphery of his vision, he was conscious of a vehicle driving slowly down the street, as if searching for an address. Some kind of official vehicle.

"What I want to say is hard to say without sounding like a complete ass, and since Gismonda here has a lock on that position—"

The men erupted in laughter.

"I will only say that I am proud to serve with such a complement of fine soldiers. That was excellent work, gentlemen. Coordinated. Tight. Swift. Intelligent..."

His smile trembled awkwardly on his face. His eyes watched the car. His mind flashed back to the incident in Rome. Three men on motorini. Guns.

His eyes flicked to the car in the road. The men noticed it too. Iucci went for his weapon.

Jesu, Scarpone thought. I have to talk to that kid. He resorts to his weapon quickly, doesn't he?

He heard Enzo's voice say, "Sir?"

The vehicle had come to a full stop in front of the terrace. A blue Audi. Two men inside. One stepped out. He was young man with close-cropped hair, a beret cocked to the side, dressed in a blue jumpsuit, black boots, black belt, and a holstered weapon.

A Swiss Guard. In day uniform.

He stood ramrod stiff by the side of his car.

Scarpone kicked back his chair.

The man addressed him from the street. "Captain Scarpone?"

Scarpone nodded.

On the far side of the table, some of Scarpone's men rose uncomfortably in their chairs to get a look at this visitor.

The Swiss Guard stepped forward, saluted, and produced a thick envelope, which he presented to Scarpone. He saluted quickly and turned to go.

"Wait," Scarpone said.

Scarpone ripped the envelope. Scanned the contents. He was being extended the courtesy of a papal audience. Bizarre. His curiosity was ripped by a wave of anger. Scarpone thrust the envelope at Enzo.

"Oh my," Enzo said. "Sir, this is wonderful! *Such* an honor."

His men were craning to look at the envelope.

Scarpone was already pointing at the Swiss Guard. "Don't go."

Scarpone seized his phone and called Fausto. The older man sounded as if the world owed him an apology. "Where the *hell* have you been, Matteo? I've been trying to reach you all day. You should expect a call from the Vatican. Every one here is up in arms. Have you seen the newspapers?"

"No," Scarpone said. "We've been busy up here."

"TV, then?" Fausto continued. "It's miraculous. Miraculous, indeed. Out of nowhere the bosses are singing the praises of the great Scarpone. They want you back here, Matteo. There will be a debriefing, first, of course. Some confidential conversation." His voice dropped to a whisper. "This could be it, Matteo. Your ticket out of that shithole."

"Why on earth? It was a simple drug bust. Montefiascone tipped us off. They've been working this thing for months."

"What are you babbling about? The *cardinal*, Matteo. That African who was shot up with you? He came out of his coma two days ago and hasn't shut up since. The bosses can't ignore someone of his stature, especially one talking to the press. He is telling the world that you saved his life."

Chapter Fifty-Nine

The hotel is near the Vatican, and the night they meet the cobblestones are slick with recent rain. Each of the stones seem to glow. My captain is dressed in street clothes. He is exhausted. Happy, triumphant, but exhausted.

He walks through the lobby with a reed-thin, elderly Nigerian man dressed in a black cassock with scarlet piping, a crimson-colored sash hanging from his waist, and a matching red skullcap on his head.

"Are you sure you can't come?" Olúdìímú says as they approach the doors. "I am permitted to bring a guest."

My captain has had three days and nights on stakeout and all he wants to do is sleep. But even that will not happen; he still must return to the station to write up his notes of the arrest of the men, the seizure of the cash, and the release of the women—Anna and eleven of her sisters found shackled together in a basement in the neighborhood of Termini, near the train station.

This visit to the cardinal is just a small courtesy, a way to say thank you to the man who has never doubted him. Some months ago, when the diplomats had ignored Scarpone's inquiries, he had turned to this man to understand human trafficking. Olúdìímú had published some policy papers on the issue of sexual slavery in his homeland. He was outspoken. He was intense. He had listened, counseled, and proffered advice that had helped Scarpone understand the massive cultural barriers he was up against.

At this point in his life, I have known my captain only one of your years. Long enough to know that he has no use for the church. Long enough to know that he does not put stock in miracles, visions, mysticism, magic. For a year he has ignored the visions welling up in his own mind. For a year already he has harbored a secret pain.

But this man—Olúdìímú—he respects.

"Regrettably, I am committed to this dinner tonight," Olúdìímú says. "But after, I can come with you. I can come to see these sisters of mine. I can minister to them in any way possible."

"That isn't necessary," my captain says. The truth is, it will be a long night for the women, too. They've already been whisked to the hospital. They'll be prodded by doctors, questioned by carabinieri, debriefed by a magistrate with an army of translators. And at the end of it all, they will have to quiet their minds enough to sleep for once in a real bed.

"I want only to show them that their nation has not forgotten them," Olúdìímú says. "That *God* has not forgotten them."

A lovely sentiment, my captain thinks.

They head for the revolving doors.

Already the captain can hear the drone of motorini outside. A buzz like angry hornets. But he dismisses this. It's Rome. Motorini are everywhere.

My captain gestures. "Please," he says to this prince of the church. "After you."

Though he has known this man for more than three months, he uses the formal form of the word *you*.

The cardinal bows slightly and enters the door first.

And so he is the first to take a bullet. It catches him in the upper chest and blows him back against my captain. The cardinal's driver, who is opening the door of the black car parked at the curb, catches a bullet in the throat. He crumples.

My captain shoves the cardinal inside the hotel, but the bleeding man fights him off, and propels himself through the doors, heading inexplicably for the street.

The motorini are closer now. Three men. Africans. Each with handguns.

They're firing as they ride but their aim is bad. The stones are slick, and they're driving one-handed.

One shot pocks the side of the hotel over my captain's left shoulder.

Flecks of stone and dust.

One of the bikes crashes against the front of the limo.

My captain shoves the cardinal down, hard. This man of seventy-six years drops, absorbing his second bullet.

My captain's Beretta is up now and firing. The assassin at the front of the car struggles to extract his pant leg from his toppled scooter. He aims at Scarpone.

My captain fires three times.

All to the man's chest.

The two scooters close in. One man hops off and runs. He's lean and fast, coming across the sidewalk at a good clip while the other circles back on the bike.

Behind him, over the runner's shoulder, my captain can see the dome of St. Peter's. Cars flow by, oblivious. Behind him, he hears glass shattering. Screams inside the lobby.

The man raises his weapon.

My captain swings the Beretta around.

They trade shots—one to the heart, one to the ribs. The runner drops.

Scarpone looks at the sidewalk.

Jesu! The cardinal is crawling across the sidewalk, arms outstretched, a trail of blood.

Where the hell does he think he's going? Scarpone wonders.

The last assassin appears over the top of the car. More meat on him. Heavier, slower. He fires. My captain shoots and misses.

He feels the sting in his shoulder. He ducks behind the car. Fires again as the heavier man comes around the back of the car.

The man starts to drop but manages to squeeze another off.

Again—a sting. Lower.

Scarpone's final round takes the man in the forehead.

Sirens in the distance.

People screaming.

My captain falls as a dead man falls. His flickering eyes rake the sidewalk. The old churchman now lies across the body of his driver. The cardinal's skullcap is missing. Blood trickles from his neck. His lips move wordlessly. Scarpone throws himself over Olúdìímú. Cradles the man's head.

Two men on top of a corpse, surrounded by a field of corpses.

Scarpone presses his hand to the cardinal's chest. This wound is the worst, no? Or it is the one at his neck? Too much blood. Not enough hands.

"Stay with me, okay?" Scarpone says.

He catches a glimpse of the cardinal's teeth. The old man appears to be smiling. "They are coming, Olúdìímú!" my captain screams over the sirens. "Just a while longer."

I have watched my captain for more than a year. In all that time, I have never touched him.

Until tonight, when I lay my hand on him.

Was it warmth he felt? I cannot say. What happened that night, I wonder still. Did some part of me pass into my captain?

"We are saved," the cardinal says. "He is already here..."

Scarpone snaps his fingers in front of the man's eyes. "Look at me!"

"We are saved...saved..." the old man murmurs.

Scarpone's eyelids slam shut but he fights them open. He cannot comprehend what the man is saying.

But I can.

Olúdìímú is looking directly into my eyes.

Chapter Sixty

He did not relish driving down to Rome on a weekday, but autumn was labor strike season, which meant the trains were completely unreliable. So he nosed his Fiat down A1 instead. By midmorning, he was ringing the bell of the commercial-ista's office on Via del Babuino with no success. Judging from the appearance of the building's lobby, the office was probably a one-man enterprise.

The holding company near Parliament was a different matter. Tony, wood-lined walls, and a tomblike air of enforced silence. My captain had dressed in his best suit, hoping to make an impression, but the woman at the desk wasn't buying it. She buzzed for a colleague in the back, an officious man with spectacles on a string who balked at his request. "*Mi dispiace,*" he said through pursed lips. "*Non è possibile.*"

It's not possible.

It's not possible.

This seemed to be the man's favorite phrase.

But the man did leave open a window of opportunity: *We must have documentation.*

Back on the street, my captain bought a newspaper, downed an espresso, and considered his options. Reveal that he was a cara-biniere? Threaten to get a warrant? That was ridiculous overkill.

Firms like theirs had evolved to shrug off the intrusion of any government authority. It was their *raison d'être.*

No choice, then. He'd have to do it. He made the call.

About an hour later, Rolando was waiting for him in the Piazza del Parlamento, as agreed.

There wasn't a speck of dust on him.

Scarpone whistled.

"So you can, when you make an effort, look presentable."

"Eat my balls," Rolando said from behind shades.

"Is that a tie?"

"I don't hear from you in weeks and this is what you demand of me, you prick? I am forced to abandon my business and my family and present myself here to be mocked?"

The two of them stared for a while at the activity behind the Parliament building. There was a security booth at one end of the square, and a green fence protecting the limos and other beautiful vehicles of the nation's top felons. Carabinieri and plainclothesmen in dark suits patrolled the area.

"I'm frankly surprised that I reached you. I thought you'd be in California by now."

"Funny thing, that," Rolando said.

"Let me guess, it hasn't panned out."

"No! It's going to happen. They just keep sending me forms. I need to fill out one for Homeland Security. What hell is that?"

"It's their terrorist agency."

"Well, is this something you can handle for me? Maybe give them a call and sort it out?"

"Are you joking?"

"All I want to do is glue rocks to the man's floor. I'm not a terrorist."

"You look like one, even in a suit."

"Piss off. Now, please, let's get down to it. This is interrupting my plans for the afternoon. I was going to sit in a bar until the games started. What's the plan?"

Scarpone presented him with a sheet of paper with five letters and a number on it. And a large wad of euros he'd withdrawn from a Bancomat thirty-five minutes ago.

"You go into that building, up to the first floor, to the offices of Venerone Finanziarie. I picked them out of the book. They're the closest so they'll have to do. You ask to see a broker. They'll present you with a stack of forms. You fill them out and buy ten shares of this stock. See the code? And the number ten?"

"I can count to ten. I'm not a moron."

"Make sure you don't leave until they give you a document certified with their seal. You'll need that document as proof that you bought the shares. Then, you'll come out, go across the street to *that* building. The office suite number is here. Liberator Holdings. You'll present the woman at the desk with your stamped buy sheet and ask for a copy of the annual report. That's a document a company produces every year—"

"I know what an annual report is. This woman. How old is she?"

"It doesn't matter."

"It does to me."

"She'll probably give you the runaround but you have to stand firm. Insist. Act insulted. Haughty. Threaten to call the cops if you have to. You're entitled to it now that you've bought the shares."

"Ten shares. What am I, a cheap bastard?"

"It's all you can afford."

"It's all *you* can afford."

"Go. Get started. I'll wait for you."

Rolando left, heading for the building across from Parliament.

Scarpone looked around. The piazza was devoid of decent cafes. He backtracked to Via in Lucina and found a new coffee bar that offered him a view of the alley leading to the piazza. But he'd have to sit at an outside table, looking like an idiot tourist the whole time. So be it. He picked his seat, ordered an espresso and tried to make fifty milliliters of dark liquid last as long as he could, which was not long. He ordered a bottle of mineral water while he paged through his newspaper a second time. Sipping, reading, watching.

It took about forty-five minutes for Rolando to reappear on the street. He paused at the head of Via in Lucina, saw Scarpone, and nodded. Then crossed the street.

Scarpone peeked into the coffee bar. The baristas were watching a TV soccer program which featured two male commentators in suits arguing while a gorgeous woman in spaghetti straps waved a mic between them.

Scarpone read the paper, cursing himself for not have the foresight to bring his paper-cutter.

A bombing in a paint factory in Palermo.

A drug seizure at a nightclub in Ancona.

A dozen Senegalese collected with counterfeit handbags.

A winning lottery ticket claimed by a mother-in-law and her estranged daughter-in-law. The son suing both for a guaranteed stipend for life, free from their interference.

Delightful.

He sipped the water and felt the bubbles burn against his tongue and throat.

Fifteen minutes later, he looked up to see Rolando striding down the alley, loosening his tie. He sat at the table across from Scarpone. The waiter appeared. Rolando ordered a coffee and slid the report across the table. It was printed on paper that felt like a custom-made suit.

"They gave it up easy. Though they did ask why I had bought so few shares."

"Who asked this? The girl?"

"Yeah. Cute, I thought. A bit heavy on the makeup."

Scarpone leafed through the report.

"What did you tell her?"

"I said I was trying to get my daughter interested in financial markets. This is bullshit. My daughter is interested in the toy market. And the food market. And the overpriced shoe market. I told the receptionist that I liked the thought of my daughter owning a piece of Rome. That's what they do, right? Real estate?"

My captain inspected the document's mission statement, expecting to see a name here, but it was merely signed from the board. Next came a list of the financial documents herein contained…

"Commercial real estate. Apartments too."

"Rich bastards. Millions, I'll bet."

Scarpone paged to the back. A list of names. Way at the bottom, he found no mention of the commercialista who'd arranged for the notary in Allerona. But there was another list of names. And a long list of subsidiaries. And there, close to the top, was the photo and the name he'd expected to see.

"Find what you need?"

"Yes."

"Great. Then we can go. The game's at two p.m."

"No. Unfortunately, it means I need to head back up."

"Balls."

Chapter Sixty-One

The two men looked up when he burst in the door of the azienda. The bookkeeper Damiano was the first to see him, but my captain couldn't be bothered with that clown. He hung a right into the foreman's office.

Adriano, the sonless man, wore a smile. "To what do we owe this..." he started to say, but the captain's manner put him off. The captain stepped behind Adriano's desk and studied the drawing hanging on the wall, pressed behind glass. Scarpone had first seen the map on the day the Albanian's body had been found. But he hadn't studied it nearly enough. It was a map of the azienda's lands.

"May I?" the captain said, gesturing.

The foreman started to speak: "What—"

Scarpone wrenched the map off the wall and smashed it on the edge of the foreman's desk. He did it just swiftly and carefully enough to send all the shards of glass in the trash bin.

"Marshal! What on earth are you doing?"

The captain slipped the map out and allowed the wooden frame clatter to the floor. He pointed to the ceiling.

"Is he here?"

"Who?"

My captain stalked toward the stairs.

At the top of the gut-like gloom, Scarpone ran into Count Cortese, who was coming out of the kitchen with a cup and saucer.

"What is this? A pleasant visit from you, Marshal? But you did not think to let them announce you?"

All Scarpone could think to say was, "There are discrepancies."

Downstairs, the bookkeeper yelled up his apologies. And Adriano was already phoning up to the count's office with news of the strange intrusion.

"It must be urgent," the count yelled down to the bookkeeper, "to warrant such an entrance. This way, Marshal."

Scarpone followed the fragrance of the man's tea into that large, sterile room that appeared almost blanched by the sun. The count went around the desk. He set down the tea, but did not sit.

"How can I help?"

"I wish only to bring your attention to certain facts. You'll need this map."

He thrust the paper at him.

"You're familiar, of course, with cadastral maps?" Scarpone said. "I regret to say that I removed the glass which held the stickers indicating your holdings. So we shall have to look for them together by referencing the lot numbers. Are you ready? Look at the map."

"I don't understand."

Scarpone flipped to a page in his notebook. "*Look at the map.* Lot number 0018657, parcel B and following, to H. Have you found it?"

"It's right here. I'm familiar with these lands, Signore."

"This one in particular is owned by Hungarians. The family Vajda."

"If you say."

"'*If you say?*' You must know them. Two minutes ago a sticker bearing your logo covered their lot. Doesn't that indicate that you have dealings with them?"

The count flashed a foxlike smile. "You know, you ought to check with the foreman on this."

"Lot 0098764, parcel G and following, to R. Do you know *that* one? Family Harrak. And lot 0988775, parcel D and following, to M."

On and on the marshal went, until he had read off the numbers pertaining to each and every parcel. His face reddened as he spoke, while the count merely stared and sipped his tea.

"I see the lots," the older man admitted, "but I don't receive your meaning."

"Five parcels in all. *All* of them planted with grapes. *All* planted with olives. *All*—and this is significant—*flat* and *contiguous*. Located on the southern plain below the borgo. All bought within the last three years from families who lost sons."

The tea cup did not rattle when the count shrugged. "What does this have to do with me? We buy from grape sellers all over the region. That's our niche. We're brokers. We take the grapes. We bear the risk. We in turn sell the grapes and juice wherever we can get the best price. So it has been as long as my father has been in the ground, God rest him. You'll have to deal with the foreman if you want to know about these landowners. I'm afraid I know little about them or how they came by their land. As long as they're good suppliers, we deal with them."

"You don't know who they are?"

Again the maddening shrug. "No. Foreigners, from the names you're spouting. May I offer you a tisane, Marshal? You seem troubled. Anxious. Overwrought."

"Overwrought, you son of a bitch?"

"Excuse me?"

"How can you sit there and say you don't know them when you in fact are the owner of all these properties? Each of the deeds are in the name of a family trust of some kind, but those trusts don't truly exist. They're dummy corporations designed to cultivate the impression that these foreigners own the property. But all those trusts lead back to Liberator Holdings, in Rome. I don't know what you told the migrants, but the ones I talked to are under the impression that they own those properties. They don't. One family showed me the deed with their family name on it. But that paper is worthless. You bought those properties with your own money, you just didn't want anyone to know about it. So you created these family trusts. Anyone who looks at the deed at town hall assumes the land belongs to the Vajdas or the Harraks or whomever, but the migrants are just paying you rent. They entrust their produce to you each season for what is supposed to be a fair price. And I'll wager they pay over-market for every other service you provide: legal assistance with work permits that allow them to stay in this country, the registration of their vehicles, their farm insurance, and so on. No, you're not a broker. You're a feudal lord, and these people are your serfs. You helped move them here, and you dun them again and again."

The count silently drained the last of his tea. "These are strange accusations."

"Are they? From the beginning I thought this was a case of accidental death. But the Albanian Demaci was known to have a source for high-grade heroin. I now think he acquired that cut in order to target five clients, and five clients only. Five young men, all from families with good, contiguous land on the plain. Every one of the boys who died is a *firstborn* son. Firstborn sons are their families' princes. So much so that Castelpietra actually has a statute on the books preventing parents from selling property without clearing it with their firstborn son or that minor child's representative."

"Oh, *that,*" the count said. "It's a foolish, antiquated law which they passed after World War II when farmers were leaving the land in droves. So what, Marshal? There's also a law that says neighbors who own adjoining property must sign off on any land you're selling. Such things are mere formalities at real estate closings."

"I agree. They're relics of an older age, but obstacles nevertheless. The citizens of your borgo grow to adulthood understanding that each generation must think of the next. In such a city, the quickest way to break a family's spirit is to kill its firstborn son. It forces parents to confront their own mortality, and plan for a different financial future. That such a string of deaths would be coincidental strains credulity. Each of those families lost sons at the hands of an Albanian man whose vehicle is registered and insured by your Rome company. That can't be coincidental, either. Don't you find that strange, Cortese?"

"*Count* Cortese."

"Do you find that strange, sir?"

"Please—we've gotten off on the wrong foot here. I rarely interact with Rome. That's an investment for me, not a passion. The firm is vast, with many partners and interests. To infer a connection from scraps and lies told by foreigners is taking Liberator's connections to unrealistic bounds. Come now, Marshal!" the handsome man said, laughing. "What you're saying is truly outrageous, almost comically so. I urge you to sit and talk first with the magistrate or perhaps a doctor before you go around accusing people. The way you're talking, you could easily have lost your mind."

"I struggled with this for a long time, until I realized that it all hinged on the thing that is most important in all the borgo."

"And what is that?"

"Land."

"Land, Marshal? Hah! Land is abundant and cheap as dirt."

"Follow me. When people look at a hill town, the focus is always on the striking panorama of a castle or church on that hill. But these towns were built on hills for protection. But their survival depended on what lay below—the farmland. The flatter the land, the more valuable, the more easily worked. You implied as much the first day we met."

"And I say again that you need only throw a rock to hit abandoned land. I can buy land anywhere I want. I need not orchestrate ridiculous land grabs and murders. That is preposterous. I have lived here all my life and I assure you our wine market is only shrinking, not growing. Nationwide, our population is dropping. We face more competition when we try to export. The entire world is overplanted with grapes. It's the reason my father got out of it, the reason I have been abstemious in cultivating new crops."

"Until three years ago, that might have been true, but then something happened that rewrote the rules of the game locally."

"And what is that?"

"The Americans came."

The count's weight shifted.

I have you, Scarpone thought.

"*Tiber Goat.* They're across the river, they need lots of grapes, and they don't much care what their quality is. They moved in three years ago, and then boys began to die. Not everyone knew what was going on when the Americans first started planting. But *you* did. You would have learned about it from your daughter. Now you had an insatiable new market. But you also knew that if *you* made overtures to the grieving families, they would become suspicious of your sudden interest. So you used the migrants as a cover. Their rent and their grapes would bring in a nice income while you waited for the real target to come within your sights."

"My God! First I'm murdering children. Then I'm chasing grapes and exploiting farmers. I am Dracul himself! Go ahead—what could possibly be my ultimate goal, Marshal? Tell me, then get the hell out of my office, you crazy son of a whore!"

Scarpone grabbed a pencil from the count's leather cup, bent to the map, and drew two parallel lines across the Little Tiber River.

"The bridge has been long delayed," Scarpone said. "But it'll be finished this year. I heard Charlie Anderson talking about it the day of the pageant. How he *loved* this side of the river. How the idea of making Lazio a tourist destination for wine interested him, mostly because the land was cheap. But to lock in one giant parcel to build an American-style winery would be tough. It would have to be near the highway. Everyone drives past on their way to Florence. Tourist buses would have to have easy access. And when the tourists were done, they could drive across the bridge to Charlie's *Umbrian* winery. It was a nice plan, Cortese. Get control of the land. Rent it out to migrants as a cover. Bide your time. Kick them off when it's time to sell to Tiber Goat. I don't for a second think Charlie and Lucia knew any of it. But you did it all, waiting for Charlie to come knocking. And if he didn't, one day one of your people would casually mention to him that the perfect parcel for his next winery was here for the taking. Killing the firstborns removed a legal obstacle, allowing you to approach the families frankly and directly. But it also had to happen for *emotional* reasons. Mostly, the boys died to satisfy you. You lost your son. Why shouldn't they lose theirs?"

"How dare you speak of my son? You, of all people?"

"You think me crazy, but you haven't reached for your phone, I notice. Shall I tell you why? It's because you want to know how much I've gotten right. It's true I don't know you, but I know that you're a liar and murderer, accustomed to profiting from the deaths of others. You prefer to work behind the scenes, and blame others for your actions. The first glimpse I had of this was months ago when one of my men told me how your father-in-law had died at his daughter's hands. The contessa's father, I gather, drowned in Bolsena Lake. The contessa jumped in to help him, or so you told the townsmen, but your father-in-law died just the same. Of course we both know that's a lie. She was incapable of drowning her father. The contessa can't swim; she's deathly afraid of water. I saw it myself. I'm guessing you leapt in, and seized the opportunity to pull the old man under. Your ex-wife was too traumatized, and your children too young, to perceive the truth. Her father died, *she* inherited, but *you* profited. That's how you operate. And years later, just as you were about to begin divorce proceedings, you planted that slander against her just as you needed to curry favor with the townspeople."

The tea cup hit the desk with a rattle. The count sat. He produced a handkerchief from the middle drawer of his desk, and used it to wipe his lips.

"Are you finished?"

"For now."

"I must say it's a troubling story, troubling more for you than me. I can't imagine you can prove a word of it. You assert a relationship between me and this Albanian. Let him come forth and give his testimony, then. Oh—he is dead. I don't know how, and I don't care. The migrants? Let an army of interpreters question them, if you can muster such a feat. They claim to be owners, you say? Sadly, they are ignorant of legal matters. I have rental leases on file at town hall that spell out the truth. They are unlikely to breathe a word against someone who, if you are right, has given them their first source of stable income in their lives. Who will speak out against such a man, if, as you say, that man is me? I can't think of anyone. Say you are able to show that these transactions went through Liberator. Circumstantial. How strange that we would buy land and rent it to tenants. That's the way of the world, Signore. Ah, but the paperwork seems labyrinthine and confusing? There is no law against it. We simply like our privacy. I can name my next corporation after my mule if I so desire. What business is it of yours? So you see, Captain? Who will speak out against the one you claim is me?"

Scarpone leaned across the desk. His face within an inch of the man's chin.

"I have the commercialista."

"What is this, you say?"

"I have your commercialista, Giorgio Albirone, who works out of an office in Via del Babuino in Rome. He was your handmaiden. He orchestrated and worked this entire operation for you. He has assured my former supervisor, Fausto, that he is willing to detail certain personal conversations with you and the Albanian and the migrant families. He will talk, Cortese, which means I have you."

The count bent to his desk, tearing his eyes away from Scarpone. "That is indeed vexing," he said.

When the man stood back up, he held something leveled at Scarpone's body.

A Beretta.

Chapter Sixty-Two

The count stepped closer to the desk and nudged the middle drawer closed with his hip.

"You see," he said, "I prefer another, more tragic story. The story of a man sent to a city not his own when he himself was still unwell. A man given to wild hypotheses, allegations of crimes where none have been committed. A man so high-strung and upset that he nearly caused the death of himself and a highly placed Vatican official. Yes, Marshal—I know that story. Did you think you'd be able to burst in here, make accusations, cart me away, and I'd have nothing to say in return?"

I feared for my captain's life. By rights he should have been panic-stricken. But I was startled to find that he was thinking much more practically.

Saying nothing is the intelligent thing to do, Cortese, Scarpone thought. But if you want to talk, talk, and let's see if I can pick anything of use from your ramblings.

You're in your mid-sixties. You've never fought in a war in your life. But you would have done your required military service. That would have been enough to teach you a lifetime of firearm skills.

There's a chance you know what you're doing.

That you've had training.

But you probably weren't issued that pistol. It's an old model, probably seventy years old. Maybe you inherited that piece. Maybe you bought it from someone who served in the last war.

How often have you fired and cleaned it?

Do you know if the spring is still good?

Do the rounds jam?

Do you know how much pressure you have to employ to depress the trigger?

Probably not—or you wouldn't be handling it so casually.

Show me the gun, Scarpone thought. Show me its left, show me its right...

"Do you know who you're dealing with?" the count said. "When there are fundraisers...when the church, the soccer team, the schools need money, do you know who they think to ask? Do you know who is at the top of their list? Do you?"

Scarpone made a show of thinking carefully. His eyes raked the ceiling, bounced to the window behind the count, and flitted over the top of his desk.

The older man's free hand massaged his lower back. *You're uncomfortable standing,* Scarpone thought. *So sit, you son of a bitch. And show me your trigger next...*

"No answer?" Cortese said. He smiled triumphantly, and slung his butt and right thigh on the desk. His torso twisted to face Scarpone. "My family built this city, Marshal. People forget that ours was the castle from which the borgo was built..."

Good, asshole. Because you chose to sit, Scarpone thought, you're now about a foot closer to me, and thus physically unstable. Your right foot probably isn't touching the ground. You've made my work easier.

"Our stones and our blood built the borgo. Do you think I would let it go? Let it go to the likes of peasant families? To migrant filth from every shithole in Europe? To a mentally unbalanced—"

Aw, to hell with it, Scarpone thought.

He swung his left arm. The arc caught the count in the throat, and sent him flying backward. His skull hit the desk. The air went out of him. As he struggled to right himself, Scarpone wrenched the gun from his hand. Grabbed his throat and slammed the back of his head once more against the desk.

Scarpone ejected the magazine and round. Stripped it. Sent all of the pieces to the floor but one, which he held up for the count's inspection.

"This model was designed with one of the more complicated safeties," he told Cortese. "It requires a 180-degree-turn. But it's worth performing if you ever need to point it at anyone again. Which you won't."

"Vaffanculo."

"On your feet."

Ten minutes later, a curious procession emerged from the offices of the azienda. The captain escorted the count down the street. The foreman and bookkeeper followed nervously from a safe distance.

Witnesses would later say that the count was obviously in handcuffs, though he hid it well under a beautiful woolen jacket. His teeth were clenched tightly in his jaw, but he held his head high. He was, if nothing else, a student of appearances, of *la bella figura*. Though he couldn't easily tip his hat magnanimously to those he met upon the street, he nevertheless bowed regally to everyone he met.

Every eye in town was upon him. The men in the coffee shop. Alessandro the barman. The ladies at the clothing and notions stores. The red-nosed, sickly patrons of the *farmacia*. The pork store girl. The family who ran the grocery, the older couple who ran the *salumeria*, the young, pinch-faced girl who ran the kitchen apparel shop, and the Internet-surfing geek who sold paperback novels and newspapers at the stationery store.

All these people and more came to the doors of their shops and marveled at the spectacle. Whispers cut like knives as the borgo's biggest name was led away by the odd, awkward stranger from Rome.

Chapter Sixty-Three

The waiter who left the coffee bar on Via del Babuino in Rome that afternoon wore a green jacket and a black bowtie. On his shoulder he bore a pewter tray bearing a few Styrofoam cups with plastic lids, a can of orange soda, and an assortment of sugar packets and plastic spoons.

Babuino is home to elegant shops, but most tourists make a beeline to the bizarre statue of a satyr—half man, half goat—that was installed in the sixteenth century. The face of the goat man proved so hideous that many simply called it a monkey. Hence the name of the street: Baboon Way.

The waiter marched past the antique shops and leather goods stores until he reached a doorway between two competing clothing stores. Obnoxious rock music pumped out of both establishments all day long.

He rang the bell for one of the upstairs offices, and headed up. On the second floor, he rang the buzzer outside apartment D and was greeted by two armed carabinieri officers. One cop took the waiter's tray while the other patted him down.

A heavy cop with feminine eyes and earlobes as long as the Buddha's waved the waiter into a cramped conference room. This fat carabiniere was on the phone, and only half-watched as the waiter set down the tray.

A few other soldiers paced around the periphery of the room, looking bored, smoking, or staring out the window at the traffic below.

Eight coffees. One soda.

The cops fell on the coffee, flipping off the lids and dumping sugar like crazy into the tiny vessels.

The only civilian in the room sat nervously twirling his hair. He seemed well suited to this rundown, badly furnished office.

He held out his hand for the soda.

The waiter accepted his *mancia,* or tip, with a melodramatic bow and dashed off.

Downstairs on the street, he tossed the tray into a green dumpster and stepped over the seat of a parked motorino. He detached the breakaway tie from his neck, and flung it into the trash, along with the green jacket.

He gunned the engine and drove away.

By then, in the conference room upstairs, the hair-twirling man had already dropped the can of soda, which splashed its contents and burned a hole into the gray, industrial carpet.

The man thrashed in his seat and grabbed at his throat. Bloody foam spewed from the man's mouth for several seconds before the fat cop dropped his phone and began screaming at the top of his lungs.

Chapter Sixty-Four

The magistrate dragged Scarpone to a room in city hall that was filled with hissing pipes, brooms, and cleaning chemicals. A dangerous room, considering Saviano was toting a cigarette.

He shoved Scarpone against the metal shelving and fished blindly in the dark for the string. Putrid yellow light rained down on them. Saviano slammed the door.

"What the hell are you doing? Are you mad? You must know we can't possibly try this case."

"I feel as if I'm always hearing that from you. You're a good man, but I think it's time you acknowledge that perhaps with age you have lost your balls."

Saviano eyed him narrowly. "You and I have been through a lot lately. I have seen that you are a man capable of strange things. Powerful things. Perhaps such power addles the mind and unmoors one's sense of logic. I cannot say. But I urge you now to think of your career. Think of your future. You don't want to pick a fight with this man. You must know that you have little evidence."

"I have the pistol he used to threaten my life."

"His lawyer has already said his client feared for his life. He is entitled to self-protection under the law if you were acting like a madman."

"Ah, this is the Scarpone-as-madman defense?"

"I understand your charges. Perhaps we can show that he is tied to those transactions. He and his lawyer will find a way to explain away these fictitious family trusts and the empty promises made to the migrants. They got a serviceable residence and land at a cheap price. Honestly, the lawyers could easily make it seem as if he's their benefactor."

"That's what he does. He's always the munificent one, isn't he? A point of fact: they don't own the land, but he owns *them*. *He* decides when or if their rent goes up. *He* controls what they get paid for their produce. *He* controls the water on those properties. *He* controls their work permits and the legality of their vehicles. That is the beauty of his plan. If, in another year, he needs them off the land, he can do it easily and sell the property to the Americans. If he can't persuade the Americans to buy or the bridge is delayed, his serfs continue paying him as before. It's slavery hidden in plain sight. If they breathe a word of their arrangement, they'll lose their work permits and be forced to leave the country."

"Listen to yourself. You're saying this man befriended a drug dealer and instructed him to kill five children—all for the sake of an *investment*. You realize what his attorneys would do in court if we pressed forward? You don't have proof that those boys were intentionally sold lethal doses at the count's behest. If he wanted to steal the land, he could have done it without killing their sons."

"Exactly right, but it fits his psychology. He toys with people. He enjoys it. He manipulated his own *daughter* in a land transaction. He cannot take pleasure from a deal unless the other party is somehow broken. Killing the boys was, to him, a satisfying way to get the families to reassess their futures and give up that soil."

"You can't prove the charge. The Albanian is dead."

"No, but I have the commercialista in Rome. He will attest that he arranged for these land deals on the count's behalf. We'll use interpreters to get those families to speak freely. The Finance Guard will tear apart his financial records. It will be hard to do, but it can be done. By law you can hold him on suspicion, pending your investigation. And I suggest you do. He is clearly a flight risk."

Saviano's eyes darkened. "We have agreed that he spends tonight in his home. He assures me on his life that he has no other weapons but a hunting rifle. Your men will collect it and stand guard over the azienda office. Tomorrow, we go through the papers and they had better make sense, Matteo. It's all we have. If they are gibberish, if these back-room arrangements are in fact poorly documented, we'll have no hope of getting Liberator to open their books."

"How many times must I tell you? It's not *just* the paper trail. We have the accountant in Rome."

"Matteo, Matteo, listen. This is what I'm trying to tell *you*. I spoke with your Fausto in Rome. A good man by all accounts. The commercialista is dead."

THEY BROUGHT THE COUNT DOWN IN THE ELEVATOR. His men—the foreman, the bookkeeper, and the first of his attorneys on the scene—were waiting just inside the double doors. They watched as D'Orazio removed the cuffs. Enzo was nearby with some papers for the lawyer.

Scarpone stood in the back of the hall leading to the front doors. He heard Saviano offer birdlike sounds of conciliation, and heard the count murmur something back. The cluster of men smelled strongly of cigarettes and unspoken stress.

The count took his jacket from his foreman and turned to go.

Then stopped.

"Outside," he told the others. They fled.

Cortese stabbed a finger toward Scarpone and said, "You—a word."

Then he leaned heavily on the doors and let himself out.

Scarpone followed him. A crowd had gathered on the far edge of the piazza near the shops. Everyone watching. Even the old men who gathered every day could not look away.

Cortese stood apart from his men, the jacket on his shoulders, sleeves flapping. He was fussing with a cigarette lighter when Scarpone reached him.

"I don't know how long you thought you'd be in this town, but from this moment forward, I'd begin to mark time, friend. It ends soon."

"I don't know how you can live with yourself," Scarpone said.

The count smiled. "You're incorrigible. A fool. And you know why? Because you have nothing to lose. This is the only reason love was invented and the only reason children are allowed to be born: so men can be controlled. A man without family is a loose cannon. If he is found worthless, he will be crushed underfoot."

"Five boys dead. For money and grapes."

"What do you know? In time those lands will do more for this town than anything those children would have contributed."

"You lost your son, so you think nothing of robbing others of theirs."

"How *dare* you?" Cortese said. "Who the hell are *you,* sir? You and I are the same. Men with nothing. At least I lost a son tragically. Do you know what that's like? You can't possibly. You, on the other hand, were a thoughtless, reckless man—a drunk, my friends in Rome say—who killed his own family in an automobile wreck."

Something broke inside the captain.

He lunged for the old man's throat. The count threw up his hands to fight him off but Scarpone knocked him back against a parked car. Dug his fingers into the cords of the man's neck. Their faces were close together. The count screamed. Spittle flew from his mouth. Their eyes locked. The captain saw into the sun-ravaged face of the old man, and peered past the snot-colored cataract over his right eyeball.

Scarpone hissed, "I condemn you!"

He slapped the man's face curtly, and ran the palm of his hand slowly down the count's cheek as if wiping away slime.

The old man struggled to shake off my captain's hand. "How dare you? Who are you? Who are you to say such a thing?"

"I condemn you," Scarpone said again. Another brisk slap and wipe.

The count spat. A large gob of saliva hung on the tip of Scarpone's nose but he would not relinquish his grip. Again and again, he wiped his hand down the old man's face.

It took six men to separate them. The men of the azienda dragged their raging employer along the cobbles, back to the office. And while the carabinieri waited for their captain to calm himself, they avoided looking him in the eye.

Chapter Sixty-Five

"It pains me to think that my recovery has occasioned difficult moments for you and your work," the cardinal said.

"I don't know that it has," Scarpone told the man. "I don't have the responsibilities I had when I last saw Your Eminence. I've been reassigned."

"So I've heard, and hence my vehement desire to see that wrong corrected."

They were in a Vatican lounge for visiting dignitaries. The audience had gone as well as those things possibly could. The pontiff's words were obviously scripted and designed to bestow sincere thanks and a blessing, but the words that washed over my captain only dashed his spirits.

He couldn't shake the feeling that he had taken a wrong turn in a labyrinthine government building and was stuck waiting in a queue while a functionary conferred a sentence upon him.

Now, at least, they could talk. The cardinal was, for the time being, confined to a wheelchair. But his prognosis was good. His doctors believed that with rehabilitative therapy, rest, and a robust diet, he would be mobile in a span of a month.

The older man reached over to take Scarpone's hands. His eyelids squeezed shut. "I can't think of it. I can, but I mustn't. It is still too horrible. But when it *does* come to me, I can only thank God our

Father that we were so lucky to have a guardian at that moment, to watch over us."

"Thank you, Your Eminence."

The cardinal squeezed his hand. "Thank *you*. But I meant another. Can you truly say that you did not feel his presence?"

"I don't know what you mean."

"A force for good that saved us from certain death."

Scarpone's collar felt tight. *Yes, yes,* he was thinking. *God is always with us. Blah, blah, blah.* He ratcheted his head and locked eyes with Enzo, who sat in another part of the room, flipping through the Vatican newspaper, *L'Osservatore Romano*.

"I'm not versed in philosophy or theology, Your Eminence. All I know is, bad men exist. And when bad men do bad things, if it's within our power to stop them, we must, even if it occasions their death or ours."

The old man nodded slowly. "I suppose you must be comfortable with that tradeoff or you cannot pursue your calling. But I choose to believe that even a man such as yourself must have divine guidance or the forces of evil would be too great. Too great indeed."

The old man sighed heavily. "I have news for you. About the young women."

He raised a shaky hand and pointed to a manila envelope sitting on the table in front of them. "One of them saw fit to contact my office, asking if you were well. And sending along a gift."

Scarpone reached for it.

"You'll be happy to know that she and some of the others have been transferred to a facility on the coast of our country, to a mission run by the good sisters. It was not thought wise to return them to their own villages for fear of reprisals. Some seek asylum in your country on the grounds that they are political refugees. I don't know where this will lead, but the sisters are looking after the majority quite well."

Scarpone opened the long, thick envelope. Inside was a folded sheet of artists' paper. Carefully, he pulled it apart and saw a charcoal sketch of the face of a young girl. Lips apart. Bright teeth and eyes. A self-portrait.

The writing at the bottom was uncertain but clear.

This is me now, Capitano.
Can you see? I am smiling.
Thank God for you,
Anna

Chapter Sixty-Six

As the cab took them from the Vatican through the heart of the city, I was struck with the powerful feeling that I had come home. Neither the soot clinging to the ancient ruins nor the murkiness of the river could dampen my enthusiasm. Once, not long ago, I had entered the captain's life here. Here was where we belonged. The borgo was a pleasing place, but it would never be a city of caesars, popes, and artists. Here, the very stones seemed to welcome us back to the land of our fathers.

The cab shot down the Lungotevere toward Testaccio. Scarpone paid the fare and led Enzo first through the outdoor market. The captain paced from stall to stall, admiring fruits and meats and bending to sniff the produce. But buying nothing.

"Why are we here, sir?" Enzo asked.

On the far side of the market tents, Scarpone stood on the sidewalk and stared up at the windows ringing the square.

"Is that..." Enzo said.

"There," Scarpone said. "That balcony was ours."

I caught a glimpse of his mind as he spoke. Behind his eyes he saw the woman in the red eyeglasses, smiling at him as she worked in the sunlight.

He stood there a long time, until the stone in his throat went away.

Then he led the way to Volpetti's, where they bought two small sandwiches. A thick slice of mortadella flecked with shaved pistachio, pressed between two thin sheets of oily focaccia. They peeled back the wax paper as they walked to the cemetery gates. They sat on the benches outside and washed down their small meal with bottles of *acqua frizzante*. The edges of the cemetery were lined with tall, thin cypress trees. Every tourist to this land imagines them as the symbols of the Tuscan countryside. But in Lazio, in Rome, cypresses are the green sentinels of death.

Scarpone checked his phone for messages. Fausto had called. Numerous times.

"They want me back, Enzo."

"Really?" Enzo paused, squinting from the glare on his spectacles.

Scarpone shrugged. "They're so anxious to bury the bad press kicked up by Olúdìímú's recovery that they're willing to post me to any squad I choose. Terrorism. Human trafficking. Antiquities. Anything."

"My God," Enzo said. "Men like us...men like me, that is...would kill to land a post like that in a decent city." He paused and lowered his eyes. "What will you do?"

My captain crunched his sandwich. "Bureaucrats. It shouldn't take a man coming out of a coma to shame them into doing what's right. So I'm staying in the borgo."

Enzo lunged forward to give the captain an awkward hug. He stopped, seeing tears form in Scarpone's eyes. "Something I said, sir?"

My captain wept.

Enzo said in a tentative voice, "Was it just as they say, Captain? Your son and his mother?"

Scarpone's eyes clenched. He nodded. "A year before the incident with the cardinal. I took time off. Then I got sucked into Anna's case. I was so sure that my head was clear. That I was ready to throw myself back into the work. Then I put the cardinal in a coma."

"You saved his life!"

Scarpone reached for the younger man's wrist. His voice croaked, "I'm so sick of putting bodies in the ground. If you were a priest, would you absolve a man such as me?"

"I'm not a priest."

"I know, but would you? Three men dead, Enzo."

"That was regrettable, sir, but it was in self-defense."

"An innocent driver. The cardinal. A family slaughtered. And now the count."

"You're mistaken. The count lives."

Scarpone smiled wanly. "Does he?" He dropped his face into his hands. "Shit. Surely, in such a small borgo, everyone knows the truth about me."

"To be perfectly honest, I'd heard some things when you came, but...it wasn't my place..."

Scarpone stood. "Give me a moment."

Enzo watched him head into the cemetery.

Chapter Sixty-Seven

The captain ascends the steps of the mausoleum.

I can feel Enzo down the path. I feel heat rising off his body, the heaviness of him.

There is the click of the key. The captain enters and sits.

And suddenly I am enclosed in darkness.

I hear his weeping. I hear his recriminations. I hear metal scraping on stone when he hunches forward in the folding chair. I hear him uttering words to the larger sarcophagus.

Then he rises. He bends at the hip and gives a light peck to the larger stone. Then he bends and kisses the smaller.

With that kiss comes a rushing of wind, and my whole being is pinned to the stone.

His breath pierces me. I'm trapped inside the block, suffocating, and cannot pull myself away. Scarpone lingers there entirely too long. He offers his apologies. I can feel his heart—real, living, palpable, and surrounded by a muddle of grief.

"I'm sorry," he says. "I'm so sorry."

Then he goes. When his lips pull away from the stone, it's as if a lance has been pulled from my body.

I hear the creak of the door. Then he is back on the path, walking away, his friend at his side.

For a long while, I lie there absorbing the truth.

I have followed this man for two of your years. I have watched him, heard him, felt him, known him.

Once, the blood of the ancient Romans, the blood of this man, flowed in my veins. I find this interesting, but merely that.

Now I know who and what I am.

In life I was the son of this man, Scarpone.

In death I am nothing, a mere shade.

I think on this until I can take it no longer. I wrench myself from my place, and follow them out. I pass through stone and door and gate to watch as they enter the cab.

Enzo's hand is at the great man's back.

How can it be, Scarpone is thinking. *How can it be?*

I don't know why, but I am not sentimental about this fresh truth. Perhaps when you pass through the veil of life you lose all ability to laugh, to cry, to grieve. But you continue to learn, to observe, to witness. And this I have done.

Like those old Romans before me, I am closer now to dust than man.

Which is why I cannot weep for my captain.

How can it be? he asks. My response is not comforting, but it is the truth: Because it can, *Babbo*. Because it can, Daddy. It can, it can, it can.

Chapter Sixty-Eight

Later that month the borgo celebrated the annual wine festival. For three days the streets turned red. Families and tourists held court by day. At night the city was turned over to its young men and women, who made asses of themselves, cheering loudly and guzzling wine from two-liter plastic bottles. Still others perched on the stone staircases of the city center and hoisted huge demijohn jugs to their lips. The borgo stunk of alcohol. Tourists who lingered long after dark wondered if they had not made a bad decision by venturing so far from Orvieto and into such a poorly lit village.

It had been a trying couple of days for the count. His lawyers had managed to beat off the prosecutor but there were still irritating requests for documents and statements.

They had not dared to arrest him again.

In keeping with the custom of the festival, the azienda erected a long table groaning with nibbles in the gateway of the compound. The count sat dressed in his white suit and hat, greeting workers who passed by, offering them a drink and a snack, and accepting—if they were so kind to offer it—a small token of their esteem and loyalty. This is called making one's *obligo,* and it was a tradition that stretched back to the birth of the borgo itself. On feast days in the past, the sires of his family had graciously accepted chickens, rabbits, wedges of cheese, bolts of cloth, jars of olives or dried fruits, and even small sacks of candied almonds.

There were few gifts this year. Workers who did stop by sipped their wine, made their excuses, and hastily departed. The foreman and the bookkeeper feared their employer's wrath in light of such a dismal turnout. But the count put on a brave face and smiled his way through the festival. On Saturday night, at a critical point in the ceremonies, when the ass-like mayor rose to say a few words, his speech was punctuated by a loud cry and the sound of collapsing furniture.

Count Cortese, proprietor of the Azienda Madonna della Sorgente, had fallen from his chair and onto the road.

A doctor was summoned. Seeing that the count was incapable of speech, the physician assumed that the man had suffered a stroke. An ambulance whisked him to the Orvieto Hospital, where doctors poked and prodded and captured their images. The following morning, with solemn urgency, they wheeled the count into a gallery where they tried to get what they could of the obscene, pulpy mass that had grown inside him. They closed him up and prescribed bed rest before sending him home.

That was the best they could do. Any nonna could have told them that as soon as the air penetrated his body, the count was as good as gone.

He lingered still, a shrinking man in clothes too large for his frame. Over the next few weeks, the foreman and bookkeeper propped him up in a wheelchair outside the walls of the compound, heavily swaddled in blankets. The count waved at townspeople, but the rheumy look of his eyes said all.

One night he insisted to his nurse and housekeeper that a dog with red eyes had parked itself on his bed and would not leave. Later, the ladies heard him moaning a single name over and over: "*Scarpone! Scarpone!*"

That morning at dawn, I saw him walk through Lucia's vineyard, completely naked, a determined grin on his face. Inside the house, Lucia had only just gotten the call. Instead of rushing over to the old man's residence, she went to her son's room, took him in her arms, and wept.

Enzo learned from Iucci, who'd taken the call at the station.

Allegra Chiostro did not need to be told. The witch of the borgo went out that morning with a smile on her face. She lowered herself onto the rocks and raised her arms in gratitude to the sun.

The day after they closed the old man's tomb, Scarpone went down to the lower chapel alone. He bought a candle and watched a while as its flame flickered across the dead man's stone. The least I can do, he thought, for a man whom I winnowed from the face of the earth.

Chapter 69

Wind came out of the hills one morning and worked its way through the valley of the Little Tiber. In Ciconia, the pathologist Cavalcanti dragged herself from the bed she shared with the dozing Gismonda and went to raise the temperature on the heater in her apartment. To her dismay, she found that the *caldaia* was dead. Gismonda, claiming to know about such things, had not performed the system's annual reset, as he had promised. This meant that the only available warmth in the dottoressa's apartment was the body of her lazy soldier. She shot her gaze out the window, thinking that if she hurried now, she would be able to sneak out for coffee, unseen by Gismonda. Much as she enjoyed their time together, she did not see this relationship lasting forever. He was not a man she could take home to Perugia. What she would do now, she didn't know. She had made a mess of things, throwing over her long-time boyfriend for this sluggard.

At the azienda, Adriano the foreman and Damiano the bookkeeper shivered in their sweaters and stacked wood in the office stove. Then they got back to work, sifting through the company's papers one by one, trying to make sense of their late employer's curious arrangements in time for the coming audit. In light of recent allegations and upon the recommendation of the magistrate, the finance police had indeed taken an interest in the count's affairs. Equally interested were the battery of Milanese accountants hired by the count's heir, or rather, the mother of the count's five-year-old heir.

The foreman and the bookkeeper frowned more than smiled these days, but they were determined to stay the course. Damiano the bookkeeper, especially, wondered if he should think about getting a new job. As prudent as this course of action might have been, he banished it from his mind as unthinkable. He'd had this job since he'd gotten out of the technical institute; if he played his cards right, he would have it till the day he died—as was only fair.

In the piazza near the church, the pork store girl locked up her uncle's store, adjusted her earbuds of her iPhone, and headed out. She hit the wall of chill and cursed herself for not having brought a sweater or jacket. She beat her arms in an effort to stay warm, and by the time she arrived at the Bar Fleming, her nipples were delightfully erect, giving the old farmers something to pretend they weren't seeing as they downed their shots of espresso.

The coffee bar was busy. Enzo and D'Orazio were taking their breakfast on the way in to relieve Puzio and Iucci. The Sbuccio brothers studied the TV for news of today's car races. The muscular brother adjusted his fanny pack and helped his slower brother break up his cornetto into pieces small enough for dunking. Alessandro the barista told the men how his wife, who had vehemently fought his acquisition of a new used car, now used it almost exclusively. The male patrons quickly grasped his tone, and began taunting the barman for being a fool. They managed to stretch this classic, battle-of-the-sexes comedy routine for a good long while as they jingled change in their pockets and waited for the day to warm up.

On the road outside town, my captain rode his bike to Lucia's just as the truck from the bakery was leaving. It was early but the workers and Lucia were already outdoors, finishing the last of the season's cleanup. Magda greeted the captain and led him into the kitchen, where the boy was already digging into a hot cornetto.

The captain accepted the coffee gratefully and went out on the terrace to wait. My Lucia beat her hands together, ridding them of dirt, and headed up to the house to take her cup. The captain had just come by to say hello, she knew, and this pleased as much as frightened her.

They stood on the terrace and watched the land. The vines looked relieved. For one, the worm that once dwelled under the vineyard had crumbled to dust. For another, the vines had given up their seasonal burden and were happy now to be left alone, happy to stretch their woody, peeling arms to the sky for just a few more weeks before they lapsed into dormancy.

Sometime soon, it would be time to turn their attention to the olive grove. My Lucia only had a hundred trees at the moment. But they would make good oil. Two or three weeks from now, she and her foreman and the workers and perhaps even my captain would climb ladders and harvest the fruit in the old way—beating the branches with canes. The fruit would fall to blue tarps, and be taken over the river and up the Umbrian hills to the stone mill co-op near Castiglione al Lago.

I stood on Lucia's hill and watched them together. My captain's skin was brown these days, his hair grayer. My Lucia smelled beautifully of expensive perfume, soil, and herself.

I wish that I could see further into their future, but I can do this no more than they can. I can only say with truth that for once my captain looks strong and hearty and content. I try to listen to their words but already my concentration fails me. This morning my mind is not what it was. The wind is in my ears. It rushes down the hills and blows right through me. Already parts of whatever I am are being turned to dust.

Piece by piece, bit by bit, I am rent by the wind.

The dust of me settles on the Little Tiber. My captain and Lucia, who have not left my sight in many of your months, are already on the horizon. I ride the blood of the river past the borgo. There is the town, there are the spires of the church, and the square tower of the old chapel.

There, high on the side of the hill town, Allegra Chiostro picks her way among the rocks. I wonder what she is foraging for today. Mushrooms, late-season wild garlic, what? But it is not for me to know.

I cannot think long enough to care.

The wind moves and she looks up. She turns to the river and raises her hand. If I had a hand I would raise it back.

The words she utters are the words of my people.

Salve, she whispers. *Ave atque vale.*

Good-bye borgo. Good-bye strega. *Ave atque vale.*

Hail and farewell.

And soon I cannot think even this.

My words hit the air and become formless. All I hear is the sound of my mind chanting the river's name: *Teverina, Teverina, Teverina.*

These waters will bear me south to the city of my fathers. There the memory of me rushes to become one with silt and stone, and my voice will be no more.

Before You Go...

If you enjoyed this book, I'd be extremely grateful if you'd **leave a brief review** at your retailer's site. Reviews are one of the best ways a reader can help an author. Reviews help other readers find out about the book.

Consider signing up for my newsletter. Building a relationship with my readers is the best thing about being an author. And the Daggyland VIP Club is the best way to stay in touch and be among the first to learn about upcoming books and deals.

As a welcome gift, you're entitled to download any or *all* of the range of ebooks in my Starter Library, completely free of charge.

Two of the stories in the collection are set in Italy. One is the very first Captain Scarpone story, which appeared in *Alfred Hitchcock's Mystery Magazine* way back in 2013!

Another free book in the Starter Library—*The Mesmerist: Aftermath* —is a short, explosive, never-before-seen chapter that was cut from the original manuscript of the novel, *The Mesmerist*. It's not sold in any store online. It's exclusively for members of the VIP Club.

Your contact info will never be sold or shared with anyone. You can easily opt-out at any time. Did I mention it's free?

VISIT JOSEPHDAGNESE.COM TO SIGN UP

Also by Joseph D'Agnese

In the Mesmerist Series

The Mesmerist

The first in a spellbinding series of thrillers about an underground culture of gifted individuals who can kill with a glance or heal with a touch. If you like noir stories and occult detectives, this is for you.

Ear of God

(Coming Soon!)

When a kidnapping attempt goes tragically wrong, occult detective Ishmael Soul fights for his life—and the life of a young psychic child. Second in the acclaimed thriller series.

King of Thinks

(Coming Soon!)

A long-rumored mastermind is killing the city's most powerful psychics, forcing them to off themselves in a battle of the minds. Can Soul stop the diabolical "king" from gaining control of the White House?

Other Fiction

Sorceress Kringle

Everything you know about Santa Claus is a lie—and that's just the way *she* likes it. A stunning fantasy epic about the story behind the world's most beloved bringer of gifts.

Murder on Book Row

Beatrice Valentine is a larger-than-life bookshop owner with a penchant for three things in abundance—delicious Italian food, *vino,* and murder. The first in a series of delightful whodunnits set in a world of rare books and copious snacks.

Jersey Heat

A gorgeous scientist. A duffle bag of cash. A tough guy's only chance to do the right thing. An action-packed, full-length thriller with all the twists, turns, savage wit, eccentric characters, and black humor found in the work of Elmore Leonard or Carl Hiaasen.

The Marshal of the Borgo

Part whodunnit, part ghost story. A troubled cop and a teenaged witch rain down vengeance in a small village in Italy. If you enjoy the work of Magdalen Nabb, Andrea Camilleri, Michael Dibdin, or Donna Leon, you will absolutely love this evocative, sun-drenched story in the career of Captain Scarpone.

Arm of Darkness

A demonic prankster visits earth to punish do-gooders and evildoers alike with equal fury. Six horrifying tales of horror in one slim volume.

Daggyland #1 & #2

The easiest and most complete way to read the author's award-winning short stories. Most of these tales first appeared the world's best mystery magazines. Some appear in print for the very first time.

Nonfiction

Signing Their Lives Away

The true story behind the 56 men who signed the Declaration of Independence. Entertaining, essential, inspiring.

Signing Their Rights Away

The true story behind the 39 men who signed the U.S. Constitution. Praised highly by the *Wall Street Journal*.

Stuff Every American Should Know

What's the difference between the Declaration and Constitution? Who invented blue jeans? What's the story behind patriotic American songs? A pocket-sized hardcover perfect for stocking stuffers or gift-giving.

The Money Book for Freelancers

A critical guide to wealth-building and debt eradication for self-employed people. The *only* personal finance system for people with not-so-regular jobs.

The Scientist & the Sociopath

Incredible true-life stories collected from the author's in-depth reporting for the world's top science magazines.

Blind Spot

A ground-breaking "Big Think" book about why we fail to perceive solutions to intractable problems—even when they're staring us right in the face.

Big Weed

A Colorado millionaire's rollicking story of life in the cutting-edge world of legal marijuana entrepreneurship.

The Underground Culinary Tour

An eye-opening account of how the restaurant industry is being quietly transformed by Big Data.

The Indiana Jones Handbook

A beautifully designed hardcover volume that delights armchair archaeologists of all ages. (Warning: Out of print and hard to find!)

For Children

Blockhead: The Life of Fibonacci

The award-winning children's picture book about the medieval mathematician famous for the number pattern that bears his name. The book the *New York Times* called "charming and accessible."

<u>*American History Comic Books*</u>

Contains 12 educational comic books for classroom use. Designed to be easily photocopied by teachers for students in grades 4 to 6. Published by Scholastic, the biggest name in classroom learning.

About the Author

Joseph D'Agnese is a journalist and author who has written for children and adults alike. He's been published in the *New York Times*, the *Wall Street Journal, Wired, Discover,* and other national publications.

In a career spanning more than twenty years, his work has been honored with awards in three vastly different areas—science journalism, children's literature, and mystery fiction.

His science articles have twice appeared in the anthology *Best American Science Writing.*

His children's book, *Blockhead: The Life of Fibonacci,* was an honoree for the Mathical Book Prize—the first-ever prize for math-themed children's books.

One of his crime stories won the 2015 Derringer Award for short mystery fiction. Another of his short stories was selected by mega-bestselling author James Patterson for inclusion in the prestigious annual anthology, *Best American Mystery Stories 2015.*

D'Agnese's crime fiction has appeared in *Shotgun Honey, Plots with Guns, Beat to a Pulp, Ellery Queen's Mystery Magazine, Mystery Weekly Magazine,* and *Alfred Hitchcock's Mystery Magazine.*

D'Agnese lives in North Carolina with his wife, the *New York Times* bestselling author Denise Kiernan (*The Girls of Atomic City*).

To claim your free Starter Library, sign up for Joe's newsletter at his website: josephdagnese.com

twitter.com/JosephDAgnese
instagram.com/JosephDAgnese
amazon.com/author/josephdagnese
bookbub.com/authors/joseph-d-agnese
goodreads.com/JosephDAgnese

Manufactured by Amazon.ca
Bolton, ON